"I NOTICED YOU ENJOY TEASING, KATHY," SAID LONGARM...

"Oh? Are you saying I've been teasing you?"

"I don't know what you've been trying to do. It's your wagon. It's your deck of cards."

"We can't play cards in the dark."

"I know. You turned the lamp out."

She started to cry. So he reached out, gathered her in, and kissed her. She responded hungrily, then pulled away. "No. I don't want to!"

"Sure you do." He kissed her again. She'd put up a better fight if he was wrong, and then he'd have to turn her loose. But meanwhile her lips were saying "go" . . .

Also in the **LONGARM** series
from Jove

TABOR EVANS

LONGARM

AND THE
GHOST DANCERS

A JOVE BOOK

First Jove edition published July 1980

10 9 8 7 6 5 4 3 2 1

Printed in the United States of America

Jove books are published by Jove Publications, Inc.,
200 Madison Avenue, New York, NY 10016

Chapter 1

It was a dull gray Sunday morning, and Denver looked dead as well as dry. A thirsty man whose health depended on it could always get a drink in Denver, city ordinance be damned. But that wasn't Longarm's reason for being up at such a ghastly hour on his day off. The tall deputy had a bottle of Maryland rye at his furnished room on the less fashionable side of Cherry Creek, so he wasn't searching for any side door to an officially closed saloon. He was on an unofficial mission for the Justice Department, or rather for his boss, Federal Marshal Billy Vail. The Justice Department might well have frowned on his spare-time activity, and Billy Vail said his wife would skin him too, if she found out about it.

Longarm sauntered up the steps of the city jail, took a deep breath, and went inside. It didn't work. Longarm had never been able to break himself of the habit of breathing, and the air inside reeked of stale tobacco smoke, disinfectant, and vomit. A desk sergeant eyed him curiously as Longarm strode to the desk, took out his wallet, and flashed his federal badge.

The Denver policeman frowned and said, "We don't have anyone in the tank that Uncle Sam could be interested in, Marshal."

Longarm wearily pushed his flat-crowned Stetson back from his forehead. "I'm only a deputy marshal in the first place, but I understand you're holding a Miss Penelope Ascot on a charge of disturbing the peace."

The desk sergeant blinked in surprise and replied, "Oh, her? Yeah, we have her in the women's tank with

5

some whores and another crazy lady. We were fixing to send her over to the county asylum for observation this afternoon. What in the hell does Uncle Sam want with a lunatic?"

"Material witness," Longarm said, soberly. He didn't elaborate. Billy had said something dumb about bailing his old friend's kid out, but the local authorities had charged her with everything but typhoid, and what was the sense of packing a badge if you couldn't use it once in a while?

The desk sergeant looked at his charge sheets and muttered, "Federal witness, huh? According to the arresting officers, Penelope Ascot was engaged in the demolition of the Dew Drop Inn when they arrived on the scene. Prior to that, she'd also heaved a brick through a couple of plate-glass windows on Larimer Street, and the folks at the Silver Dollar want to know who's going to pay for a mirror and seventeen bottles that used to stand behind their bar."

"She's a caution," Longarm agreed amiably, "but what the hell, it's not like she killed anybody, and I have to report back with her." He saw the hesitation in the cop's eyes and added flatly, "I'm sort of in a hurry, friend."

The desk sergeant looked unhappy and said, "I don't know. You'll have to clear it with my captain. That crazy little gal owes a lot of money to the community for what she did."

"Where's your captain, then?"

"It's Sunday. He's off duty today. I think he said something about taking his kids to Cheeseman Park."

Longarm had known this before his arrival, but he looked surprised and sounded disgusted as he snapped, "Jesus H. Christ! You mean to hold a federal witness incommunicado while your captain takes his kids to the *zoo*? What's his name, Sergeant? If I don't show up with my witness, a federal grand jury figures to cloud all up and rain fire and salt on somebody. I sure don't mean to be the one standing underneath without a slicker, if you take my meaning."

The sergeant blanched visibly. "Hold your horses,

6

damn it! I never said it was *impossible* for you to have her. I just said *some* damn body will have to pay for the damage she did last night!"

Longarm pasted a reasonable smile across his tanned face and said, "Hell, she's a member of the Women's Christian Temperance whatever, ain't she?"

"That's for damned sure! Those crazy ladies from the WCTU have been temperate as hell with their bricks and hatchets, lately."

"I know. But they're a nationally chartered organization, right?"

"I reckon so, but that still don't give them no call to go around busting up saloons, does it?"

"You're right as rain, Sergeant," Longarm agreed equably. "If I were you, I'd send a bill to the national headquarters of the WCTU for each and every bottle Miss Ascot busted last night!"

The sergeant brightened. "By jimmies, I never thought of that! Her outfit must have more in their safe than she had in her purse when we picked her up!"

"There you go, old son. Look how you'll be saving the county the expense of a sanity hearing and such, too."

The desk sergeant punched the call bell on his blotter as he said, "I'll mention that to the captain. Where's this here federal hearing being held, in case he asks?"

Longarm hesitated before he said, truthfully enough, "I can't say for certain. Like you said, it's Sunday. We'll get her statement from her this afternoon, of course, but it's hard to say when she'll be called before the jury."

A weary-looking turnkey limped into view and the desk sergeant said, "Gimpy, we're turning that WCTU gal over to this here federal man."

Gimpy breathed an audible sigh of relief. "Praise God from whom all blessings flow! Maybe we'll have some peace and quiet back there now."

As he turned away, Longarm followed. He knew the usual procedure was for them to bring a prisoner out to him, but the more he hung around the desk, the more lies he'd have to tell. The sergeant hadn't asked

7

for his warrant, and with luck he might not even have to sign for her. He'd pointed this out to Billy Vail when the worried marshal had said the regular officers he knew might not be on duty over the weekend.

As he followed the limping turnkey back to the cell blocks, Longarm heard a young but strident voice, singing, "Lips That Touch Liquor Never Shall Touch Mine."

Off-key.

Gimpy stopped before the barred cell that the awful caterwauling was coming from and said, "Shove a sock in it and put your bonnet on, Miss Ascot. Uncle Sam has just taken you off our hands and tortured ears!"

As Gimpy unlocked the door, Longarm peered in at the five women in the gloomy cell. The one standing up was a surprisingly pretty little redhead in a severe black dress that almost completely concealed her figure. As she pinned her black sunbonnet on, covering her flaming mop of hair, she announced loudly, "I welcome my chance to stand trial, and I glory in my coming martyrdom!"

Gimpy told Longarm, "She's been talking like that ever since they brought her in last night. What charge are you boys holding her on?"

"Suspicion of bootlegging," said Longarm, soberly. He saw that Gimpy didn't have a sense of humor, so he quickly added, "You know that Lydia Whatsitsname that ladies take for female complaints? Well, we have evidence that it's eighty-proof alcohol and they've never paid a cent of the federal excise tax. Internal Revenue asked us to look into it."

Gimpy agreed, "Well, she's a female and she sure does complain a lot," as Penelope Ascot stepped grandly from the cell to face Longarm with a look of lofty superiority. Gimpy asked, "Do you aim to handcuff her, Deputy?"

Longarm smiled down at the tiny flame-haired terror and said, "I reckon she'll come quietly. How about it, Miss Ascot?"

She replied stiffly, "You have tobacco on your breath. Where are you taking me, sir?"

8

Longarm sighed and said, "I'll explain along the way. I can promise you it won't be a saloon. Let's go out front and get your belongings."

As Penelope Ascot walked between the two men, trying to look taller than either, a whore from the cell she'd just left yelled, "You're on the right track, sister! You just keep giving 'em hell, hear?"

"Convert of yours, ma'am?" asked Longarm.

Penelope sniffed and said, "Poor Flossy is another downtrodden victim of Demon Rum and men like yourself."

Longarm let it go. He could have said he didn't have to pay for it, and that if he did, he'd pick something better than Flossy, but he just wanted to get out of here with the crazy little gal.

Considering that he was getting her out of jail, she sniped like hell all through the business of recovering her belongings and signing her out. The damned desk sergeant did insist on getting Longarm's John Hancock. How he and Billy were going to explain any of this to Washington was up for grabs. He knew he could get the owner of the Silver Dollar to drop the charges, but Billy was going to have to spring for some busted glass on the q.t.

They finally got outside and Longarm exhaled a long, relieved sigh as he took her elbow and said, "I hired a surrey for us. It's hitched just down the street."

"Where are you taking me, you brute?" Penelope asked.

He said, "I wish you'd stop mean-mouthing folks and *listen* to them once in a while, Penny!"

"Penny? How dare you call me by my childhood nickname, even as you drag me to durance vile! Have you been drinking? You look like a drinking man."

He gritted his teeth and hung onto her elbow as he half-led and half-shoved her toward the parked carriage. He said, "I called you Penny because that's who you were when Billy Vail was riding with your father for the Texas Rangers. I ain't taking you anywhere all that vile, and I sure aim to have a good stiff belt of Maryland rye when I get you there!"

9

Penelope gasped, "Oh, are you a friend of dear Uncle Billy's?"

He growled, "I *work* for Billy Vail, who, lucky for you, is the U.S. district marshal here in Denver. He had a fit when he heard about his little Penny going crazy last night on Larimer Street."

"Sir, I assure you I was perfectly rational when I attacked the forces of evil and corruption upon my arrival."

"Get in the surrey, ma'am. I'll unhitch the critter."

Penelope allowed him to boost her up behind the dashboard, and sat primly as he untethered the bay gelding's reins and joined her. He backed away from the high sandstone curb and clucked the horse east toward Capitol Hill, up the street. He was dying for a smoke, but he'd been trying to cut down anyway, and this looked like as good a time as any to resist temptation. The little gal beside him seemed to be studying his profile as he drove. Finally she nodded as if satisfied, and said, "I didn't think Uncle Billy would hire a drinking man. You were just joshing me, weren't you?"

Longarm had lied enough that morning, so to change the subject, he asked, "How does Captain Buckeye Ascot of the Texas Rangers feel about his daughter running around scaring folks, ma'am?"

"My father, alas, died six years ago this fall. Surely Uncle Billy told you of his weakness, sir?"

Longarm shook his head and said, "No, ma'am. To hear Billy tell it, his old sidekick, Buckeye, didn't *have* any weaknesses. I'm sorry to hear he ain't with us anymore, but he must have been quite a man in his day. Billy never gets tired of jawing about the time the two of them stood off the whole Comanche Nation on the Staked Plains. I reckon that's why Billy wasn't happy about seeing you in jail."

"My father drank," said Penelope Ascot, flatly.

Longarm didn't answer. She'd already told him part of what was eating at her. He didn't remember hearing Billy say that Captain Buckeye Ascot was a drunk, but Penelope's father had been retired for some time since they'd ridden together, and it figured that a worn-out

10

and cast-aside man might want to steady his nerves more than most folks might approve. Penelope was saying, "The doctor said it was cancer. They always cover up to spare the feelings of a drunkard's kin."

Longarm knew better. "Most of the death certificates like that read 'heart failure,' ma'am. Have you considered that your dad might really have had a cancer? A thing like that could account for any man drinking a mite, if folks took a charitable view."

Penelope wrinkled her pert little nose and insisted, "He drank when I was little. I used to smell the liquor on his breath when he came to tuck me in and kiss me good night."

Longarm shrugged and drove on. He'd already been told that she took her temperance work seriously. Penelope suddenly nudged him and said, "Stop! Did you see that saloon back there?"

Longarm reined in, puzzled, and asked, "Which one? We've passed a couple just now."

"*That* one, back there on the other side of the street, is *open!*"

Longarm said, "No it ain't, ma'am. The front door's locked with a grill and there's a 'closed' sign hanging in the window."

Penelope sprang down from the surrey with surprising grace and an ominous look in her eye as she insisted, "I saw men inside, through the plate glass! They were *drinking!*"

"Hey, come back here!" He called, as the little redhead strode grimly across the street with a ramrod up her spine, not looking back. He swore and ran the surrey to a curbside hitch rail before he jumped down and quickly hitched up. By the time he'd followed her halfway, Penelope had bent to one knee near the far curb and was gathering loose cobblestones from the poorly paved street. Longarm broke into a run and called, "No! Don't do it!" as Penelope straightened up, cocked her right arm, and pitched a rock right through the saloon's front window!

There was an explosion of broken glass as two-thirds of the window shattered. Penelope wound up and fired

11

an amazingly accurate pitch at the glass that was still left, to leave the offending saloon's window gaping open as though in empty wonderment. As Longarm got to her side, he said, "I sure wish you'd stop that, ma'am."

The door was locked and grated, but men appeared in the new opening, and a man in a white apron shook his fist and yelled, "I'll kill you for this, you maniacs!"

Penelope threw again, and the bartender ducked as a paving block sizzled through the space his head had just occupied. His customers took cover too, as Penelope's barrage continued. From somewhere inside came the mournful sound of more glass smashing.

Longarm reached for her, but Penelope was advancing on the foe, singing. Off-key.

Longarm dove after her, missed, and groaned aloud as the little temperance fighter mounted the curb to stand in front of the busted-out window as she wound up again. It seemed impossible that she still had rocks left in that daintily hoisted skirt, but she'd armed herself with a mess of them, and seemed unaware that her striped stockings were showing above her high-button shoes. She threw the rock and spattered glass and liquor under the shattered mirror over the bar. But then Longarm grabbed her from behind and picked her up bodily to shake out the rocks she still had in her skirt.

She gasped, "Put me down! I've hardly started!"

Longarm lowered her to the ground, but hung on as he said, "Honey, you have just finished for sure, and it's time to vamoose!"

Then the bartender appeared at the window again with a double-barreled, sawed-off shotgun.

Longarm let go of the girl with one hand to draw his own double-action .44 as he said pleasantly, "I'd take it kindly if you'd point that scattergun somewhere more neighborly, friend."

The bartender roared, "You son of a bitch! First you bust my window, and now you're hiding behind a woman's skirts!"

Longarm said, "I never threw those rocks, old son. I've been trying to make this gal stop."

"Well, step away from her and let's have it out anyway. I'm so riled I just have to kill somebody, and gals don't count!"

Longarm said, "I know just how you feel, neighbor. But we'll be backing off now."

"You yellow-bellied bastard! You know I can't shoot you with that gal in front of you!"

"It's unfair as hell," Longarm agreed amiably. Then he added, "*You* don't have any cover at all and, mad or not, this ain't a popgun I'm pointing your way. Don't you reckon we'd best quit while we're both ahead?"

"Who's ahead, goddamnit? Look what you two lunatics just did to my saloon!"

"I'll chide her about it as soon as we're out of range," Longarm assured the infuriated barkeep. Then he let his voice drop a mite as he added, "It never would have happened if you hadn't busted the Sunday blue law, and I could see it as my duty to arrest you. But what the hell, I see you paid the fine already, so we'll just be on our way."

Considering that he'd just saved her life after getting her out of jail, Penelope Ascot sure sulked a lot. She hadn't said a word since he'd handcuffed her to the seat of the surrey so they could drive up Golfax Avenue in a more civilized manner.

He didn't drive her to Marshal Vail's home. Billy had some sort of arrangement with a widow woman who lived on Sherman Avenue, and he'd asked Longarm to meet him there.

Longarm drove into the backyard of the spacious brownstone, and was tethering the horse to a cast-iron post when Billy popped out of the back door to join them. The bald, pink-faced chief marshal grinned as he shouted, "I knew I could count on you, Longarm! How are you, Penny? My Lord, if you haven't grown up pretty as a—" He broke off, and his bushy black eyebrows met in a frown. "Longarm, what in thunder is Penny doing in those handcuffs?"

"She throws things," Longarm said. "I'll unlock her now, if you can swear you don't have a decanter of Madeira on the premises."

As Longarm freed her, Penelope nodded at Vail and said, "It's good to see you again after all these years, Uncle Billy, but I want you to fire this deputy. He actually laid hands on me and interfered with me as I was striving to uphold the law."

Billy looked dubiously at Longarm, who said, "I never laid hands anywhere important, and she was heaving paving blocks through windows at the time. You can fire me all you want. I'd rather herd *sheep* than escort her on my own time."

"Let's go inside," Vail suggested, taking Penelope by the arm to help her down as he added, "Lord have mercy, how you've grown, child. The last I heard of you, you'd married up and were living in St. Louis."

As the three of them walked to the back door, Penelope held her head defiantly and snapped, "If you must know, I'm divorced. They make beer in St. Louis, and the man I married seemed intent on drinking all of it!"

The two men shot appraising looks at one another over her sunbonnet. Penelope was starting to make more sense, if you wanted to call it sensible to wreck saloons.

Longarm had been inside the house before, but he hadn't asked, so he didn't know just what was going on between his boss and the attractive widow who met them at the door. He'd been told her name the first time they'd been introduced, but he'd forgotten it on purpose and had been sincerely glad that he had when, a month or so back, Billy Vail's wife had asked him in a desperately casual tone if he'd ever met Mrs. So-and-so. Longarm had looked sincerely blank. He'd been halfway home before he remembered that the name Vail's wife had asked about went with the somewhat younger and much prettier gal on Sherman Avenue.

So he studied the Boston ferns and maroon wallpaper, and tried not to listen as Billy introduced little Penelope to the graying but active-looking widow. He

14

found the whole situation a mite distasteful, even though he knew human nature and himself too well to offer a moral judgement. He didn't care if other men fooled around on their wives, but he resented being drawn into a sticky bedroom farce in which he didn't get to sleep with any of the ladies involved.

As Longarm was trying not to hear their introductions, Penelope asked the widow, "Are you Uncle Billy's mistress, ma'am?"

The widow drew herself up like the Denver dowager she was and asked sweetly, "How would you like a punch in the nose, dear?"

Billy Vail said, "I told you Penny was sort of odd, honey."

But the widow said, "Impertinent would be a more accurate appraisal. Get her out of here, Bill."

Before Vail could answer, Penelope said, "Heavens, I wasn't trying to insult anyone. I just wanted to know. As a devoted follower of Miss Victoria Woodhull, I approve of free love."

"It's *drinking* she can't abide," Longarm offered laconically.

Vail said, "I'm sure you gals will hit it off, once you get to know each other. Why don't you sip some tea or something while me and Longarm have a private talk in the study?"

The widow looked grimly at the younger, smaller woman and said, "Come with me, dear. I'm sure there's some rat poison in the kitchen, if I really look for it."

Vail took Longarm's arm and steered him out of the room as the tall deputy murmured, "Billy, they're going to kill each other."

But Vail shook his head. "Naw. Jo's a sensible gal. You can see now why I didn't want you to bring Penny to my house, though. My old woman's sort of old-fashioned, and even as a child, little Penny was sort of outspoken."

As he followed Vail into the study, Longarm said, "Crazy would be more like it. What in hell do you aim to *do* with that little redhead, Billy?"

"Send her back to St. Louis, of course. Forget Penny.

15

Me and Jo will see that she stays out of trouble, now that you've rescued her. I have a more important problem on my plate, and you're the one man I can think of who might be able to help me with it."

Longarm remained standing as Vail sat down in an overstuffed chair. He fished out a cheroot and a sulfur match and lit up before he said flatly, "It's my day off and I've had my fill of old friend's daughters, Billy. If you have anyone else you want me to get out of jail, forget it."

Vail said, "Sit down and shut up. I told you me and Jo had a handle on Buckeye Ascot's kid. This other problem is official."

Longarm sat gingerly on another chair and blew a thoughtful smoke ring before he muttered, "It's still my day off."

Vail nodded. "I know. You'll have time for that date you have with that Mexican gal tonight. I can't send you until we get the travel vouchers and such for you, tomorrow morning. I just figured as long as you were here . . ."

Longarm straightened abruptly, and his easygoing manner disappeared. "Just back up and let's talk some more about my love life," he said. "I've been polite as hell about the way other gents spend their time off duty, considering. Who in thunder gave you the right to spy on me?"

Vail shifted uncomfortably. "Damn it, Longarm, nobody's been spying on anybody, on duty or off. But a man hears gossip, and you have to admit that Mexican gal is sort of spectacular."

Longarm looked more annoyed than mollified by the compliment as he replied, "Well, in the first place, she's a single gal, and in the second place, she ain't Mexican. Tell your office gossips to take a better look before they carry tales to teacher. Everybody who has any call to mention the lady's name knows she's an Arapaho breed."

Vail brightened. "Do tell? That's even better. You going with an Indian gal, I mean. I told the War Department you got along with Indians better than any deputy I have on the payroll."

Longarm's eyes narrowed and Vail added quickly, "I didn't mention you going out with Indian gals, old son. I just said you spoke some of the lingos and had worked well with the Indian bureau in the past."

"Get to the point," said Longarm. "What sort of a mess have you got me into with the army, this time?"

Vail took out a smoke for himself and lit up with maddening deliberation before he said, "They're worried about that Paiute Messiah, Wovoka."

"The self-appointed leader of the Ghost Dance religion? Hell, I'm a lawman, not a missionary, Billy."

Vail shook his head and said, "Don't act so modest. You nipped some Ghost Dance trouble in the bud just a little while ago at the Blackfoot reservation, remember?"

Longarm looked pained and said, "*I* remember, but *you* sure don't! I only stumbled over one of Wovoka's Dream Singers while I was working on another case up there."

"Well, the point is, you put a sudden end to the son of a bitch."

Longarm protested, "I never did any such thing! One of the Indian police officers I had under me sort of got rid of the rascal on his own, and had I been able to prove it, I'd have had to arrest him."

Vail nodded and said, "I know your views on rough justice, old son. Officially, I'm only sending you up to Pine Ridge for a powwow with Sitting Bull." He flicked the ash from his cigar and added, "Of course, if the Sioux refuse to see reason . . ."

"Now hold on," Longarm cut in. "I'm not a missionary and I'm not the U.S. Army, either. If the War Department wants Wovoka or Tatanka Iyotake gunned, they have plenty of troopers drawing thirteen dollars a month and all the beans they can eat. Let them earn their keep for a change."

Marshal Vail looked confused and asked, "Who in hell are you talking about, old son? I wanted you to start by questioning Sitting Bull!"

17

"That's what I mean. Neither you nor the War Department knows the poor old geezer's name, and you're accusing him of all sorts of things."

Vail still looked puzzled, so Longarm said, "Tatanka Iyotake is what the Lakota call the gent you know as Sitting Bull."

Vail looked relieved and said, "Oh, right, the Heap Big Chief of the Sioux. We've heard the Ghost Dancers have been seen on the Pine Ridge Reservation, and Washington's worried as hell about it. I said I'd send you up there to straighten out Sitting Bull and his Sioux."

Longarm groaned aloud and muttered, "Jesus H. Christ. To start with, no Lakota's about to jaw with any white man dumb enough to call him a Sioux. Sioux means something between 'nigger' and 'enemy' in Chippewa, and the Lakota don't think much of the Chippewa, either."

Vail nodded sagely and said, "That's right. I forgot they call themselves Dakota."

"Lakota, damn it. Dakota is another white man's word. If you'd let me finish, I'd get to the second point, which is that Tatanka Iyotake is not and never has been a chief."

"Hell, what is he if he's not the chief of the Dakota, Lakota, whatever?"

"He's what we call a medicine man. It doesn't translate too well. You might say the man we call Sitting Bull is somewhere between a judge and a priest."

"But he led his warriors against Custer at the Little Big Horn, didn't he?"

"No. I got it from some Lakota I know that he was nowhere near the battle. I got it from some Crow too, and since the Crow hate the Lakota, I'd say it was true."

Vail looked unhappy as he flicked away another ash and said, "Well. I know you're partial to Indians, but whatever the old bastard is, he's a troublemaker."

Longarm smiled thinly. "I'll pass on that remark about my being partial to Indians, since I've left a few squaws keening their dead in my time. But accusing

Tatanka Iyotake of being a Ghost Dancer is dumb, even for the army. I just got through telling you he's a high priest of Wokan Tonka."

Vail said, "I know who the Great Spirit is. But Wovoka is an Indian religious leader too. So don't it figure they'd be in cahoots?"

Longarm shook his head and said, "I'll buy that when I hear that the Pope is plotting with the Grand Mufti of Islam. Wovoka's a *Paiute*, Billy. He talks a different lingo and prays to other spirits. None of the Lakota elders are likely to buy his fool notions about medicine shirts and such."

Vail got up with the expression of a cat that had the combination to the lock on the canary's cage, and stepped over to a sideboard to open a drawer.

"You're right at home here," Longarm observed.

Vail said, "Never mind about me and old Jo. I'd tell you it was platonic, if I wasn't so tired of you looking so damned know-it-all."

He took out a wadded-up leather bundle and spread it on a nearby table before he added mildly, "Tell me what this is and I'll tell you where they found it."

Longarm stared soberly at the painted buckskin garment, and took a drag on his cheroot. "That's a medicine shirt, or I've forgotten Wovoka's handwriting. Now you're fixing to tell me it comes from the Pine Ridge reservation, right?"

"It's tedious talking to a man who has all the answers. The Pine Ridge agency says there's more where this one came from, only the Indians get sort of truculent when a white man asks about them."

Longarm nodded and said, "All right. So some medicine-shirted Ghost Dancers have been to Pine Ridge. I still say none of the elders up there take Wovoka's nonsense seriously."

Vail asked, "What about the youngsters? The Sioux who claims he lifted Custer's hair was fourteen at the time. The Sioux haven't had a good licking for a while, and meanwhile, a lot of sullen kids have grown a few inches. I told the War Department I was sending you to investigate and report back to me, pronto."

Longarm protested. "Billy, I don't talk Lakota well enough to get laid. I got lucky up at the Blackfoot reservation that time because I do savvy a few words of Algonquin, and because the men I was after turned out to be white. Sending me to jaw with Tatanka Iyotake is a pure waste of time."

Vail said, "Time may be just the ticket, old son. I may not know as much about Indians as you do, but I'm a fair-minded man, and we both know President Hayes keeps turning down the army's inflated budget."

"The President's a fair-minded man too, but get to the point, Billy."

Vail sat down again and said, "The point is that if somebody like you can't nip this Ghost Dance foolishness in the bud by making a few judicious arrests, the army will ride in whooping and hollering to do the job *their* way! There's more to this than the usual feud between Justice and the War Department, Longarm. We're both sworn peace officers, and there won't be a lick of peace this summer if we don't clean up this infernal mess before somebody, on either side, gets hurt."

Longarm sighed and said, "You just touched a nerve. I scouted for the army one time, when I was young and foolish. I'll mosey up there and see if I can find anything out. But I sure hope you haven't any money riding on me doing any good."

Vail grinned and said, "There you go, old son. I knew I could depend on you."

Longarm rose to his feet and answered. "You must know something I don't, then. I'm only willing to give it a try because I remember what the army did at Sand Creek and the Washita."

Vail walked with him to the door as he said, "I'm counting on you to keep innocent Indians from being massacred, Longarm."

Longarm shrugged and said. "Innocent Indians are only half of it, Billy. I remember what happened to a mess of white settlers at Spirit Lake, too."

Chapter 2

Longarm boarded the northbound train late the next morning. He'd just had time to make it to the office and pick up his travel orders and warrants. He packed his Winchester and saddlebags aboard the coach with him for safekeeping, but his saddle and other heavy gear were riding up ahead in the baggage car. He found an empty plush seat and sat down to have a smoke and glance over the hastily typed arrest orders. Then, as the train chugged out of the yards, he muttered, "What the hell?"

Neither Wovoka nor any other Indian he'd ever heard of was listed on the warrants, and Marshal Vail had tucked a coy note in among the papers before handing them to him on the fly. It read: "Indian religious matters are before the Supreme Court on constitutional grounds at the moment. So the judge refused us on Wovoka and other big medicine men. You'll have to get something more than praying and gourd-rattling on him if you mean to make a sensitive arrest."

Longarm swore and stared out the window at the passing prairie grass as he muttered, "Shit, the train's going too fast to jump, and my possibles are up forward, too."

What, he wondered, was he supposed to do when he arrived in Pine Ridge? The Indian police would have arrested the small potatoes on his federal wants by now, if they were anywhere near Pine Ridge and giving their right names.

He knew most Indians had more than one name. They gave one to the Indian agent when they came in for flour and beef; they used another name among their friends; they had a secret familiar name only close

21

relatives knew; and, of course, they never told *anyone* the "real" name the spirits had revealed to them at puberty initiations.

How in hell was a strange white man to get a pissed-off Indian to admit that a name on a wanted notice was one he'd used, one time, to another white man?

He was on a fool's errand for sure, this time, the daddy of all fool's errands; he didn't have the foggiest notion of what he was supposed to do!

He could go through the motions. He'd pick up a mount from the agency police and ride around in circles until somebody was kind enough to confess all to a strange white who didn't even speak the local language.

He wondered how soon he could come back without getting fired. Billy was used to his spending a month or more on a tough case. But a month at Pine Ridge would be tedious as hell, even for an Indian. There'd be nothing to drink, and it was a federal crime to make love to a federal ward, even if the Lakota weren't one of the unfriendliest tribes west of the Missouri.

As he sat there staring out the window, someone sat down next to him. There were other empty seats, but he moved his rifle to make room anyway. Then Penelope Ascot said, "Uncle Billy's girlfriend sure is strange."

Longarm swung to face the little redhead with a puzzled smile as he said. "Howdy, ma'am. If you thought this was the train to St. Louis, I'll help you transfer at the next stop."

"Pooh, who wants to go to St. Louis?" she replied contemptuously.

He said, "Billy said that was where they aimed to send you, ma'am."

"Pooh again. I'm a grown woman and I go where my mission calls me."

He didn't answer. He was too busy trying to remember whether there was a saloon car on this train. He relaxed a bit as he remembered there wasn't. The candy butcher who'd be coming down the aisle in a while served warm beer as well as warm soda pop and oranges, but Penelope didn't have any paving blocks in her lap. She seemed, in fact, to be in a better mood than the last time he'd seen her.

She said, "It's sort of romantic, in a sad way. But when you get right down to it, equality like that is what we women have been fighting for."

Longarm regarded her with a puzzled smile. "I hope you won't take this personal, ma'am, but I have no idea what you're talking about."

She sighed and said, "Uncle Billy and Jo. They're not lovers. I think *she'd* be willing, but he's sort of old-fashioned about free love."

"If you say so, ma'am. I can't say I pay that much attention to other folks' business."

"Oh, I never pried. Jo told me all about it after she decided she wasn't angry with me after all. You see, Uncle Billy loves his wife, but she's one of those dull women who never want to talk about anything but children and the price of food."

"Mrs. Vail's a fine cook," Longarm allowed. "I've eaten with them a few times."

"I know. I met her as a child. I seem to disturb her for some reason, so Uncle Billy thought I'd get on better with his other woman."

Then she wrinkled her nose and said, "There, I've even done it myself. But what *do* you call the other woman, when a man's not her lover?"

"A sidekick?" Longarm suggested with a shrug.

"Uncle Billy says she's his friend. You see, he loves his wife, but she can't give him all he wants. I don't mean in bed. His wife seems quite capable of satisfying his animal needs."

"Ma'am, I sure wish you'd change the subject."

"Pooh, I'm not saying anything dirty. I'm sure Uncle Billy has never touched his other woman. You'll never believe what it is he sees in her."

"She has a green thumb?" Longarm guessed.

"No. She likes to *talk*. I mean, she likes to talk about things a man is interested in. She said she and Uncle Billy used to have long conversations when her husband was still alive. So after she became a widow woman, it

23

just seemed natural that he should keep coming by. His wife is terribly jealous and refuses to understand. But, of course, if *she* talked to him about things, he wouldn't need to visit Jo."

Interested despite himself, Longarm asked, "What do you reckon they talk about?"

She said, "I've no idea. But it sounds so romantic. I wish *I* had some man who'd treat me as a fellow conversationalist instead of a household servant and slab of meat."

Longarm decided to talk as little as possible until the little crazy lady got off the train. But she asked, "What time will we arrive at Pine Ridge, Mr. Long?"

Longarm looked at her incredulously. "I'm sorry, I must have misunderstood you. It sounded like you were asking about Pine Ridge."

"I was. That's where I'm going."

"Come on, Pine Ridge ain't a town, it's an Indian reservation."

"I know. Uncle Billy was telling us last night about his reasons for sending you there. You know, of course, that Demon Rum is the cause of all this Indian trouble?"

He rolled his eyes heavenward and muttered, "Thanks a lot, Lord." Then he lowered his gaze and looked Penelope in the eye. "Ma'am, I'm not going after drunken Indians. They have their own reservation police for that, should the need arise."

She nodded and said, "All the more reason for me to be there, then. If I find any firewater at the trading post, I'll just do my Christian duty and put an end to it."

He said, "Ma'am, I'd strongly advise against throwing rocks at a likkered-up gent of *any* race. But if I just had to heave a rock at a drunk, the last one I'd pick would be a drunk Lakota! They don't like us much when they're cold sober."

She shrugged and insisted, "I'll do as I must, once we arrive at the reservation."

He said, "No you won't. You're changing to an eastbound train at the next stop, ma'am. I've enough on my plate already without folks throwing rocks at men I only aim to question politely."

Penelope Ascot set her little jaw stubbornly and insisted, "Pooh, it's a free country and I mind I can go anywhere I like."

He said, "Yes, ma'am, anywhere but the Pine Ridge Reservation, with Ghost Dancers skulking about and war talk in the air."

"Are you connected with the Bureau of Indian Affairs, sir?"

"No, but . . ."

"But me no buts, Mr. Long. My duty calls and my mind is made up. I am bound for Pine Ridge to spread the word and preach against the evils of Demon Rum. No mortal man of woman born is going to stop me!"

Longarm didn't answer. Penelope waited for a time as the wheels clicked under them before she asked, "Well?"

"Well what, ma'am?"

"Weren't you going to say how you intended to stop me?"

Longarm sighed. "There has to be a way, but I'm still trying to figure it out."

"Pooh, why can't you men ever admit it when a woman gets the better of you?"

It was a good question. Longarm didn't have the answer to that one, either.

The town of Hat Creek didn't even have a sensible name to offer, but Longarm got off there when the train stopped. It was as close to the Pine Ridge Agency as the Burlington Line got. This still left him over fifty miles from his destination, and he'd been telling Penelope Ascot all the way from Denver that he wasn't about to take her with him, but she got off the train too.

Longarm picked up his saddle and gear and tried to ignore her as he took bigger steps than usual out of the depot and up the dusty main drag with the load braced on one shoulder. The diminutive redhead almost had to trot as she tagged after him, but he could see her reflection ghosting him as he passed shop windows, and she looked determined as hell. He figured he could leave her behind in a flat run, even packing his load, but that figured to look just plain ridiculous. Folks were already looking at him sort of funny.

He bulled his way past two roughly dressed hands lounging near a watering trough, and glared at them as they stared innocently through him and the little dark shadow on his trail. He spotted the hotel he was aiming for and quickened his pace as, behind him, Penelope yelled, "Mr. Long! Duck!" and things got even more embarrassing.

Penelope was certainly tedious, but there was something in the way she'd yelled that made him step to one side as he turned. A bullet parted the air where his shoulder blades had just been. He threw the load to one side as he crabbed the other way, drawing as he saw that one of the two men he'd just passed was lying facedown in the dust for some reason, and the other was pointing a smoking gun at him. Longarm cursed as he saw that the fool girl was in his line of fire behind the gunslick. As he kept moving sideways, the fellow fired again and nicked the brim of Longarm's Stetson. Then, as Longarm saw that he had Penelope out of his line of fire and was about to return the compliment, the man trying to kill him buckled at the knees and pitched forward into a pile of horse shit as Penelope wound up to throw another rock.

As she shrugged and lowered her arm, Longarm grinned. "You sure throw rocks good, ma'am."

"They were trying to kill you!" she replied, staring down in wonderment at the two men she'd put on the ground. Longarm said, "I noticed. I'll be hanged if I know what those boys had against me, but I owe you for saving the taxpayers of these United States a funeral."

The gunplay had pretty well cleared the street, but a man wearing a tin star and an uncertain look cut across to stop near one of the unconscious men as he said, "I sure wish somebody would sort of fill me in on what all that shooting was about."

Longarm's gunhand was lowered politely, but he didn't put his Colt away as he nodded down at the two at his feet to reply, "I'm a mite confused myself, constable. My name is Custis Long and I'm a deputy U.S. marshal. I reckon it's safe to assume these two gents ain't."

Other townies, observing that the tall stranger and the little crazy lady were talking politely with the local law, were edging forward to hear better. The town lawman rolled one of the downed gunmen over with a thoughtful boot and opined, "They ain't from hereabouts, neither. This one's still breathing."

Longarm nodded and said, "I suspicion they'll both survive, thanks to my guardian angel here."

He saw that the constable was expecting more information, so he added, "Her name is Miss Ascot and her daddy was a Texas Ranger, and if there's a saloon in the immediate vicinity, don't tell her where it is."

The constable shook his head sympathetically. "My first wife had a drinking problem too." Then he turned to the townies who'd formed a circle all around. "Any of you boys ever see these two sleeping beauties before?"

One man volunteered, "I was drinking next to them the other evening. They was sort of sullen jaspers, but I heard one call the other by name. The one with the fancy spurs is called Culpepper."

Longarm looked relieved as the youth helped him get the saddle on his shoulder again. He said, "That explains their manners, then. I sent a road agent called Culpepper to the gallows a year ago this summer. He said at the time that his kid brother would get me. For a minute I thought this might be a serious situation."

"Don't you call it serious when two men try to gun you, deputy?"

"Shucks, that happens all the time, and as you see, these poor benighted saddle tramps were dumb enough to turn their backs on a woman. What I meant was that I'm on government business and might have gotten hung

27

up here in Hat Creek, had they turned out to be important owlhoots."

The constable turned toward the four closest townies. "You boys drag these rascals over to the lockup and tell Sandy to let 'em recover in the tank." Turning back to Longarm, he asked, "I take it that any papers posted on these gents don't interest you?"

Longarm grinned and said, "They're yours to keep and cherish, constable. I know for a fact there's no federal paper out on either one. But if the one who answers to Culpepper is anything like his big brother, he's doubtless wanted on a robbery charge or two. I'm afraid I ain't allowed to file for rewards. So, if I were you, I'd put my arrest on the wire and see if I get lucky."

"*My* arrest, deputy?"

"Hell, you just arrested them, didn't you?"

The constable grinned boyishly, then glowered at the bystanders. "What's the matter with you boys? Can't you see these folks are guests of the community? Take that fool McClellan saddle off that gent and escort him right to wheresoever he might be headed."

The crowd closed in jovially, and one man even took Penelope's carpetbag as others relieved Longarm of every burden but his guns and hat. One of them asked where they wanted to go, and Longarm said the hotel would do nicely, so the crowd almost carried the two of them in that direction. The one packing Penelope's bag said, "This sure is heavy, little lady. What are you toting in your bag, rocks?"

Penelope replied sweetly, "I always travel with a few pounds of railroad ballast. It pays to be prepared."

The townies deposited the two of them inside the hotel, and as Longarm signed the register, the room clerk asked him, "Is this lady with you?"

"Not hardly. I am on official U.S. Government business, and I'll be staying here until somebody sends me a mount from the remount station north of town."

Penelope said, "We require separate accommodations, sir. But I will be staying the same length of time.

28

I shall be riding with Mr. Long, out to the Indian agency at Pine Ridge."

Longarm started to tell her she was crazy, but it hardly seemed polite to say a thing like that in front of folks, to a lady who'd just saved his life.

Later that evening, as the sun was setting over the mountain range to the west, Longarm was beginning to worry about other things than Penelope Ascot. He'd wired ahead to the army remount station that he'd be arriving on that train, then he'd sent another wire since he'd settled in at the hotel. But he didn't have a horse and he hadn't even received an answer. The army was like that sometimes. Remount hated to part with a critter for another federal agency. It looked as though he was going to have to hire a livery nag and mosey down the creek to have a personal discussion with some hard-ass cavalry gents. But the damned station was a two hours' ride and he'd have to wait until sunrise. The hotel room he'd hired was tolerable for a trail town, but he was restless instead of tired after the long ride on the Burlington, and Hat Creek looked like one of those towns that rolled its sidewalks up for the night at suppertime.

He locked his room and stuck a match stick between the door and the jamb, where an intruder wouldn't notice it, then he went downstairs to see what action Hat Creek might afford a restless gent. He found little Penelope Ascot perched like a blackbird on a lobby chair, near a wilted Boston fern. He asked her what she was doing there and the pert prohibitionist replied, "I'm waiting for those horses you mentioned, of course."

He sighed and said, "*Horse*, ma'am. Singular, not plural."

"Do you expect me to ride pillion all the way to Pine Ridge?"

"No, ma'am. I know this is hard for you to grasp, but I'll try again. You can't come with me to the Pine Ridge Agency. I am on a mission for Uncle Sam and you don't work for him." He saw the hurt look in her

29

eye and softened it a mite by adding, "I know you have a mission of your own and I admire your gumption. But you just don't know what you'd be letting yourself in for. The Indians are on the prod, and even if they weren't, it's a long, dusty ride to a miserable place. The agency ain't a town, it's a mess of shanties and a garbage dump. You know that Mexican slum down by Cherry Creek in Denver?"

"A slum's a slum, Mr. Long. I've done some work with the poor."

"Go back and do some more, then. Those unemployed Mexicans in Denver are living high on the hog, next to what's left of the Lakota Confederacy. Shiftless, drunken Mexicans are ten times more civilized than anyone you'll likely meet on the Pine Ridge Reservation. Most Mexicans are Christians, and the Alamo was a long time ago. The Indians don't *want* folks coming among them to do good. They'd like white folks to leave them the hell *alone*."

"They need proper guidance," she insisted, primly.

He said, "The Seventh Cav is giving them all the guidance they can tolerate, ma'am. They guide them back across the reservation line every time they happen to stray. We're losing at least one trooper and five Indians a season that way. If troublemaking Ghost Dancers are really on the reservation now, the wastage toll figures to climb."

She sat even straighter as she insisted, "Can't you see that's why I'm needed out there, Mr. Long? Everyone knows that firewater is the cause of all this Indian trouble!"

Longarm sighed deeply. "Firewater ain't the cause, ma'am, it's a symptom. The disease is something deeper and harder to cure."

"But, don't you see, we *have* to find the cure. There must be some way that we whites can make the Indians see the advantages of our higher civilization!"

"I'll pass on which race had the higher civilization when Columbus took that wrong turn on his way to India. I've never seen an Indian build a locomotive, but I've never seen a nine-year-old Indian kid working

30

in a cotton mill, either. I don't have any pat answers, which likely makes me smarter than either the army or the Bureau of Indian Affairs."

"Then why are we going out to the reservation, if you don't intend to help the Indians?"

"Ma'am, *we* ain't going any such place. *I'm* going because they're sending me. I'm a peace officer, not a missionary. My job is to find out who is disturbing said peace and make them stop."

"But can't you see that your job will be easier if the Indians are sober and attentive?" she persisted.

"Ma'am, I don't care if they're sober or not. You're the one who ain't paying attention. We're talking in a tedious circle, and since we've both had our say, I'm going out to see if I can find something to read or whatever."

As he touched his hatbrim to her and headed for the door, she called after him, "Mind you don't start drinking, Mr. Long!"

He didn't answer as he stepped out onto the plank walk, but she'd just given him an idea and he was grinning like a weasel in a hen house by the time he got to the swinging doors of the nearest saloon and pushed his way inside.

The town constable was there with a couple of deputies. As Longarm bellied up to the bar, the local lawman said, "Your money's no good tonight, Long. Omaha is sending us five hundred dollars on them rascals in the lockup, and you are late to the celebrating!"

So Longarm helped himself to the bottle of redeye someone slid down the bar to him. The trade liquor was raw and smelled worse than it tasted, which was terrible, but he swished it around in his mouth and spilled some down the front of his shirt for luck. The next time he met up with Penelope Ascot, he aimed to smell like a Larimer Street drunk. He'd tried reasoning with the pesky little gal; maybe *disgusting* her was the answer!

But Longarm was a big man with a considerable capacity for redeye, and as he made himself disgusting

31

he asked the others what they knew about the trouble out at Pine Ridge.

One of the deputies said, "We're ready for 'em. Hat Creek ain't Spirit Lake, and if those pesky redskins jump the reservation again, they'll be conducted direct to the Happy Hunting Ground!"

Another townie said, "Hell, they'll never make her this far. The Seventh Cav has them new Hotchkiss guns and they're spoiling for another crack at the Sioux. The Seventh is still sore about poor Custer."

Somebody said, "Custer was an asshole." The first townie nodded and said, "I know, but he was still a white man and the Sioux made the Seventh look bad. I was talking to some troopers the other day and they said the army is just praying the Sioux are serious about that Ghost Dance shit. They can't get *at* the Sioux unless they leave the sheltering wings of the agent out there."

Longarm asked, "Does anybody know if Tatanka Iyotake himself is taking any interest in that new Paiute religion?"

There was a pause and someone asked, *"Who?"*

"Sitting Bull. He's still their pope, ain't he?"

The constable said, "Beats the shit out of me. I don't know why they let the old red rascal live when they rounded them up after the Little Big Horn."

Longarm took another sip of the awful redeye. "I reckon it had something to do with the peace treaty we signed with them. The reason I'm interested is because Wovoka's new religion won't convert enough to matter unless Tatanka Yatanka and the other tribal elders go along with it."

Someone said, "That's why I say we ought to kill ever' goddamn Sioux old enough to vote. We're never gonna make 'em behave till we give each and ever' one a bath and teach 'em to talk English. If it was up to me I'd have the Indian problem solved in six weeks."

Longarm resisted the impulse to ask him when he intended to get on a boat for Europe. The boys were trying to be friendly, and while his tongue was feeling pins and needles, he was too sober to get into a discussion of the Indian problem; he'd seen too many barroom brawls start that way. No two white men west of the Big Muddy had the same solution, but each one was truculently sure he had the one right answer.

He knew the army wanted the Indians disarmed and scattered in small bands that would be easier to manage, while the Indian bureau favored consolidated county-sized reservations with central schools, model farms, and such. There was something to be said for either plan, but both wouldn't work at the same time, and since Indians weren't allowed to vote, none of the folks trying to help them saw fit to ask them for suggestions.

He saw that the locals didn't know how to help the Indians either, and he knew he'd wake up as sick as a dog if he drank enough of that redeye to matter. So he excused himself from the tedious conversation and went out to see what else was going on in Hat Creek.

Nothing was. The distant tinkle of a piano told him there was another saloon down the street, but it was getting dark and the piano was playing "Garry Owen," off-key. That meant they were likely jawing about the recent Indian troubles down that way too. Longarm decided reluctantly to call it a night. The drinks he'd had had settled his nerves a mite and he figured to catch a good night's sleep and get an early jump on the remount officer by showing up for that mount before they were wide awake, come morning.

Back at the hotel, he was surprised to see Penelope Ascot still keeping company with that same potted fern. He was afraid that if he asked her why she was still sitting in the lobby, she might tell him, so he nodded politely and went on upstairs. As he checked the matchstick and was unlocking his door, he saw that she'd followed him.

She sniffed and said, "I think you've been *drinking*!"

"Yes, ma'am," he replied evenly. "I smoke cheroots and gamble at cards too."

"Oh, Mr. Long, how could you?"

"It wasn't all that hard, ma'am. I just kept picking up the bottle and pouring until my shotglass was full."

33

"Oh dear, you smell like a brewery. I thought you had more character."

"To be exact, ma'am, I suspicion I smell more like a distillery than a brewery. As for my character, I don't reckon I have any. I am a weak-willed, shiftless skunk who ought to be tarred and feathered just for talking to a lady. So you'd best head elsewhere. I would walk you to your own room, but I'm so drunk I might fall down and disgrace you when they found me lying outside your door in the cruel gray light of dawn."

He opened the door and went inside. She followed him. He struck a match and lit the candle stub on the nightstand after making certain the blinds were drawn. She looked like a lost, friendless pup in the soft, wan light. He had to remind himself there was kindness in his cruelty as he stared owlishly at her, sat down on the bed, and said, "I don't know why in thunder you're here, little lady, but if you aim to get laid, you have come to the wrong place. I am so drunk I couldn't get it up with a block and tackle."

He'd expected her to flinch and run for the hills. Instead, she sighed and said, "You poor man, you don't know what you're saying. I can see that Demon Rum has made you take leave of your senses."

He nodded contritely. "That's true. When I get likkered up, I get so ornery I curdle milk just passing the cow. I am half-hoss and half-alligator and so mean that folks board up their windows when they hear I'm in the county."

She was still standing there, so he started shucking himself out of his duds as he continued, "You'd best stand clear, ma'am. I ain't had a bath for a year and the sight of me naked has driven strong women gray-headed."

"You surely don't intend to get undressed with me standing here, do you?"

"I sleep in the raw whether folks are looking or not. You'd best leave, if any of this is a shock to your delicate nature."

He took off his coat and unstrapped his gunbelt to hang it over a bedpost. He was surprised as she stood her ground while he unbuttoned his vest and started on his hickory shirt. She licked her lips and said, "I wanted to talk to you about how we are to get out to the reservation."

He took off his shirt, wadded it up, and threw it across the room. Then he started hauling off his boots. The girl stamped her foot and said, "You're not listening to me!"

He finished shucking the boots before he stared down at the rug, blinking his eyes and muttering, "This sure is a noisy place, wherever I may be."

"I want you to promise you'll take me with you in the morning."

Longarm got to his feet, looked at her in mock surprise, and said, "Well, howdy, little darling. They never told me a gal went with this room, but I'm ready if you are."

"Mr. Long, you're so drunk you can hardly stand! You should be ashamed of yourself!"

"I know. My mama always said I'd come to a bad end amongst tobacco, strong drink, and weak women."

Then he started taking off his pants. It made him feel foolish, but if that didn't do it, nothing would.

It didn't. Penelope stepped over and snuffed the candle as she said in a disgusted voice, "You're exposing yourself, you idiot."

Then, as he saw that she was moving toward the door, he sighed with relief and sank down naked on the bed. Penelope didn't go out the door. She closed it. Then she came back and sat down beside him. "Are you ready to be good now?"

He put an arm around her waist, braced himself for the inevitable slap, and tried to sound dirty as he leered, "Who wants to be good? I'm feeling wicked as hell and I aim to have my way with you, my proud damsel!"

She said, "Oh, all right, but let me get undressed first."

Longarm moved away, abashed, and gasped, "Beg pardon, ma'am?"

Her voice was mingled with the silken sound of

clothing being shed as she replied, "I said it was all right. But I do so hate to have my chemise ripped, and you must admit you're too drunk to undress a girl properly."

He frowned in the darkness and dropped the drunk act as he said, "Penny, this is getting past fooling around! I thought you hated men who drank."

"Poor silly. It's Demon Rum I hate, not its poor victims. I *love* people. And I'm sure you'll find the natural pleasures the Lord gave us even nicer, once I reform you."

And then she crawled over to nestle in his arms, stark naked, as she purred, "Now, isn't this ever so much more pleasant than drinking in a dirty old saloon?"

He didn't want to respond, but she was an exciting little bundle of nudity and he felt his free hand exploring her even as he protested, "This is sure a peculiar way to reform folks, Penny!"

She guided his hand in place over a small, firm breast as she answered, "Pooh, sex and Demon Rum have nothing to do with one another. You didn't think I was one of those poor, dried-up puritan types, did you?"

"I don't *now*! But this sort of takes getting used to."

She reached down between them to fondle him as she giggled and said, "So I noticed. Is it that awful stuff you've been abusing yourself with, or are you just shy, dear?"

"Uh, a little of both, I suspicion. You did say something on the train about being an admirer of Virginia Woodhull, but I thought all that free love stuff was just talk."

She began to stroke him as she crooned, "I thought by now you'd know I'm a woman who suits actions to her words." Then she slid her head down to join her hand, and since she couldn't talk with her mouth full, she offered no further explanations.

Longarm was a couple of miles outside of town the next morning, when he reined in the hired livery mare and stared thoughtfully up at the telegraph pole by the trail. He was riding alone to the remount station down the wire. Penny had made him promise to come back, but he'd cross that bridge once he forked an army bronc. The severed copper wire swung slightly in the morning breeze and he muttered, "All right, I'm sorry I said all those mean things about you, remount."

He rode on. He couldn't tell if the wire had been cut or just torn loose by the wind. Either way, it was sort of surprising that nobody from the Signal Corps was out here fixing it.

The remount station was said to be an easy ride from Hat Creek, and even a livery nag was frisky in the morning, so Longarm heeled it into a lope, scanning the horizon as he rode.

The foothills of the Rockies rose to his left. Rolling prairie groped eight hundred miles to the Missouri over the horizon to his right. He topped a rise and reined in again, shifting the Winchester across his knees as he studied the smoke-talk to the north.

The rising puffs of green-wood smoke hung twenty miles or more away against the cobalt sky of the high plains. Longarm couldn't read the smoke talk. No white man or strange Indian could. He knew it wasn't a code like Morse. The rising signals were prearranged each time a war party rode out in paint. He was too far away for the smoke to be talking about him, so he rode on.

He knew it could be kid stuff. White kids weren't the only ones who liked to play cowboys and Indians. If it wasn't some kids practicing to be Dog Soldiers when they grew up, it could still be a hunting party. The north herd was pretty well shot off lately, but he knew the Indian bureau issued rifles and ammunition to their wards to supplement their government rations.

It made the army mad as hell.

He figured to hear about it when he reached the remount station. He sometimes wondered about the way folks thought in Washington. Had it been left to him, he'd have picked another regiment to police these parts. The Seventh Cav was good, and its officers and men were likely as fair-minded as most, but it seemed presumptuous to expect the men who marched to "Garry Owen" to forget certain misunderstandings on the Rosebud, the Little Big Horn, and other places too numerous to mention or forgive.

He rode on, musing, until he topped another rise and spotted the remount station ahead—or what was left of it.

Longarm walked his hired horse down the slope toward the burned-out cluster of frame buildings near the empty corral by the trail. He reined in, dismounted, and tethered the mare to a cottonwood a good distance away. Horses were funny about the smell of blood or barbecued flesh.

Cocking the Winchester, Longarm walked the rest of the way in. He spotted the first body in the doorway of the gutted office. The sergeant was lying facedown with an arrow in his back. He had been scalped and they'd cut off both of his hands. Another arrow was imbedded in the door jamb above him. Longarm nodded to the cadaver and said, "It was cut-and-run, all right. They'd have taken time to recover their arrows if there'd been more time."

But where was everybody? Longarm circled the building and found a Negro wrangler in civilian dress draped over a corral rail out back. He had two arrows in him, but they hadn't stopped to scalp him. Longarm knelt to scoop up some fresh brass, glanced at the cartridge bases, and mused, "Army issue. They lured the sergeant to the door and grabbed him before the others suspicioned there was anything amiss. Then they shot a volley of fire arrows and lit out. This wrangler likely broke cover when he saw that they meant to take the ponies with them." To the dead Negro he said, "You shouldn't have done that, old son."

He was still scouting for a sign when he heard the drumming of hooves and looked up to see a quartet of men in army blue bearing down on him. As they reined in, the corporal in command snapped, "This is U.S. Government property, mister!"

Longarm nodded. "I noticed. I'm government property too. My name is Long and I'm a deputy U.S. marshal. Was this your outfit?"

"You're goddamned right, and it still is! We chased those Sioux sons of bitches till we lost their trail. Now we aim to wire for help and wipe the whole damned tribe out!"

"They cut your wire before they hit you, in case you hadn't noticed," Longarm pointed out. "I can see I'll never get the horse I came out here for, but I'll be proud to wire the story in for you. I'd say you need a burial detail and a sharper look at the sign they left before you go accusing anyone, though."

The corporal dismounted as Longarm stepped over to the door jamb to tug the arrow loose. The corporal said, "I reckon I read sign as well as you do, mister. If that ain't a Sioux arrow, I'll eat it."

"Would you like to spread some mustard on it first, or do you eat your arrows raw? Don't you see those blue stripes there, near the feathers?"

The soldier grimaced. "Of course I do. There's one just like it in poor Sarge. Everybody knows the Sioux paint stripes on their damned arrows, mister."

"*Red* stripes," Longarm corrected him. "Blue paint is favored by Cheyenne and Blackfoot. Arapaho like green, for some fool reason."

"You mean Sarge and Peanuts were killed by maybe Cheyenne or Blackfoot?"

"If Peanuts is that colored gent out back, he was killed by Cheyenne. So was your sergeant here. There ain't any Blackfoot in these parts, for one thing, and they cut his hands off, for another."

The corporal looked down at the murdered NCO and swallowed before he said, "Jesus, they sure messed him up, didn't they? We were having breakfast when there was this knock at the door and he got up to—"

"I read what happened," Longarm cut in. "The Cheyenne are called the finger-cutters by the other Indians because they're the only tribe that mutilates a dead enemy's hands like that. They learned scalping from the Lakota, but their old-time religion teaches them to take hands or fingers, sometimes a whole arm."

"Jesus Christ, what would they want with Sarge's hands?"

"I don't know. What did King Henry want with Anne Boleyn's head? The point I'm making is that you boys are blaming the wrong Indians. You weren't hit by Sioux. The party was Cheynne, and while we're on the subject, how many of them were there and what did they look like?"

"What did they look like? Hell and damnation, they looked like *Indians!*"

One of the other troopers joined them to say, "I got a shot off at them as they drove off the ponies, mister. There was maybe a dozen of 'em and I couldn't see their faces 'cause they was going the other way. I don't know one tribe from another, but I did notice they all had on the same outfits."

"What sort of outfits?"

"*Funny* outfits. Some wore jeans and others rode bare-legged, but they all had on them same buckskin shirts, all painted with pictures. They looked like what you'd get if you skinned a tattooed man and wore his hide as a shirt. Ain't that a bitch?"

"It is. They were wearing medicine shirts."

The corporal asked, "What in hell's a medicine shirt?"

"Magic," Longarm replied. "Bulletproof. Those medicine signs are supposed to protect the wearer from any white man's bullet."

"That's the dumbest notion I ever heard! No painted picture can make a buckskin shirt bulletproof, damn it!"

Longarm pushed his Stetson back on his forehead, narrowing his eyes. "They might not agree with you. You boys didn't *shoot* anybody wearing a medicine shirt, did you?"

Chapter 3

Penny had been right. She was better in a bedroll on the prairie than in the hotel's creaky bed. But all good things must come to an end, and it only took them three days and two nights to get to the Pine Ridge Agency.

He'd hired them two livery mounts, which accounted for the slow ride. It had seemed sort of mean to make Penny walk, considering, so he'd put her mount on the expense account as a pack animal. It was no lie that he was packing nice baggage on the second pony. But he'd told her that once they arrived, she'd have to turn the critter in and rustle up another for herself. He meant to commandeer a decent mount from the Indian police at Pine Ridge, and there was just no way the taxpayers were going to give her one too. She'd promised she'd be good, and she had been, especially at night. It came as a pleasant surprise that she was a good campfire cook too.

They topped a rise and spied chimney smoke ahead. He and Penny had grown right friendly in the past few days, but she still had this stubborn cross-grained notion about reforming folks. So he said, "Yonder's the agency, and I really should be horsewhipped for bringing you this far."

"Pooh, you know I'd have come anyway, even if I'd had to walk."

"I know. You ain't listening, honey. You've got to understand that the Indians up ahead already have a legal guardian. So go easy on your reforming notions. I might get jealous if you reform any Indian the way you reformed me, and they'll likely kill us if you hit anybody with a rock."

41

"As long as I can satisfy myself that there's no fire-water being sold to the poor Indians, you have nothing to fear, darling."

"Well, I doubt you'll find them selling Old Crow at the trading post, but you still ain't listening, girl. The agent up ahead is already enforcing such temperance as the Sioux will stand for. I told you back in Hat Creek that the agent is the law out here. If he tells me to arrest you for disturbing the peace, I'll have to do it."

"Surely you jest, Custis. I thought you were the ranking lawman out here."

"You thought wrong, then. The agent is like a territorial governor. He can arrest *me*, if he's of a mind to. I'm here to investigate and to help. You're here because . . . because I can't think of a civilized way to keep you away from those poor Indians. But now that we're about to bust in on them, I want you to promise me you won't do or say a thing before you check with me. Do we have a deal?"

"Suppose I say no?"

"The Indian police have a jail up yonder."

"Custis, you wouldn't dare, after all we've meant to each other!"

Exasperated, he slapped his thigh. His horse huffed noisily and rolled an eye back toward him in annoyance. "That's the trouble with you emancipated gals. You say you aim to meet us on our own terms, then you go all dewy-eyed on us when we treat you like sensible human beings. The fact that we are lovers has nothing to do with the fact that it smarts like hell to get scalped."

"Darling, you know I have a mission."

"Hush. I have a mission too, and it's more important. I'm sorry as hell that some folks ruin their lives with strong drink, but it makes me even sorrier when I see folks killed in a war."

"But if we save the Indians from their evil habits, dear . . ."

"Jesus, don't you ever listen? You've never seen a war, girl. I have, more than once, and every one was ugly as hell. I threw up the first time I saw a burned-out wagon train. I threw up again at a burned-out Indian camp. A dead baby is one ugly sight, no matter what color its mama was. I'm a peace officer, and I aim to keep the peace in these parts. If you or anybody else starts trouble where we're headed, I am going to cloud up and rain all over you."

"What if some Indian gets fresh with me?"

"I'll chide him. It was your idea to tag along, so, when in Rome you're to act like a Roman. I don't expect any Indian to start up with you, as long as you behave."

"But if they do?"

"I'll have to study on it. I begged you not to come along. I know this sounds hard, Penny, but if it's a toss-up between you and an all-out Indian war, you lose."

The agency was a clutter of buildings too large to be called a ranch and too small to be called a town. The white agent lived in a painted frame house; the Indians who resided there lived in unpainted cabins. This was not because the Great White Father was too cheap to issue paint, but because the Indians thought that painting wood was silly. Paint flakes off, but if you leave the wood alone, nature weathers it to a nice silvery gray.

Longarm knew that what a white might have thought were signs of poverty were often simply indicative of a different way of living, while luxuries the taxpayers might begrudge the Indians were, to the Indians, the useless trappings of an alien culture. So he withheld judgment, and when Penny commented that the settlement "smelled funny," he said, "They think we smell funny too, and remember what I said about Rome."

They were greeted at the agency door by the agent's wife and a tall, pretty blonde in a white nurse's uniform. They seemed overjoyed to see another white gal, and gathered Penny in as Longarm tethered the ponies. They said the agent was across the way with some army man, looking for Sitting Bull. So Longarm left Penny to fill them in as he walked the way the women had pointed.

A lean, dark figure fell in at Longarm's side and said, "You will not find the old man in his cabin. Have you come to arrest him?"

Longarm glanced at the federal badge on the Indian's blue tunic, then up at his solemn dark eyes, shadowed under the wide brim of a round-topped black hat, and shook his head. "I'm not here to arrest anybody, if I can help it. They call me Longarm and I just want to have a talk with Tatanka Iyotake, if it's all right with you."

The Indian police officer looked almost pleased as he replied, "I have heard of you, Longarm. It is said you are a good person, and though your Lakota accent is terrible, you make an effort to call Tatanka Iyotake by his true name. Do you have any idea why other white men call him Sitting Bull?"

Longarm said, "No. But I don't think they mean it unkindly. You folks give your kids names too long for us to remember. It's easier to call a man Red Cloud than to say The Sun Shines Red Above the Mountain Mists. But if you'll give me your handle, I'll do my best with it."

The Indian smiled and said, "Call me Simon Peter. That is the name the Black Robes gave me."

"Oh, are you a Catholic, Simon Peter?"

"No, but the Black Robes think I am. I enjoyed coloring the books at the Black Robes' mission, and no white man can pronounce my real name. I am a Hunkpapa and I counted coup at the Greasy Grass."

"I wasn't there, but we call it Little Big Horn."

"I know. It was good fight by any name. I don't fight with you people anymore. After we gave up, Tatanka Iyotake said we had to learn to get along with you. Do you think we are going to have another war?"

"I hope not. Are you a Ghost Dancer, Simon Peter?"

The Indian shook his head emphatically. "No. Tatanka Iyotake says they are crazy. I don't think the other white men believe this. They keep saying the old man is a troublemaker."

They'd almost reached the Indian cabins now, and Longarm saw an army officer and a civilian coming their way from a doorway. He asked the Indian, "Is that why your medicine man lit out, Simon Peter?"

"No. He is hiding from a crazy white lady."

Before he could elaborate, they were joined by the other whites. Longarm introduced himself to the agent, who said, "This here is Captain Kehoe of the Seventh Cav."

Longarm was too polite to say he didn't believe in ghosts, but Kehoe was used to odd looks and added quickly, "Not *that* Captain Kehoe, damn it. Custer's troop commander was a cousin of mine."

Longarm nodded and said, "I heard the Seventh was a family outfit."

The officer shot a hard look at the Indian next to Longarm as he said grimly, "You heard right. I lost a brother at Little Big Horn too. And now that sly old rascal, Sitting Bull, is out somewhere brewing up more devilment."

Longarm said, "My fellow officer here said something about him having woman-trouble."

Simon Peter nodded and said, "That is true. Some crazy white woman is trying to marry him. Tatanka Iyotake is hiding from her."

The agent laughed and said, "Oh, I know about that. A few years ago the Sioux captured a schoolteacher. Sitting Bull adopted her and let her go after a while. She's been a real pain to the agency ever since."

"She writes letters to the old man," Simon Peter explained. "When she heard about more trouble out here, she wrote and said she was coming out to protect Tatanka Iyotake. She said she would never forget how he protected her, and now she wants to be his wife. But he says he doesn't want any more wives."

Longarm frowned and asked, "Are you sure this white lady is proposing marriage, Simon Peter?"

"I don't know what she wants. She never writes letters to *me*. But she told Tatanka Iyotake that she loves him and won't let anyone hurt him. She said she would do anything he wanted her to do. Doesn't that sound like a woman who is serious about a man?"

"Let's go over to the house," the agent said. "The gal they're talking about is one of them do-gooders. When the Sioux treated her decent and let her go that time, she became a convert to the cause of the Noble Savage. Here I am, trying to make farmers out of them, and she keeps writing to the newspapers that we're abusing the hell out of her friends." He turned to Simon Peter and asked, "Do you feel abused, Pete?"

The Indian said, "Yes, but I think you mean well. I liked it better when we got to fight the Crow and hunt the buffalo, but I don't see what good a white wife will do Tatanka Iyotake. He would be much happier if all of you would leave him alone."

The agent sighed and said, "I'll go along with that. Buffalo Bill keeps pestering him to join a Wild West show, too. The poor old gent must be as confused as hell."

"I wish I shared your sentiments, sir," Kehoe said. "But I never rode out here to save Sitting Bull from a shotgun marriage. I still want to talk to him about that attack on our post near Hat Creek the other day."

Longarm's eyebrows rose in surprise. "Didn't those boys tell you they were jumped by Cheyenne, Captain?"

"Cheyenne? Why would Cheyenne attack us? These Sioux have been behind every rising since Little Crow rose during the Civil War!"

Longarm explained that he'd been on the scene at the remount station and added, "I aim to ask the Cheyenne why they did it, but the men who hit your post weren't Sioux. I told your soldiers that at the time. Do you mean to say they put it on the wire as a Sioux attack?"

Kehoe said uncertainly, "Look, an Indian is an Indian, damn it."

"Yeah, and I remember what Phil Sheridan said about *good* Indians, too. But fair is fair, and it's not like there's a shortage of Indians in these parts. Do you remember Sand Creek?"

Kehoe snorted derisively. "The regular army had

nothing to do with that misunderstanding at Sand Creek. Those idiots were Colorado Militia."

"That's true, to the everlasting credit of the army. But those Indians murdered at Sand Creek for what another band had done are still dead, and their kinfolks are still sore as hell about it. The Sand Creek band were Cheyenne, too. It ain't impossible that the attack the other morning was a returned compliment. I'd study some before I smoked up any more innocent bystanders."

Kehoe's face was starting to turn red. "I'd hardly call Sitting Bull an innocent bystander, damn it!"

"I don't care what you call him. But at the moment he's a ward of the U.S. Government, and as such, he's under my protection until I say different."

Kehoe stopped and swung around in his tracks, dumbfounded. He stared at Longarm and gasped, "Are you threatening me, Deputy?"

"Nope. Just telling you where we stand. I've got enough on my plate right now, so until some Sioux really rise, I want you to stay the hell away from them."

"You maniac! I happen to command a whole troop of cavalry!"

"You command 'em all you want, Captain. But keep them away from here until I see some need for a display of force. I promise I'll whistle for you if I want you."

"And if I decide to ride in, banners flying and the band piping 'Garry Owen'?"

"I'll arrest you for disturbing the peace."

Kehoe laughed. "A whole cavalry troop, Deputy?"

Longarm smiled back, but his eyes gleamed like blue gunmetal. "If I have to."

"You damned fool. I've a good mind to take you up on that."

"Do what you're of a mind to," Longarm told him. "I'll likely go down against a whole troop, but I swear to God I'll take you with me."

Captain Kehoe rode off to wherever pissed-off cavalry officers go, and the agent led Longarm inside, where they found the three women having a hen party in the kitchen. Longarm already knew the agent's name was Gatewood and that he was a Hayes appointee. The latter was both good and bad. President Hayes had replaced most of Grant's corrupt "Indian Ring" with honest men, but few had ever seen an Indian that wasn't standing in front of a cigar store before he got the job.

It took no effort to remember that the motherly-looking woman serving tea and muffins was Mrs. Gatewood, and Longarm already knew Penny Ascot, so he only had to remember the nurse's name. It was Olga Swensen and she hailed from Wisconsin. He'd have known she was a Swede anyway. Her bound-up hair was the color of a new manila saddle rope and her eyes were cornflower blue. She'd picked up a tan from out-door living, and had cheekbones that would have passed her for a right pretty Squaw if her eyes and hair had been darker. She shook hands like a man when Long-arm was introduced to her, then she asked him, "Have you been vaccinated yet?"

He said, "Yes, ma'am. They did it in the army."

"You'd better let me do it again," she told him. "The serum we have now is better."

"Another time, maybe. Right now I have to let my boss know I'm still alive." He smiled crookedly. It was peculiar, he reflected; he'd been shot and stabbed and hit plenty and painfully in his time, but he purely *hated* needles.

As Gatewood led him out of the kitchen, Olga called after them, "The Mandans were wiped out by smallpox not long ago, you know!"

Out in the hall, Gatewood sighed and said, "She made me and the missus roll up *our* sleeves, too. Telegraph shack's just down yonder."

They entered the well-appointed combination post office and telegraph shack attached to the main house, and Longarm said he'd send. As he sat on the bentwood chair in front of the key, Gatewood reached over him and threw some switches, saying, "I'm patching you in to Western Union. We have direct lines to the army and the Interior Department in Washington, and a private net to the various police posts on the reservation. I hope you'll make your message sort of short and sweet. We have to pay Western Union."

Longarm told the agent he'd reverse the charges, then he got on the line, addressed a collect wire to Billy Vail in Denver, and sent: ARRIVED STOP INVESTIGATING STOP LONG. "Well," he said as he stood up, "that ought to hold him."

Gatewood chuckled. "You were a mite more long-winded when you chased poor Kehoe off the reservation just now."

"Well, my boss knows me, Kehoe doesn't. So I had to explain some. You didn't *want* them parading about out here, did you?"

"Lord, no! He was making me nervous even before I learned from you that they were chasing the wrong Indians. As usual. Let's go back and join the ladies, shall we?"

"Uh, I'd rather we didn't for a spell. I may have sounded like I knew what I was talking about outside, but I'd like to get a better handle on the situation here, and it's hard to carry on a serious conversation in front of women and teapots. Can we set somewhere else and powwow some?"

Gatewood nodded and led him out to the front porch, where they sat on the steps and lit up two of Longarm's cheroots. Gatewood started explaining the layout of the county-sized reservation and Longarm cut in, "I've had time to study my survey map. Tell me more about the town sites I see on it."

"We've got seven trading post and police station layouts spread across the reservation. The government built cabins around each town site, but of course the Indians have their own notions and seldom stay in the cabins unless it's cold as hell. They'll send their kids to school as long as we push them, but as soon as we ease up . . ."

"I spotted some tipis in a draw as we rode in. Are all your reservation police Sioux?"

"Yes. Acting under my orders, of course."

"What if their old chiefs gave them different orders?"

"I frankly don't know. It hasn't happened yet."

Longarm blew a thoughtful smoke ring as he digested this. Then he said, "Tell me what you know about the Ghost Dancers you reported."

Gatewood replied soberly, "Ghost is a good name for whatever in hell is going on. You see, some of the Indians are sort of sullen, and even when they come in for their rations they pretend they don't speak English. Others tend to suck up to us, doubtless hoping to get in good with the Great White Father."

"I went to grammar school. It's the teacher's pets who told you Wovoka's missionaries are out there in the hidden draws, right?"

"Of course. But I didn't get hysterical about idle rumors. The white sutlers at the trading posts have reported drumbeats and mysterious glows at night. Some of the more notorious troublemakers have been acting cockier than usual. A couple of Sioux I suppose you could call teacher's pets are missing. And you saw yourself that Indians hit an army post the other day."

"They were Cheyenne and it was a long ride from here. What I'm most interested in is your Indian police. What do *they* say is going on?"

Gatewood waved a hand in a gesture of dismissal. "They say it's kid stuff. Simon Peter tells me none of the tribal elders have endorsed Wovoka's Ghost Dance movement yet."

"Yet?"

"Yes. As you may have noticed, Simon Peter is a bright and somewhat sardonic type. He says we whites are encouraging the Ghost Dance by the way we react to it. I'm not sure I understand."

"I do," Longarm said. "Most Indians set a lot of store by a calm disposition. A grizzly doesn't get excited when a cub growls at him. Back in the Shining Times, the old chiefs sat and smoked sort of silent while the young braves pranced about yelling all sorts of crazy advice. Then the chiefs told the tribe what to do and they generally did it. The way a sub-chief got a following was to get the old chiefs to pay attention to him."

50

"Hmm, do you mean that if we just ignore the Ghost Dance, it will go away?"

Longarm tugged pensively at a corner of his mustache. "I don't know. That's what I'm here to find out. It might be too late. You see, Wovoka is a Paiute—what we call a Digger Indian. Up until damned recently, no horse-Indian would have listened if a Paiute only wanted to give him the right time. But we've taken their horses away some, and kicked a lot of pride out of every tribe. The way it works in a regular jail, two gents who might never have spoken to one another on the outside tend to get together as they plan a break."

Gatewood's sallow face reflected perplexity. "But Simon Peter says none of the old chiefs like Sitting Bull are paying any attention to the Ghost Dance. He says the only Sioux he's heard talking about it are just kids."

"He might be fibbing," Longarm suggested, "or he might be telling the truth. They say the Sioux who counted coup on Custer's body was thirteen years old at the time. You see, while Crazy Horse was mounting his main charge along that ridge above the Little Big Horn, a mess of ragtag kids from the village tore up the slope on foot, anxious to show their mamas they were old enough to go a-courting or something. Later, Crazy Horse allowed they'd been a big help to him. His mounted charge just rolled up the trooper's skirmish line like a rug while they were busy aiming down the slope at what must have seemed like an infantry attack to them."

Longarm stopped as he caught himself getting wound up on the subject, and added simply, "Kids are the ones you have to worry about in a war. They die like flies, but they can take you with 'em, fighting foolish."

Gatewood grimaced knowingly. "I was with the First Ohio in the war. What are we to do, Longarm?"

"*We* ain't going to do anything. Your best bet is to just go on running things as usual while I have a look around. If I can catch Paiute missionaries stirring up trouble, I'll just arrest 'em for trespassing, since they don't belong on this reservation."

"I understand you ran some Ghost Dancers off the Blackfoot reserve a while ago."

Longarm sighed deeply. It had been nasty business, and the memory didn't warm him. "That's the trouble with gossip. A man drops a can of peaches and by the time they hear about it on the other side of town it's gotten to be a wagonload of watermelons. A Ghost Dancer did get killed up there while I was investigating something else. I didn't kill him and I didn't run him off. I didn't take his notions all that seriously at the time."

"What about *this* time?" Gatewood asked.

"I still might not think it was more than kid games, if I hadn't seen some dead men with my own two eyes. Those Cheyenne *were* wearing medicine shirts and the Cheyenne did ride with the Sioux in the Shining Times. But so far, there's no evidence that the Sioux are getting ready for a rematch, and I hope to keep it that way."

Longarm saw that his views were only upsetting an already worried Gatewood, and that the agent couldn't tell him a thing he didn't already know. So he stubbed out his smoke and suggested they join the ladies now.

They went back to the kitchen, where they saw that the women were still sipping tea. Longarm had never figured out how gals did that. He knew no man could imbibe that much liquid without having to piss. Women likely had stronger kidneys. He wondered why thinking of that blonde nurse's kidneys made his pants feel itchy. It wasn't like he was hard up, In fact, Penny was sitting right there smiling at him. She said, "Olga says her Indians haven't been drinking, but that I can help her vaccinate them."

Longarm sat down at the table beside her and said, "That sounds like fun."

As Mrs. Gatewood poured him some tea, the nurse across the table said, "What I really need is a roping team. I've vaccinated some of the tamer ones here at the agency, but the rest run away when they see my uniform. I don't think they understand that I'm only trying to help them."

"They can be sort of cross-grained about us offering

52

to help 'em," Longarm agreed. "The way the Great White Father diddled them out of the Black Hills might have something to do with it. We told them *that* was for their own good too."

"I'm not up on Indian history," Olga said, "but I do know smallpox has killed more Indians than all the fighting since the Pilgrims arrived. The Mandans were completely wiped out by the plague in the late thirties."

Longarm nodded again and said, "Don't forget the cholera. The reason the forty-niners had so much trouble crossing the plains was that the medicine men said the wagons brought the cholera with them."

Olga nodded emphatically. "The medicine men were right. More whites as well as Indians were killed by disease than in all those battles too. But we know how to prevent cholera and smallpox now. If only I could get some cooperation from these savages!"

Longarm didn't comment on her attitude. He knew the Seventh Cav thought they were savages too, even though Olga's shots figured to cause less heartbreak. He caught himself about to offer some suggestions on getting along with Indians, but it wasn't his chore. He sipped his tea and looked at the calendar on the wall above Olga's blonde head instead of suggesting that she'd do better if she shucked that white uniform. He could have told her Indians were leery of a medicine color like white. It made *him* feel funny too, when he thought of her peeling those white duds off that big hourglass shape of hers.

Penny was saying something, and he swung around to smile at her fit to bust. Penny was as pretty as a picture and he knew he deserved to be tarred and feathered for having such a fickle, dirty mind. He was looking forward to another private session with the little temperance gal, as soon as he could figure how to get her alone without it looking indecent. So what in thunder did it matter what Olga looked like with her clothes off? He surely couldn't get the *two* of them in his bedroll, could he?

This train of thought was going to start raising clouds

of steam pretty soon, so he excused himself and rose to go out for a look around.

Simon Peter called a halt as the two of them topped a grassy rise above a cottonwood-lined creek to the northeast. The Indian police officer pointed with his narrow chin at the blue haze of smoke above the trees and said, "You stay here. I will ride in and see if the old ones want to talk to you."

"Do you think Tatanka Iyotake is camped down there?"

"I don't know. It is the camp of Tipisota's band. Tipisota and Tatanka Iyotake are name-brothers. They hung together on the Sun Dance pole in the Shining Times. If anyone knows where the man you call Sitting Bull might be . . ."

"Go ahead. I'll stay up here polite while they look me over."

Simon Peter's long pigtails bobbed beneath his round-topped hat as he rode down the slope to vanish into the trees. Longarm knew he'd have time for a smoke, so he dismounted and lit up a cheroot as he let his spotted Indian pony graze. It was a clear, crisp day and he felt sort of wistful as he swept his eyes around the empty horizon. It was ideal hunting weather, and when he'd first come out here after the War, those tawny hills had been dotted with buffalo. Of course, even then, you didn't see buffalo every day on every rise. So the land hadn't changed that much. The only difference was that, these days, you knew you *wouldn't* see buffalo, no matter how long you waited.

An arrow thudded into the sod near Longarm's right boot. He saw that it was a kid's quail arrow, so he didn't turn around. He kept staring down at the trees as he held the reins and puffed slowly at his cheroot. After a time, a high-pitched voice called out, "How do you make circles with your smoke like that?" and Longarm turned around. It represented no loss of dignity to notice someone who spoke English to you.

A raggedy-trousered Indian kid of about ten was standing there with a toy bow. Longarm blew another smoke ring and said, "It just takes practice. I don't know why your elders don't blow smoke rings. It ain't all that hard. I reckon they just never thought about it."

The boy said, "My white name is Joseph. I am the grandson of Tipisota. In the Shining Times he killed many of you Americans. Is that why you are scouting his camp?"

Longarm knew the Lakota called U.S. soldiers "Americans," so he told the kid, "I'm not an American, I'm a civilian. I'm waiting here to see if your grandfather wants to talk with me. I rode out with Simon Peter. Do you know him?"

"Simon Peter is one of my uncles, but he has two hearts. He works for the Great White Father. My mother says she is ashamed of him. But he has never been cruel to me. I think I have two hearts for him, too."

Longarm didn't pursue the matter, but made a mental note that the others found the Indian police officer too loyal to the agency for their taste. It meant Simon Peter was likely telling the truth, most times. But it meant his fellow Hunkpapa lied to him a lot, too.

Longarm spotted the Indian they'd just been talking about waving to him from the trees, so he led his borrowed pinto down the slope as young Joseph tagged along after retrieving his toy arrow.

As they joined Simon Peter, the policeman told Longarm, "The old man is not here, but Tipisota and the other elders are willing to smoke with you. I think they must be very worried about something."

Longarm followed Simon Peter through the cottonwoods to a circle of lodges set up in a clearing by the creek. Simon Peter said something to Joseph in their own high-pitched lingo, and the boy took the reins of Longarm's mount as the tall lawman was led to a plain white canvas-covered lodge. They ducked inside. It was dark, and the haze of smoke made it even harder to see. The smoke hurt Longarm's eyes. He knew Indians suffered in old age from more eye trouble than white people did, but they said smoke kept bugs and evil spirits away, so what the hell.

Longarm hunkered down in the space they'd made for him, and was handed a calumet to smoke as Simon Peter introduced him in Lakota. As Longarm's eyes adjusted, he saw that there were a half-dozen old Indians in there with him.

The one in the position of honor, facing the entrance, raised a weary hand and said, "We will speak English. We know who Longarm is. He knows that we know. Longarm is one of the few Wasichus who can tell a Cheyenne from a Lakota."

Longarm passed the pipe as he had a better look at Tipisota. The old Hunkpapa's face was wrinkled like a dried brown apple, and he was wearing a white man's wool coat, held across his chest with a safety pin. There were no feathers in Tipisota's iron-gray hair. That gave Longarm an opening and he said, "Tipisota is entitled to a full bonnet of coup feathers, but he does not need them among real men. All men know of Tipisota's deeds in the Shining Times."

Tipisota nodded modestly. "If Wasichus wore coup feathers, Longarm's would drag on the earth behind him as he walked. We have heard about the dishonest Indian agent you arrested for cheating the Utes. In the Shining Times the Utes were our favorite enemies. When evil white men were killing Blackfoot on another reservation, Longarm went after them too."

Another Indian said something in their own tongue. It didn't sound as friendly. Tipisota sighed and said, "My brother wants to know if it is true you fought us too, once."

Longarm nodded gravely. "I have killed Lakota. I have killed Cheyenne. I have killed Shoshone and Nadene too. I do not apologize. I killed them in good fights."

"I believe you. Would you fight us, if we rose again?"

"Yes. My brother knows I work for the Great White Father. I have come here to find out if we are going to have another war. What are my brother's words?"

Tipisota's steady gaze did not waver, but his expression grew more concerned. "Hear me. We are not bad people. We did not want to fight you the last time.

We had given you all our lands but the Paha Sapa—what you call the Black Hills—and the Great White Father said the Paha Sapa was to be ours forever. Our God, Wakan Tonka, used to speak to us in words of thunder among the peaks of the Paha Sapa, and the Great White Father said he understood this. He said the Paha Sapa would be ours forever. But then men found the yellow iron in the Paha Sapa, and when we tried to drive them away, the Americans came to kill us. We did not wish to fight."

Longarm knew that, despite the protestations, the old man was still on his brag. So he nodded and said, "For men who did not wish to fight, you did all right on the Rosebud and the Little Big Horn."

Tipisota nodded, pleased again by the compliment, but his eyes were moist as he said, "Those were good fights. But even then, we knew we had lost. Many of our people were frightened when they saw what we had done. How were we to know the Custer soldiers were going to let themselves be butchered like rabbits? It had never happened before! We ran up into Canada, but the Red Coats of the Great White Mother said we couldn't stay there. The Great White Mother spoke for us with the Great White Father and he said he would not punish us if we came to this place and obeyed him. So once again we made marks on papers and agreed to all the terms. My brother Longarm knows this to be true."

Longarm nodded gravely and took a drag on the calumet as it came his way again. He let out the smoke and said, "My heart soars to see that my brothers have kept the peace."

"We want to," said Tipisota, "but again the Great White Father is breaking his words. Can't he read? *I* can read the words they made us agree to on those papers. Why does the Great White Father ignore them?"

Longarm said, "My brother knows that my people choose new leaders every few years, true?"

"Yes. It is what you call demo-something. You do not let *us* vote for a new Great White Father, though."

"Someday we may. Meantime, the men we call politicians do not feel bound by the words other politicians wrote long ago on a paper. Some of my people don't like this either, but that's the way it is. Just what is it that you're complaining about? Has the Indian agent been cheating you?"

Tipisota shook his head. "No. Gatewood is a good person and if we have to take the warpath we will try to spare him. Last winter, when his wife learned that one of our women had used up her ration and was sick, she took the woman and her children in the big house and treated them like her children. She cried when one of the babies died. We will let her and her husband live, if we can."

Longarm nodded and said, "I think Gatewood means well too. But who are you mad at, the soldiers?"

"No. The Americans are like you. They do what they are told. They would like to have a war with us because they are young. Our young men, too, wish another war. They do not remember the last one. They have been raised on proud legends, told by old men who should know better."

"Just what is it that troubles my brothers, then?" Longarm asked.

Tipisota sighed. "The words on the paper keep changing. First they say we are to get one ration, then they tell us we are to get another ration. They say one time that we are free to pray to our old gods. Then they build churches and schools and give our children Christian names!"

"Aren't you free to use your own Indian names?"

"They say we are. Have you ever tried to sign for your allotment with a name the white man does not have on record? Now a crazy white woman has come to stick pins in our children's arms. Was there anything about *that* in the peace treaty?"

"Maybe not, but don't you see that some of these changes are meant to help your people?"

"There was nothing in the words on paper about changes! Why do your people want to keep changing things all the time? Isn't the world confusing enough if you leave it alone? Hear me! We have changed

58

enough! Once we ruled the plains from the Great Sweet Waters to the Shining Mountains and there was no need for a man to keep learning new things. Each season was much like the one before, and once a young man learned how everything worked he could grow old with dignity. Do you know, my own granddaughter laughed at me the other day because they'd taught her some crazy thing at the mission school about the world being round, like a ball? When I told her that the Paha Sapa was the hub of a wheel-shaped world, she laughed at me and said I was an ignorant person! My own grand-daughter! What are they teaching our children in those schools?"

Longarm didn't answer. The other old Indians had been sitting quietly, but he knew Tipisota wouldn't be speaking straight English if nobody else in the lodge did, and there were few Indians who got to be very old if they didn't know such English phrases as "Drop that gun," or "Come out with your hands up." So he wasn't surprised when a moon-faced old gent suddenly blurted out, "What is a Wild West Show?"

Longarm managed to keep a straight face, but it wasn't easy. He said, "Back in the East there are people like me who have never seen people like you. They pay money to sit and watch mock battles between cowboys and Indians."

"But cowboys seldom fight Indians. First the Americans drive all the buffalo and Indians away, and then the cowboys come with their cattle to graze the empty land. Don't they know this, back East?"

"No. They think white men out here dress in fringed buckskin and woolly chaps and ride around shooting at rubber balloons on strings. But why should this worry you? Nobody's trying to make you watch a Wild West show, is he?"

Tipisota said, "They have not invited us to watch. They want some of us to join them. A white man named Cody is after Tatanka Iyotake to sign another paper he calls a contract. He says he wants to take Tatanka Iyotake to a place called London and introduce him to the Great White Mother, Victoria."

"Do you reckon he's going?"

"I don't think so. I think he is frightened. The last time we spoke, he said he was riding out alone to fast and seek a vision. He doesn't understand why the white people can't leave him alone! They keep calling him a war chief, which he never was, and keep after him to speak for his people."

"Doesn't Tatanka Iyotake speak for his people? The Hunkpapa, at least?"

"Of course not. That's another thing about you people that we can't understand. You get one old man drunk and make him sign a paper he can't read, and then you say the whole nation is bound by his word. Does that make any sense?"

Longarm shifted his weight awkwardly. "I don't know much about treaties. I'll allow both sides have broken some in the past, but let's stick to the here and now."

Tipisota nodded. "Good. Go tell the Great White Father to leave us alone. That is all we want. He can have the rest of the country. He can even keep the Paha Sapa, even though he never paid us the money he promised us for it. But hear me, we will stand for no more changes!"

The moon-faced one across the tent said something in Lakota, and when there was a general nod of agreement Tipisota added, "We won't mind if they change our allotments for the better. Many children have been born since we agreed on how much each family should get. We still get the same allowances. Sometimes they send us more than one monthly amount and sometimes they send nothing and tell us we were supposed to save the extra food and spending money. Our women do not understand this. In the Shining Times, when the hunting was good, we ate fat cow. When the hunting was bad, we did without. Now, when they have to do without, our women yell at us. They tell us to get off our lazy rumps and go get more food and money. When we say we don't know where to get more food and money they say scornful things about our manhood."

Tipisota took the calumet from the man next to him, puffed it quickly, and passed it on before he said,

"We are worried about the young people drinking too much, too. The Great White Father passed a law against his red children buying firewater, and we elders agreed this was a good idea. But when white men sell our young people firewater, nobody kills them. Some people say the Great White Father is paid to look the other way by the men who make firewater. What does my brother Longarm say to this?"

It was a ticklish question. Longarm tended to believe that such scoundrels who made a profit from turning Indians into alcoholics should be shot at the very least. On the other hand, he knew that the Indians considered him—correctly—a servant of the Great White Father, no matter what his private opinion might be. If he showed any lack of respect, these men would not trust him.

After a moment, he said, "Hear me. The Great White Father before this one was a good person, but he was not wise and he had bad men for friends. They were called the Indian Ring. They are not in power now, so isn't it true that my brothers no longer get condemned beef or Confederate money they can't spend at the trading post?"

"We have not been cheated like that recently," Tipisota admitted. "But they say you are getting ready to choose a new Great White Father. Is this true?"

"Yes, it's an election year."

"Then how are we to know we won't get another bad man for our Great White Father? What if the new people you elect decide to cheat us again?" There were tears in the old man's eyes now. "Can't you see how this makes us look to our women and the young people? In the Shining Times, when we told them something, it was so!"

Longarm nodded sadly. "Sometimes I see bad things that I'm helpless to do anything about, and it makes me want to cry tears of blood. Sometimes I feel that *my* world is changing too fast, too. But the Shining Times are over. We live in times when even a strong man has to act like Brother Coyote instead of Real Bear. Do you remember how the trickster Coyote always got his way without getting hurt?"

Tipisota perked up and replied, "I didn't know white men knew the stories of Brother Coyote."

Longarm said, "He is in our stories too, by other names. You see, our world has been complicated longer than yours. I will tell the Great White Father about your complaints. I will tell him you are worried about the sudden shifts in his Indian policy. But you will have to learn to live with those changes nobody can do anything about. You have many friends among my people, but you have many enemies too. You are afraid of our strange ways, but many of my people are afraid of your ways too."

Tipisota frowned, confused. "What are you talking about? Our ways are not hard to understand. We have always followed the same path. *We* are not the ones who keep changing the rules!"

It was the opening Longarm had been groping for. He took the calumet and inhaled deeply before he let the smoke trickle out and said, "Hear me. In the Shining Times there was the Lakota Confederacy, and the Americans knew who they were having good fights with. There were you Hunkpapa, and Teton, Oglala, and others we called Sioux. There were your Cheyenne and Arapaho allies. Sometimes the Blackfoot joined you and sometimes they fought us alone when the rest of you decided on a truce for a while. Is this not the truth?"

Tipisota smiled wistfully. "Yes, those were good times."

"The Americans enjoyed them too," Longarm said. "But now it is *you*, my red brothers, who have changed the rules."

There was a unanimous gasp of indignation, and Tipisota snapped, "That is a terrible thing to say! Explain yourself!"

Longarm said, "We used to fight with all the cards on the table. Our young men wore blue and your young men wore the paint of honorable enemies we knew about. Now we hear that men who never stood against us like the brave Lakota in the Shining Times are talking of another war. But they do it like women, gossiping in the dark. A man from a tribe that never fought bravely against anyone is stirring up your young men with foolish talk."

"You speak of Wovoka."

"I speak of a mission Indian who never heard a shot fired in anger. I speak of a Paiute telling High Plains warriors what to do. You talk to me about changes? Is there anything in your old traditions about a Digger Indian leading Dog Soldiers or Crooked Lances into battle? Has Wovoka purified himself of fear on the Sun Dance pole?"

Tipisota stared sullenly down and muttered, "The Sun Dance has been forbidden by the Great White Father."

Longarm nodded sympathetically. "I know, but is there an old warrior here who has no scars on his chest? How many ponies has Wovoka tamed? How many coup feathers does he wear? How did a despised enemy come to speak for the great Lakota?"

Tipisota roared, "Hear me! I am getting very cross with you! Wovoka is not our leader. We think he is crazy too. Don't you give us credit for any sense at all?"

The moon-faced man across the tent began to sob softly to himself as he drew a knife from the folds of his robe and slowly cut a long red gash on his own forearm, for reasons Longarm figured only another Indian might understand. He ignored the self-mutilation of the old sage and said, "My heart soars to hear my brother's words. But if you elders are not listening to Wovoka's message, who is?"

Tipisota looked uncomfortable as he answered, "Nobody important. Wovoka's tales of spirits helping us are for children's ears. Some of our young men don't remember how the Americans shoot. They have nothing to do but drink and brood, these days. They scorn our advice because, they say, we lost all our fights. They say maybe Wovoka's medicine is stronger than ours."

"So you *do* have Ghost Dancers on this reservation?"

"A few. Not many. Those people who attacked the

63

Americans were Cheyenne, like you told the Americans."

"Do you know which band they were from?"

"The Cheyenne are our friends. None of the Cheyenne elders were in on it. You must forgive the young men who did it. They were drunk and they wanted to try out the medicine shirts they'd bought."

"I thought so. Is Wovoka himself on the reservation now?"

"No. He is hiding over in the Great Basin. He says the spirits have revealed that there is a warrant out for his arrest. The Ghost Dance leader who told those Cheyenne to do bad things is named Kamono and he lives in a medicine wagon as he travels from camp to camp. We can't tell you where he is right now."

"You can't, or you won't?" Longarm asked.

Simon Peter, who had been sitting quietly by the entrance all this time, said, "They can't, Longarm. The reservation police have been looking for that wagon too. Kamono has strong medicine. People say it is a big wagon, painted red, but it must be able to fly. Many times we have tried to cut the traveling Ghost Dancer off when we got word he was on the reservation. We have lost his sign on open prairie. It is very annoying."

Longarm was a bit taken aback by this news. "How come you never reported that to Gatewood, Simon Peter?"

"Does a man brag when he returns empty-handed from a hunt? Besides, I don't like to make a Paiute look good. He's already telling everyone how easy it is to fool you white men. If word gets around that not even an Indian can track him in a big red wagon . . ."

"I follow your drift. I see what the situation is, now. You and the other men of authority are against his new notions, but you can't stop him from stirring up the kids. How long do you think we have?"

Simon Peter glanced at his senior, Tipisota. The old chief sighed and said, almost in a whisper, "Not long. Each year there are fewer of us old men, and more young men come of age who do not remember the

64

Shining Times. In ten years even the tribal elders will be men who were at most only warriors when we followed the old ways. Already, men who were only children when we fought at the Greasy Grass are boasting that they were war chiefs."

"Are we going to have peace this summer?"

"This summer? I think so. The Ghost Dancers will have to count coup on more easy wins, like the one at the remount station, before anyone important will follow them."

Longarm had to remind himself that his hosts didn't consider killing two men a war, and that running off a remuda of army horses was their idea of youthful highjinks. He nodded gravely and said, "I will tell the Great White Father to keep his own young men under control. But if any more white people are killed I won't be able to stop what you all know will happen."

"I know," Tipisota replied. "The Americans will swoop down on us cursing and saying bad things. They will knock down lodgepoles as they search for weapons and firewater. Our women and dogs will make a lot of noise and someone on one side or the other will get excited and start shooting. Then we will have a war whether we want one or not."

"We all know about Washita and Sand Creek. Will you elders help me put a stop to the Ghost Dance movement before it gets out of hand?"

Tipisota smiled thinly. "We have been trying since before you got here. But our feathers have wilted, our limbs have grown weak, and nobody listens to our words anymore."

Chapter 4

As he rode back toward the agency with Simon Peter, Longarm was too polite to voice his suspicions that the moon-faced old man in the lodge back there had been Sitting Bull. He knew he could be wrong and that Tatanka Iyotake really might be out communing with his spirits like they said. On the other hand, the white race didn't have a monopoly on fibbing, and the old medicine man might have had his own good reasons for not wanting to make himself known to a lawman. More than one public figure who considered himself an expert on Indian affairs had suggested in print that it might be a good idea to lock Sitting Bull up, and the old man could read.

Longarm noticed that they were being trailed, but he didn't comment on that either. He knew his Indian companion had spotted that fool kid, Joseph, scouting them on his bitty buckskin pony. Longarm had been a kid once, so he understood the game the boy was playing. He just hoped Joseph would outgrow it before some white man who took mounted Indians more seriously blew Joseph off his pony to make a good Indian out of him.

If Simon Peter had lied about where Sitting Bull was, he might just be fibbing about that big red wagon. It sounded too much like Heap Big Medicine to be true. In his scouting days, Longarm had been trailed by Sioux. He'd had one hell of a time hiding his own ass from them. He doubted like hell that he'd have been able to lose them while driving a big red wagon. He'd said mean things about Digger Indians back there because it was his job to drive a wedge between

Wovoka and others, but he knew Paiutes were better than most at covering their tracks.

He asked Simon Peter, "Have you ever seen this big red medicine wagon?" "No," the Indian replied. "I would have arrested Kamono for trespassing if I had."

"Then you don't know for a fact that he's traipsing about in a big red wagon."

Simon Peter snorted and asked, "Do you think my people are color-blind, too? Some white doctor wrote that we are color-blind because we have one word in our language for blue and black. But we can see as good as anyone. Red is a color everyone knows. When my people say they saw a red wagon, they didn't mean pink or purple, damn it."

"Now don't get your bowels in an uproar, old son. I don't think the folks who told you they saw a red wagon are color-blind. But it's just possible they were fibbing."

"Why should my people lie to me?"

"*My* people lie to *me*, all the time. It goes with the job when a gent wears a badge. This Ghost Dance missionary hasn't been putting on his medicine show for his *enemies*, you know. So ain't it just possible that his friends would want to throw you off with a false description?" Simon Peter rode in silent thought as Longarm continued, "When a lawman is faced with two possible answers, it's best go with the one that's least impossible. What we've got here is either a big red wagon that can vanish in a puff of smoke, or some folks bullshitting the law, which has been known to happen. I've never seen a man make a big red wagon vanish in thin air, have you?"

"We followed its tracks a couple of times," Simon Peter pointed out.

"Sure you did. Red wagons make tracks a heap different from just any old wagon, don't they? How many plain old farm wagons would you say there are on this reservation, Simon Peter?"

"Many. I have never counted all of them."

"There you go. You've got roads between the town

67

sites and a mess of wagons moving up and down to make deliveries and carry folks to the trading post and such. So you and your boys follow the mystery tracks until they get lost in others and then you circle out, scouting for a bright red dot on the horizon, right?"

"True. But we never see it. Hear me, I know I ride faster than anyone can drive a wagon. Several times we have posted men along the reservation line as soon as we heard the Ghost Dancer was back. Then we have made a sweep. We have never caught him. The young men laugh at us because of this. It is very annoying."

"You don't have the manpower to post a guard every few yards around your borders. What do you do, set a scout up on every rise?"

"Of course. You can see how open the country is. A man on a rise can see for miles. There are no caves or anything like that, and we have searched the few forested areas with care." He rode in exasperated silence for a time before continuing, "I think you may be right. The young men may be lying when they say their friend's wagon is big and red. But that is not fair. They have no right to laugh at us for failing, if they tell us we are looking for something else."

Longarm thought about that before he answered. He knew that while stealth and what his own kind called treachery formed part of the warrior's code, it was considered sort of cheating to hand even an enemy a bare-faced lie. Most Indians had a better sense of humor and a greater gift of sarcasm and double-meaning than white folks gave them credit for. In their tales of Coyote, the trickster liked to give the other spirits a hint of his plans in advance, or make them look foolish with a promise he could keep to the letter, while meaning something else. Longarm remembered the childish riddle about a thing that was black and white and red all over. He asked the Indian, "Do you have puns in your lingo, Simon Peter?"

"Puns? You mean words that have two meanings?"

"Yeah. Could there be a way of saying 'wagon' and meaning something else?"

Simon Peter shook his head and said, "No. Wagon is the word we use. The only Lakota word that sounds like it is *wakan*. That means 'spirit.' "

Longarm pushed his Stetson forward and scratched the back of his neck. "Hmm, could they be telling you to search for a great red spirit instead of a big red wagon?"

"That's crazy."

"So is a bulletproof shirt made out of deerhide. This Kamono might be telling folks he's riding with the Great Spirit of the Red Man, and folks are sort of twisting the meaning a mite."

"But his wagon leaves tracks!"

"Of course it does. This reservation is too blamed big for him to walk across. But let's study on where he goes between visits. Most Cheyenne are over on the Rosebud Reservation to the east, these days. Can you drive direct to there from here?"

"Almost. The corners of our reservation meet. But there is a white man's county between us and the Rosebud Reservation. It is called Bennett County. We seldom go there. They get excited and call the soldiers."

Longarm had left his survey map at the agency with his other possibles, but he had a pretty good picture of the layout. "There's another incorporated county northeast of where the reservations rub corners. So any Indian passing from one to the other would have to pass through a bottleneck. Is it safe to assume you've got it staked out?"

Simon Peter nodded and said, "Yes. But Kamono has been on the Rosebud Reservation. He has been north to talk to the people at Standing Rock too. No police officers have seen him."

"Ain't there a Cheyenne reservation between here and Standing Rock?"

"Yes. The Cheyenne say he has not been among them. Do you think they could be lying?"

"Anybody could be lying. It's easy. It was Cheyenne who jumped those troopers the other day. Meanwhile, I aim to set up a lookout for that big red wagon."

"But you just said there might not *be* a big red wagon."

"I know what I said. Sometimes Coyote tricks his enemies by telling them the truth. But an Indian driving a big red wagon sure figures to stand out, driving through all those white settlements and ranch-lands."

By now they'd reached the agency, and Simon Peter peeled off to ride to his own cabin and eat his noon dinner. The kid, Joseph, was still tagging along as Longarm rode up to the corral behind Gatewood's place.

As Longarm dismounted, he saw Olga Swensen on the back porch with the sleeves of her white outfit rolled up, apparently trying to drown an Indian baby. She had the kid in a tub of soapy water, and it was hollering fit to bust. Longarm tethered his pony and walked over to her. "Howdy," he said. "Wouldn't it be simpler to just shoot the little rascal?"

Olga dunked the kid's head some more and said, "She has nits. I found her playing alone on the garbage dump, poor thing. She can't be more than two."

Longarm turned and swept his eyes around the compound, but aside from young Joseph, who was drawing a bead on them from a corner of the feed shed, he didn't see anyone else. Turning back to the blonde nurse, he said, "You might have tried to get her mama's permission, Miss Olga. *I* can see you ain't really trying to murder her, but some squaws have been known to be a mite protective."

"This child's mother certainly isn't! I told you she was playing in the garbage, stark naked, filthy, and covered with vermin."

"That is sort of unusual. Where are the Gatewoods and Miss Penny? Couldn't they stand to watch?"

Olga laughed. "The agent and his wife drove into town, so Penny decided she'd go with them. They said they'd be back this evening."

"What town is that, ma'am? I've got reasons for asking."

"They went down to Whiteclay, just outside the reservation. Why are you so worried about that?"

70

"I ain't worried, ma'am, just thoughtful. I had a talk with the tribal elders just now. They admitted they ain't in control of things here."

"Heavens, do you think our friends are in danger?"

Slowly, he answered, "Well, as I remember, Whiteclay's just over the Nebraska line and only five miles or so at most. I'll mosey down that way towards evening. Do the Indians know where they headed? More important, do they know when to expect them back?"

The screaming baby bit Olga as she lifted it from the tub in a big fluffy towel, but she didn't seem perturbed as she replied, "I really don't know. Mr. Gatewood heard that some beef cattle he'd ordered were there, and said he was going to see why they hadn't been delivered. His wife and Penny decided to go with him on the spur of the moment. There's a notions shop in Whiteclay. You're certainly making the whole thing sound dreadfully complicated, Mr. Long."

"We live in a complicated world. What do you aim to do with that kid, now that it's scrubbed down and all?"

Olga looked down at the little Indian in her arms with a puzzled frown. The child had decided it wasn't being executed and had snuggled against her in the towel, sucking its thumb. Olga said, "I certainly can't put it down in the dust again. But somebody must be responsible for it."

Longarm turned and shouted, "Hey, Joe? Come over here, kid."

Joseph ducked out of sight, and Longarm called, "Game's over, boy! I need me a Dog Soldier on the double. Do you want to be a Dog Soldier or do you aim to play peek-a-boo like a bitty gal?"

Joseph stepped from cover, scowling, and smote his skinny chest as he approached, chanting, "Hear me! I am Joseph and I count coup! I have trailed the American all the way from Tipisota's and he never saw me once!"

"Yeah. Take a look at this baby, Joe. Us Dog Soldiers have to keep order in the camp, and this big white squaw can't find the baby's mother."

71

The Indian boy frowned down at the waif in Olga's arms.

Longarm asked, "Who does she belong to, Joe? You know, don't you?"

The boy said, "If you give her to me, I will ride back to my own lodge and see if my mother wants her."

"Joe, your mother must be a fine woman, but she's already got her own kids. This baby can't have walked far. What's the story?"

Joseph looked away. Longarm said, "Joseph, I've been talking to you man-to-man. Are you going to act like a sulky girl baby or are you going to speak when you are spoken to?"

"I am ashamed," Joseph said. "You two are white people and my little cousin's mother is a bad person."

"I've met up with bad white mothers too, Joseph. Will you show us where she lives?"

The boy sighed resignedly. "All right. But remember, the woman is not from my clan. Her father was, but he is dead. The woman you are looking for was given the name Mary by the Black Robes. She has no Lakota name. The other women do not speak to her."

Longarm and Olga followed Joseph with the baby. He saw a curtain move in a cabin window as they passed. So he knew, now, why no Indians had shown any visible interest while Olga washed the screaming kid in plain sight of the whole community.

Joseph stopped at the door of a cottonwood-log shack. He said, "The bad woman lives here."

Olga moved toward the door, but Longarm stopped her, saying, "Stand back, ma'am." Then he took a deep breath and opened the door. The sickly sweet smell was worse inside. He stood in the doorway staring in at the dark, fetid interior as his eyes adjusted. He saw the pale form of a naked woman spread-eagled on a cot in one corner. Olga, despite his warning, peered over his shoulder. "My God," she gasped. "She's a white woman, and she's moving!"

Longarm shoved her out and slammed the door behind him. "No, she ain't. Joseph, you'd best go tell the Dream Singers they're needed. I know what she was, but she's dead now, and they might feel it in their hearts to bury her Lakota."

The boy nodded and trotted away as Olga insisted, "She was *moving*, I tell you. I smelled the decomposition, I'm a nurse. But her chest was rising and falling and—"

"Maggots," Longarm cut in, flatly. "She must have been laying there like that for days. Covered head to toe with blowfly larva. The kid here has been living on scraps like the camp dogs."

Olga's big blue eyes widened and she looked like she wanted to faint, but to her credit she hung onto the kid and her sanity long enough for Longarm to reach out and steady her. She swallowed and said, "Oh Jesus, what am I doing here? They *told* me these savages were beyond hope or help."

"You just helped that baby by finding her and caring for her when nobody else saw fit to, ma'am. So I'd hardly say your day was wasted."

"But, my God, it's all so pointless. What kind of people would murder a woman and leave a child to fend for herself on a garbage dump?"

"Let's eat this apple a bite at a time, ma'am. Nobody killed that gal in there. I smelled trade liquor and acetone too."

"Acetone? You mean she was a diabetic?"

"You're the trained nurse. What would a fifth of alcohol do to a diabetic so far gone that you could smell acetone on her breath after she's been dead a spell?"

Olga gagged and said, "God, one good stiff drink can hit a terminal diabetic like a bullet in the brain."

"There you go. She was the town drunk, and Indians are afraid of sickness even when they're on good terms with a person the evil spirits are after."

"But this child, abandoned . . ."

"That's another bite of the apple," Longarm cut in, explaining, "They were used to seeing the kid neglected, and Indian women mind their own business. They couldn't shame her into acting decent, so they tried to pretend she wasn't there. They didn't know she was dead. They just thought she was a bad mother, like Joseph said."

"That's no excuse. They should have seen the child was neglected."

"Yes, ma'am, they should have. Back East where you were reared, I reckon ladies stopped dead on the street and adopted any dirty barefoot kid they happened to notice."

Olga looked sheepishly at the ground and said, "You're right. I suppose you think I'm a hypocrite and a snob."

"No," he replied gently. "I think you're a right pretty human being. You just have to learn that these folks you came out here to help are neither Noble Savages nor Savage Brutes. They're folks. They make the same mistakes the rest of us do."

Young Joseph returned with an old Indian wrapped in a blanket, trailed by a couple of bawling squaws. The old man stopped and stared gravely at the two whites by the door. He said, "They say the bad woman lives no more."

Longarm nodded and said, "She isn't being bad now. She's a dead Lakota. The spirits that made her weak have left her to Wakan Tonka. Do you want us to bury her for you, or has she been forgiven?"

The Dream Singer said, "No living person has the right to judge the dead. Her spirit has gone to the lodge of Old Woman, under the Northern Lights. We will bury her as the Lakota maid she once was."

"My elder brother's words are those of a good person. What will become of this baby, now that it has no mother?"

One of the squaws stepped forward, sobbing, and as Olga handed the child to her, the Dream Singer said, "She has a mother now. I know who you are, Longarm. I do not wish to be rude, but this is no longer a white man's business."

Longarm nodded, took Olga by one arm, and led her away, saying, "Don't look back. They don't want us in their church right now."

"What are they going to do?"

"Nothing all that mysterious. It's bad luck to take a body out the door, so they'll chop a hole through the wall and slide her out after dark as they sing some. They don't like outsiders watching. Some whites in the past have said dumb things at Indian funerals."

"Will they really bury her in a tree?"

"Don't know. I doubt it. There's a burial ground over to the west, and they always have buried folks in the ground more than the professors think."

When they reached the house, Longarm suggested, "Let's go in and stay out of sight. It's a blessing that Gatewood ain't here. He'd fluster them with making out reports and such. I'm glad Penny went with them too."

Olga said, "So am I."

They went into the parlor to sit down. Longarm wasn't sure about her meaning, so he chuckled and said, "I meant the way Penny gets excited about drinking. In a little while we're going to hear some tomtoms and yelling that may be partly inspired by spirits other than Indian."

Olga sat on the settee and patted it in invitation as she nodded and said, "Penny told me her views on Demon Rum. She said she'd saved you from it too."

As he sat down beside her, suddenly aware of how little room there was on the settee, she added, "It's odd, but you don't *look* like an alcoholic."

Longarm moved his arm behind her shoulders to leave more room between their hips as he laughed and said, "Penny's ideas on the subject tend to go a mite far. One beer can lead straight to the devil, to hear her. Has there been any serious drinking here on the reservation since you arrived?"

Olga said, "Well, we obviously didn't know a squaw had drunk herself to death within gunshot of the back door. Mr. Gatewood says he's keeping an eye on it. There's a man in Black Pipe who's been known to sell firewater to the Indians, but he's being watched."

Longarm squinted as he formed a mental map. Then he nodded and said, "I know where Black Pipe is. That white-held county, smack between two reservations, would be a handy place for a bootlegger to set up shop."

But Olga wasn't listening. The pupils in her big blue eyes were dilated and she was breathing irregularly as she asked, "Are you and Penny engaged, Custis?"

He looked surprised and said, "Shucks, I hardly ever get engaged, ma'am."

"Call me Olga. I like little Penny, but she does seem to have a possessive attitude. She said a very odd thing as they were leaving for town."

"Oh?" said Longarm, cautiously. "What was that, ma'am—I mean, Olga?"

Olga laughed and said, "She told me to keep away from you. Wasn't that a silly thing to say?"

He kept his face blank as he agreed, "Sort of. I didn't know you were after me."

"I wasn't, until she pointed out that the two of us would be alone out here all afternoon. I mean, you're a nice-looking man, and a girl my size doesn't meet many men tall enough to look up to, but I really hadn't thought about being—well, naughty, until she warned me not to even think of it."

Longarm nodded and said, "I remember this old gent who lived down the road, back home. We passed his orchard on the way to school and he'd posted it with a 'keep out' sign."

"And of course you and the other boys swiped his apples?"

"Every chance we got. The hell of it was, we all *had* apple trees in our own backyards. But there was something about that old gent telling us we couldn't have any of his . . ."

"I know. I'd have swiped his apples too. I never have been one to resist a dare."

Then she half-rose, turned, and sat in his lap. There was one hell of a lot of her and he had to grab her and hang on to keep her from sliding off as he considered his options. "I reckon you've made your point. But let's not get carried away."

"Are you afraid Penny will beat you up?"

"No, but she might throw rocks at us. This ain't

very delicate, Olga, and I don't generally talk behind a lady's back, but—"

"I see. You have been making love to her, then."

"Well, sort of. But like I said before, I ain't too serious about such matters, and no decent gal should be sitting in my lap. You see, I'm one of those rascals that gals' mothers warn them about."

"I was hoping you would be," said Olga. Then she bent to kiss him full on the lips. She weighed a ton, but she kissed mighty fine.

After a while, she saw that he wasn't going to pick her up and dash off anywhere with her, so she let him come up for air as she asked, "Don't you like me?"

He said, "Hell, I'm busting a gut trying not to like you better! But I don't want you getting yourself in trouble over a dare, honey."

"I won't get in trouble. I'm a nurse. What's the matter with you? Am I too big and fat for you?"

"Lord, no! I'm fighting temptation fire and tongs!"

"Why do we have to fight anything? We're all alone. We have the whole afternoon ahead of us. Am I too heavy for you? I notice your leg is starting to throb."

"That ain't my leg, but let's say no more about it. You're twisting a confession out of me with cruel and unusual punishment, but I have to say it. Penny saw me first."

"Oh, that's *not* your leg I feel! Don't you think there's enough of you for two girls to share?"

"I don't suspicion Penny is the sharing kind, Olga. I know you're bigger than her, but she's one tough little gal."

Olga squirmed her ample derriere into a more receptive position and he knew she wasn't wearing anything under that starched white uniform. She kissed him again and said, "We don't have to tell anybody our little secret, do we?"

"Some secrets are hard as hell to keep," Longarm observed.

"Try me," she said. "Cross my heart and hope to

die. Penny can have anything that's left all to herself, tonight."

Longarm figured Olga likely meant it. He'd met women like her before. It was the quiet ones who looked like butter wouldn't melt in their mouths who really screwed all the boys the saucy gals got blamed for.

He knew he was doomed either way. Olga was more likely to make trouble with Penny if she was mad at him than if she had a chance to play her own Mona Lisa games at the supper table. And the longer he held back, the more danger there was of Penny getting back before he'd satisfied this amazon.

So he rose, picking her up as he did so, though it wasn't easy. Olga giggled and said, "Oh, you're so strong! I feel light as a feather in your arms!"

"Which way is your room? I purely don't aim to use mine!"

She sighed and said, "Second door to the right down the hall. Oh, I feel so little and feminine in your arms! Take me and make me your little love kitten, you brute."

Longarm muttered, "Aw, shit!" under his breath as he toted the load to its destination, which was a brass bedstead that he sure hoped was stouter than it looked.

It was. He lowered her gently to the bedspread, risking a slipped disc in the process, and sat down to start shucking his duds. Olga said, "Oh, we can't take off our clothes. It's broad daylight!"

He started to say that he aimed at the least to remove his coat and gunbelt. Then he shrugged and said, "I noticed there was more light in here. Broad daylight's sort of cruel to the great ideas we get in more romantic light."

He started to rise, but she reached out to grab him, and when Olga grabbed a man he knew it. "What's the matter?" she asked. "I didn't say I wanted to *stop*!"

He turned and smiled down at her wistfully. "Honey, you don't know *what* you want. I've been down this trail before, so I don't get as riled about it as some gents. It's all right. You made your point. We both know I want you bad enough. From here on it just gets tedious."

She started to cry. He said, "You don't have to do that, honey. I didn't recognize you at first, so I acted the usual fool. But I ain't sore."

She stared up at him in total confusion and blurted, "What are you talking about? We've never met before!"

He smiled down at her. "Sure we have. You sat next to me in grammar school. There's one like you on every army post, and we've met at many a dance. There ain't a man on this earth who ain't met you, and there ain't a gal who's never crossed swords with you."

She said, "Penny was right. You *are* a drunk!"

He said, "Let's not talk mean, honey. I told you I wasn't sore. I used to get sore at gals like you. But after I grew up a mite, I got sort of philosophical about your cruel hobby."

"Are you accusing me of being a *tease*?"

"That's what other men might call you. I said I was philosophical. I figured out why you were doing it a long time ago. I think you were a flirty little army wife, that time. I chased you out on the veranda and showed you I was so excited about you that I clean forgot your husband and the gal I'd brought. So after batting your eyes at me all evening and saying dirty things on the fandango floor, you were stuck with getting out of it once we were alone."

"Custis, have you gone stark raving mad? I'm not married and it's cruel of you to twit me about my size!"

"Yeah, I figured your being bigger than most gals might have something to do with you being a mite bolder than most at the game. You like to boss Indians too. So I reckon this was a good day for you. You got to take charge of one gal's baby and then you stole another gal's gent and proved you were queen of the hive. So we'll say no more about it."

She licked her lips and said, "Don't you want me, Custis?"

He said, "Sure, I want you. I could likely get a teasing taste of your honey if I wanted to wrestle and

79

beg like a kid. Being a nurse, as well as stronger than most men, you likely go a mite farther than the usual temptress. But, while I'll allow I'm the fool you took me for, I'm a grown-up fool. So let's both admit you won and quit this grubby kid game."

He tried to rise again, and this time he meant it, so Olga couldn't stop him, as strong as she was. He said something about seeing to his pony as he headed for the door, but Olga shouted, "Stop!" and when he heard a button pop, he did, and turned around. Olga was shucking her white duds as fast as she was able. He saw a big pink breast peeking out of her bodice at him as she rose to haul the uniform off over her head and cast it aside. Then she stood facing him defiantly in nothing but her blue cotton stockings and high-button shoes as she blushed beet-red and stammered, "There, are you satisfied?"

He grinned at her big shapely form as he took off his coat, let it fall anywhere it had a mind to, and reached for his belt buckle. He made her blush harder by staring down at the triangle of light blonde thatch between her ample thighs as he said, "Not yet, but I soon aim to be."

Olga fell back on the bed and blubbered, "I didn't want you to see how fat I am!"

He got on the bedspread with her as he finished peeling, and soothed her, "There ain't an ounce on you that ain't pure female, honey, and I aim to pleasure it all!"

He kissed her, got a grip on one of her huge breasts, and rolled into the saddle before she could act up again. She gasped and started to resist as she felt him entering her, but he knew she was one of those undecided old gals and she couldn't buck him off.

She got used to being naked in broad daylight after her first screaming orgasm, and while he held her, moving gently as they started for a second one, she suddenly laughed lewdly and said, "You bastard! *You* were the one who was playing games! All that mean talk about me being a tease was just so you could dominate me completely, wasn't it?"

He kissed her neck and said, "Yeah, I'm a sneaky old cuss. But don't you like it better, civilized?"

"I love it. But I've never let a man see me naked before. Are you sure you don't think I'm a big fat Swenska?"

"You're built just fine. I ain't exactly a shrimp, you know."

"Oh, do I ever know it! But what are we going to tell Penny?"

He stopped in mid-stroke and said, "*We* ain't going to tell her shit! You can brag about this to her, if you still have to prove you're the prettiest gal at the dance. But I'll just say you were likely out in the sun too long and we won't be friends anymore."

"Do you like her better than me? Is she better in bed?"

"Everybody's better in bed, at the time. Right now you are the only woman on earth, and I'm about to prove it again."

"Are you in love with her?"

"No, but I don't want Penny hurt. She takes this sort of fun as serious as you, and it ain't fair to bully little kids."

"That's a cruel thing to say, darling."

"I know. You've got a mean streak too. You got me here by saying it was a secret deal we had. I don't play with folks who welsh in a card game, either."

"I see. Now that I've given myself to you like a fool, you mean to cast me aside like a toy. I might have known you liked her best!"

He closed his eyes, started moving faster, and murmured, "Oh, Powder River and let her buck!" as they came together. Neither moved or spoke for a moment as they shared the afterglow. Then Longarm said, "As I was about to say when I was so rudely interrupted, I aim to do right by *all* my friends. I'll play your game of stolen kisses on the veranda if you'll let Penny have things her way."

"You can't really hope to service two warm-natured women at once!"

"No. You'll have to take turns. That is, you will unless you play dirty and force me to make a choice."

"But don't you see I *want* you to make a choice?"

"I do. And I think it's mean as hell of you. Are we doing this because of your warm nature or because you have to prove you're a natural-born bully who keeps all the marbles?"

She sighed and said, "I'm so confused I don't know what I'm doing, but can we do it some more?"

"Sure. Let's change positions. How do you like it dog-style?"

"My God, in broad daylight? I feel like a cow!"

"All right, let's do her cow-style. I'll be the bull."

He got off and rolled her over, as she protested that he was being brutal. But he knew she liked it brutal. Olga was one of those gals who got a secret thrill from raw and dirty loving, and he knew he'd lose control over her the minute he treated her like a lady. He forced her into position on her hands and knees. The sight of her big pink rump was sort of awesome as well as stimulating. He grabbed a hipbone on either side and entered her from the rear. She hissed in pure animal pleasure and arched her back to receive it all as she gasped, "Oh, that *is* nice! I've never met a man who mastered me like this before!"

He'd already figured as much. Olga wasn't a bad old girl. She just had queer notions about her size that made her want to act like a bully. It had likely started in school when she'd found out that she could make smaller gals stop teasing her by swatting them like flies. Growing up, she'd learned more womanly tricks to play on the pretty little things she was so jealous of. Down deep, she wanted to *be* a bitty helpless thing. So he pounded her brutally, the way he knew she needed it. He knew he was on the right track when she suddenly fell forward and rolled over, spread-eagled and unashamed, and gasped, "Take me! I want to come in your arms!"

And so he did, and she never mentioned Penny as she gave herself completely.

● ● ●

The rolling prairie was gold and purple in the sunset as Longarm sat his pinto on a rise near the reservation's invisible southern boundary. He knew he was only a spit and a holler from the trail town of Whiteclay, to the south. But Gatewood's buckboard was nowhere to be seen, and they'd said they'd be back in time for supper.

Longarm heeled his mount forward, glad he hadn't brought Simon Peter after all. He'd looked for the Indian policeman, but the man's wife had said he was out scouting a rumor that there was something funny going on in another settlement. So he wouldn't have to protect his fellow lawman from the nervous whites ahead. It was tedious, just waiting like this.

As he started riding all the way, Longarm spotted a smoke plume, pink against the purple eastern sky, and muttered, "What the hell?"

The town couldn't be over that way. Whiteclay was supposed to be due south.

Then he saw that the smoke was rising in dots and dashes and knew it wasn't from a white man's chimney. It was smoke-talk.

Longarm heeled his pony to a mile-eating lope. This was no time for a lone white man to admire the pretty prairie flowers. He topped a rise and saw the little cluster of frame buildings spread across the trail ahead. There was nobody driving a buckboard toward him. He figured they must have spotted the smoke talk too. That explained why Gatewood was late getting home. Gatewood was smart, for an Easterner.

Behind him, somebody called out, "Ah-ta-nag-hree-tah-wa-hen-dee!"

Longarm muttered, "Oh shit!" as he heeled his mount into a full gallop and levered a round into his Winchester's chamber before looking back.

There were eight of them, wearing feathers and paint as well as flapping medicine shirts. They were riding flat-out, too, so he missed as he fired one-handed, to teach them some manners.

A bullet hummed past his ear to return the compliment, and he made a mental note that the brave on the

83

gray pony was the best shot, as other clouds of gun-smoke blossomed in the ruddy light to send lead wider of the mark, which seemed to be him.

He would have reined in to fort up behind his own pony, had he been jumped alone on open prairie. But a man was committed for keeps, once he made his stand, and his best bet was the cover just ahead. So he laid his head along the pony's mane and bored on into Whiteclay, and the Indians started dropping back, as he'd expected. He'd just reinforced the legend of those bulletproof shirts by missing like a dude, but they weren't ready to take a whole town on, just yet.

A gun went off nearby, but he figured nobody was shooting at him as he passed the town line and swerved behind a cabin and reined to a sliding stop. He rolled off, Winchester in hand, and ran back to join the others who were smoking up the Indians from the cover of the buildings. He joined a man firing from behind a rain barrel and dropped down beside him, saying, "Howdy. Nice night, ain't it?"

The other white man fired, cursed, and said, "We thought you was a goner. You can call me Hank."

"You can call me Longarm and I thought I was a goner too. How long they had you folks circled up?"

"Since about three this afternoon. There's about five scattered bands. They send one bunch in to draw us all to one side whilst some others try the other side of the settlement."

There was a rattle of small-arms fire from down the street behind them, and Hank said, "See what I mean?"

"Yep. It sometimes works on greenhorns. I came looking for some friends of mine. Do you know Gatewood, the Sioux agent?"

"Sure. He still has his hair. Him and a couple of womenfolk are holed up in the general store. Gatewood's on the roof with the marshal and some other riflemen. We figure the hostiles are after the cattle penned behind the store. But them red rascals picked themselves the wrong little town to tangle with."

"I can see you boys ain't sissies. You don't need me here, so I'd best mosey over to the store and see what the agent knows about this foolishness."

Longarm ran across the dusty street and along the plank walk to the only important-looking building in the little settlement. As he ducked inside, Gatewood's wife spotted him from where she'd huddled in a corner with some other gals and a mess of kids. She called out, "Oh, Marshal Long! We've been so worried about you! My husband said you might be riding out to meet us."

"As you can see, I did. Where's Penny?"

"Up on the roof with her bag of rocks. The men told her not to act so foolish, but she sure is a stubborn little thing."

Longarm saw a ladder leading up to an open hatchway, so he clambered up it. On the rooftop, he found Penny and Gatewood with four other men. Penny wasn't throwing rocks. One of the townies lay on the tarpaper with part of his skull blown away, and Penny had picked up his Henry rifle. She ran over to him, sobbing, "I thought that was you, riding in! Are you all right, darling?"

"Yeah," he said, "but let's not get mushy about it. I want you down below with the other gals, and I don't aim to say it twice."

"Custis, we need all the good shots we can get up here."

"Damn it, you've made me say it twice. Do I have to pick you up and throw you down that ladder?"

Gatewood followed a distant figure with the muzzle of his own rifle, gave it up as a hopeless target, and said, "Save your breath, Longarm. The town marshal here has been threatening to lock her up and she just won't listen." He pointed with his chin at the portly, black-bearded man next to him and said, "This is Marshal Perkins. The other two survivors are Bates and Jones. The dead man's name was Watson."

"It's a blessing he was single," added the marshal. Longarm nodded politely and gave up on Penny as he swept the horizon line in the gathering dusk. The latest attack had fallen back to a circle of black dots all around. "Have *they* lost anybody?" Longarm asked, and one of the men said, "I'm right sure I winged one, a while back."

Someone always said that. Longarm said, "I know," as he stared down at the milling cows in the corral below.

Gatewood followed his glance and said, "As we rolled in, they told us why they hadn't driven the herd out to us."

"They were lucky to get here alive," Perkins said. "We've been seeing smoke signals all afternoon. I've never seed such crazy Indians, and I've been out here for a spell." He spat and added, "Even when Red Cloud was on the warpath back in '76, they never rode agin' a *town*!"

"I've been trying to tell these boys those are not my Sioux out there," Gatewood said.

Perkins spat again. "It don't matter what reservation they just jumped. Whoever they be, they've jumped it good! I figure they'll move in again for them cows as soon as she gets dark."

One of the other men said, "I've always heard Indians don't attack at night."

Perkins just looked disgusted.

Longarm said, "We might save some needless excitement by turning those cows loose."

"And let the Indians have them?"

"Hell, it's Indian beef, ain't it?"

Gatewood said, "If we let those Ghost Dancers run those cows off, won't my tame Sioux have to do without?"

"Sure they will. It ought to make them mad as hell. I think the Romans called it 'divide and conquer' or something. It's one thing to cover up for a wild cousin. It's another thing entire to go hungry for him."

Gatewood nodded, but said, "Won't those renegades gain a lot to brag about if we let them run the cows off on us?"

Longarm said, "Hell, they're already bragging fit to bust. We just helped them prove those fool medicine shirts are everything they're cracked up to be in a firefight. Indians set great store by showing folks how brave they are. But Indians have contempt for a selfish man who lets other folks go hungry when he's living fat cow. So unless those rascals *share* the beef, the old chiefs will gain the upper hand on Wovoka's missionaries. Wovoka keeps promising a return to the Shining Times. In the Shining Times, when a warrior ate, everybody ate."

"But if they invite *all* the Indians to a big feed . . . Jesus, let's stop talking about it and turn that herd loose!"

But before anyone could move to put the plan in motion, Penny called out, "Oh, look! Over there on that rise!"

Longarm stared morosely the way she was pointing and muttered, "Damn," as the others perked up and started waving their hats. A column of cavalry was riding in, guidon fluttering and brass buttons glowing ruby in the sunset. The bugler was blowing the charge, for reasons best known to himself, since every Indian within miles was long gone.

Gatewood said, "We even saved our beef," and Longarm wanted to kick him. But he knew the retreating Ghost Dancers wouldn't stop to round up any now, even if he turned them loose.

Perkins said something about a stretcher for the dead man, and Longarm helped Penny down the ladder. The store below was deserted, as all the women and children had gone out to watch the parade. So after Penny kissed him a couple of times, he led her out on the walk to watch it too.

It was Captain Kehoe's troop, which came as no great surprise. The captain rode a white horse and reined in as his sergeants dismounted their men and fanned them out to secure the perimeter by the numbers.

Kehoe got down stiffly as the townies crowded around to congratulate him on his gallant rescue. He spotted Longarm and marched toward him, beaming.

"Ah, we meet again. What's the situation here, Deputy?"

"They went thataway. As you must have guessed, all that shooting and smoke-talk was just getting interesting. I make it about two dozen young bucks in those crazy shirts Wovoka peddles. You'd be wasting your time trying to track 'em in the dark."

"I'll wager a month's pay that Sitting Bull was leading them!"

"You'll lose. They fought like kids. That's why I'm here to tell it to you. They jumped me on the trail like raw recruits. Had a battle-wise chief been leading them, they'd have cut me off from the cover of this town, instead of singing out to me before I spotted 'em. They were chasing me like a pup snapping at a wagon wheel."

Marshal Perkins had joined them and he spat and said, "Longarm's right. They was mean and likely likkered up, but I have 'em down as kids trying to count coup."

Captain Kehoe was too well-bred to sneer at his elders, so he smiled and said, "I'm sure you're an expert in such matters, Marshal Perkins."

"I am," Perkins replied equably. "I scouted for Terry on the Rosebud, and I was at the Wagon Box Fight when Red Cloud led the attack. Next question?"

"I'll accept your opinion, sir. But that still leaves us with a war party off the reservation. We'll secure things here, and in the morning we'll ride into Pine Ridge and—"

"Don't you reckon it might be a good idea to find out which reservation they jumped?" Longarm cut in. "I just left Pine Ridge."

"I don't doubt that. Isn't it obvious that you were followed from there by those Ghost Dancers?"

"No, it ain't. An Indian lady died out there this afternoon." He saw that Gatewood was confused. "It was that Mary with the drinking problem. They ought to be holding her funeral about now."

Penny said, "I *knew* there was firewater out there!"

Kehoe asked, "What has a dead squaw to do with the attack on this town?"

Longarm said, "Nothing. No Indian would be out raiding when one of his people was in greater need of his services. The old ones are sending her off with good medicine. The young folks are expected to help with respectful long faces and some polite keening as they make her ready for the journey. Every Sioux who ever spoke to old Mary will be there. And she was Hunkpapa."

"Now just what is that supposed to mean?" Kehoe snapped.

"That the Indians we just tangled with ain't. Neither Sitting Bull nor any other Hunkpapa would be a mile away from Mary and her funeral rites this evening. Those Ghost Dancers may have been Sioux; They yelled a Lakota war cry after me. But they weren't from the bunch around the agency; it wouldn't have been decent."

Kehoe brightened at this. "Then if we rode in right now, we'd find Sitting Bull at the funeral with the other war chiefs!"

"You would, but you weren't invited, so you ain't to go."

"Oh, for God's sake, Longarm. I'm getting very tired of your bluff. You know damned well you can't stop me."

"Maybe not. But when I was in the army, we had a saying you might know. I may not be able to stop you, but I can make you wish to God you stopped! If you bust up a sacred ceremony with a cavalry charge, I'll have your bars for breakfast. I'll wire the War Department that you ignored the advice of seasoned Indian-fighters and started the battle for your own damn fool reasons."

Marshal Perkins shifted his plug of chewing tobacco, spat, and said, "I'll back Marshal Long. They likely remember me from the Wagon Box fight. There wasn't all that many of us left when it was over. I'm sore as hell about them killing Watson, but Longarm's right. You lead white troops into a funeral dance and I'll have to say the likely results was premeditated murder, if not suicide."

Kehoe looked at Gatewood, and the Indian agent said, "I'm no expert, but what they say makes sense, Captain. I can't give you permission to annoy my wards without probable cause."

A peach-fuzz lieutenant joined them in front of the store. He saluted the captain and said, "All posted and awaiting further orders, sir."

Kehoe muttered, "Carry on. It's feed 'em in the winter and fight 'em in the summer as usual, Lieutenant."

"Sir?"

"Never mind. I don't understand the policy either."

Longarm, despite certain authoritarian habits, was not a natural bully, and since Kehoe was willing to be civilized, he decided to give him a chip. He said, "You and your men did arrive at a good time, Captain, and I'll see about setting up a peaceable powwow with Sitting Bull for you, as soon as I can find him myself."

Kehoe's nostrils flared and he looked like a man with some hard words stuck in his craw, but he was adult enough to nod and say, "Very well. There's nothing any of us can do tonight but dig in and hope for the best. Is there a telegraph line here in town, Marshal Perkins?"

Perkins said, "There used to be. The Indians cut it. We can likely fix it, come sunrise. Meanwhile, I don't know about you folks, but I've had a long day and I mean to get some shut-eye. They might be back, and tired folks don't shoot so good."

Chapter 5

"Oh, Custis, you're so passionate tonight!" Penny said as they made love in his bedroll on the rooftop. He didn't answer. He knew part of his renewed desire was attributable to the contrast of her tiny torso with Olga's, and another part was guilt. He hadn't really worried about getting it up, but there'd been a moment of panic as he shucked his pants for a second time in only a few hours. Olga had done her best to wring him out like a dishrag that afternoon, but as he snuggled into the bedroll with the little temperance teacher, he discovered it was easy to rise to the occasion with such a pretty gal.

Penny seemed almost as interested in the sky above as she was in what was going on here below, as she wriggled under him. She'd mentioned on the trail, coming out from Hat Creek, how romantic she thought it was.

She suddenly went limp and sighed, "Oh, that was so nice. But can we rest a moment? With all the excitement we've had today, I'm afraid I might not be able to satisfy you fully tonight, darling."

He rolled over and groped in his coat pocket next to the bedroll for a smoke and a sulfur match as he said, "You're doing fine, honey. I had a long day too."

As he lit up, she giggled and said, "I was worried about how we'd manage this tonight, at the agency. You realize, of course, that it's almost impossible to do a thing like this out there?"

"Oh, I don't know. Anything's possible, to a determined couple of folks. It's a big reservation. We'll likely find some corner where we can work something out."

"We'll have to be very careful. I'd just die if Olga found out."

"Oh?" he answered, cautiously, lying back, facing the starry sky.

Penny said, "I think she suspects we're lovers, and she must be jealous, the poor old cow."

Longarm felt a trifle better about his two-timing, now. He said, "Fair is fair, Penny. Miss Swensen's not a bad-looking gal. I wouldn't be too surprised if she got a man now and then."

"Oh, she's sort of pretty, I'll allow, but can you imagine making love to a woman with a rump like that?"

He regarded her from the corner of his eye. "I did notice she had what you might call a full figure, now that you mention it."

Penny snuggled closer and giggled as she observed, "I bet it would take a stallion to service her."

"That's not a neighborly way to talk about another gal, Penny."

"Oh pooh, I like Olga. I just feel sorry for her."

"Sorry, or superior?"

"Well, I'll admit it's a comfort to me that I don't have any real competition out here to worry about."

He decided to let her be comforted, so he didn't reply.

Penny started to fondle him as she said, "I know you said you weren't ready to settle down. But I broke you of some other bad habits, and I want all this to myself for as long as I can hang onto it."

"I wish you'd watch out with those nails."

"Am I hurting you? It doesn't feel like it's seriously injured. Do you want me to kiss it and make it well?"

He snuffed out his cheroot and said, "Hold your fire. There's something funny about the way those cows down there are milling."

She gasped and asked, "Can you see anything?"

"No, but we'd better get dressed anyway. It'll save a lot of explaining in a minute if I'm right."

"My God, is someone liable to come up here? I'd die if they caught me like this!"

"That's what I just said. Forget your drawers and just slip on the dress."

He left his own underwear in the roll as he sat up and started clawing on his duds. Penny snapped a fastening and whispered, "Damn! What's happening down there?"

"Beats the hell out of me. I thought those soldier boys were supposed to be standing guard!"

Then all hell broke loose. Cattle were bawling and guns were shooting and folks all around were hollering fit to bust. Longarm told Penny, "Stay here. That's an order. I ought to be back directly, but I sure won't make love to you no more if you ain't here."

Then, without waiting for an answer, he leaped up and ran over to the hatchway, strapping on his gunbelt. He left the Winchester with Penny.

Out on the street, he spied a man running toward him with a lantern. "Douse that light, you fool!" he yelled, and ran past him without waiting to make sure the fellow did it. He whipped around the corner of the store and almost ran over a soldier in the moonlight. The cavalry trooper blurted, puzzled, "The Indians have run off the cattle!"

This news was no great surprise.

He found Captain Kehoe in the empty corral, cussing a blue streak in the dust-filled moonlight. Gatewood arrived with Perkins, stared about in wonder, and asked, "Where are my cows?"

Longarm asked, "Was anybody hurt?"

Kehoe took his hat off, threw it on the ground, and kicked it. "No, goddamnit! I'll have the corporal of the guard court-martialed for this!"

Longarm assumed that the frightened-looking NCO standing at attention by the open gate was who the captain had in mind. He said, "If it's any comfort, I was, uh, on guard on the roof up there. They slipped in mighty quiet."

"Good," Kehoe replied with malicious delight. "You can be a witness at the court-martial. Do you have any idea what this is going to look like when I have to report it to regimental headquarters? We're Seventh Cav, goddamnit! Those savages are making a habit out of making us look like greenhorns!"

Perkins spat and said, "It do get tedious. But don't be too hard on your men, Cap. Indian kids is raised sneaky. I've known a buck to slip in and swipe an officer's sword with his hound dog asleep in the same tent."

Kehoe said, "Oh, that will look fine in my report, won't it? 'Dear Colonel: I hate to tell you this, but last night after I posted a full guard detail, some drunken Indian made off with a herd of government beef from under our guns!'"

Longarm held up a hand, palm forward. "Just hold on, now. I'm a mite confused. Didn't you and Agent Gatewood here *plan* this ruse?"

Kehoe blinked in confusion. "Ruse? What the hell are you talking about?"

"I distinctly remember how you two talked about letting those Ghost Dancers steal the cattle in order to track them to their hideout. Ain't that the way *you* heard it, Marshal Perkins?"

Perkins grinned broadly under his thick black whiskers. "It sure was. I remember thinking at the time it sounded pretty slick."

Gatewood caught on and added quickly, "Right. I assigned that beef to the army to use as bait. It's all coming back to me now."

The lieutenant and some other troopers came running, followed by some townies. The junior officer asked what had happened and Longarm, seeing that the captain was still confused, said, "It's all right, boys. The captain just slickered the Indians into leaving a trail for you to follow."

Kehoe was staring at Longarm like a condemned man who'd just been pardoned. "Carry on, Lieutenant," he stammered. "Boots and saddles will blow at five-thirty sharp." Then, as the junior officer left to make his rounds, Kehoe held out his hand to Longarm. "I had you wrong, sir."

Longarm shook the proffered hand and said, "Maybe we were both a trifle hasty. Does that poor corporal have to stand like that all night?"

The captain turned to the rigid corporal and said,

"As you were. How much of this have you heard, *Private* Riggins?"

"Every word, sir. It was a trick you planned to play on the Indians. You told me not to tell the others, but to let the Ghost Dancers steal some cows as long as they were polite about it and didn't lift no hair."

"Carry on, *Corporal* Riggins. I don't expect them back tonight, but we're still on full alert."

The corporal saluted and marched off to gather his scattered squad.

Kehoe said, "I think you made another friend there, Longarm. I'll have to admit I acted like an idiot."

Longarm shrugged and said, "Let's not carry modesty to bragging. They were trying to rile you into charging like a bull, and I notice you never did it."

"Can I buy you a drink? I want to hear some more of your unusual views on Indian fighting. Either I'm going crazy or you're starting to make sense!"

"Custer has been treated unfairly in the papers," Kehoe was saying as he and Longarm lounged against the only bar in town. Longarm nodded sympathetically. He'd have been surprised as hell to hear a Seventh Cav man say Custer was an idiot. He sipped his drink and said, "I've read it both ways. But since I'm here, you know I wasn't there. I reckon Custer and his boys did the best they knew how. Most men do."

He didn't want to rehash the Little Big Horn; he wanted to go back to bed. Even if Penny hadn't been waiting for him, it made more sense to get some honest rest than to figure out the rights and wrongs of an old fight.

Kehoe continued, "Writers who've never seen the High Plains fault poor old George for things he had no control over. Sure, he might have done better, had they issued him a crystal ball. It's easy any Sunday morning to know what we should have done Saturday night. I'll bet you think you'd have come out of that mess alive, had you been in command that day, right?"

"I said I wasn't there. Had I been, I'm not sure I'd

have split my squadron into three columns the way he did."

Kehoe shook his head and said, "You're wrong. You'd have sent Reno scouting off to your one flank and Benteen off to the other for the same reason George did. You'd have been carrying out the orders of a superior officer."

"I thought Custer *was* the commanding officer," Longarm said, taking a cheroot from his coat pocket.

"I know. A lot of top brass were anxious to give George all the credit, when the whole campaign went wrong. But let me tell you something, Longarm. Custer was never in command of that expedition. He and his under-strength squadron were ordered to scout ahead of General Terry's main columns. Custer wasn't looking for that fight; he was *sent* into it."

Longarm struck a sulfur match on the edge of the bar. "I've always wondered how the man who wrote the army manual on High Plains tactics seemed to ignore the advice of his scouts. But he still divided his small force, knowing he was riding into enemy territory," he said as he touched the flame to his cheroot.

"You're not paying attention," Kehoe said. "Custer was ahead of the main column on a scouting mission. His orders weren't to *fight* the Indians. General Terry told him to ride out and *locate* them. Custer's men were spread out because scouts are supposed to spread out. You don't locate shit, riding bunched up. Can't you see where that left George?"

"Sure. It left him dead, along with the troopers riding with him."

"No argument about that. Custer made contact with the enemy, as they'd ordered him to do, and the enemy was too strong for him. Nobody knew the Indians had gathered on the Little Big Horn. It might have been Benteen who ran into them, and we'd be talking about Benteen's last stand. George just drew the short straw. Once a skeleton troop of light cavalry made contact with the enemy, it was all over. They were outnumbered more than ten to one on the enemy's ground. There wasn't a damned thing Custer or any other officer could have done to change the outcome. I've heard all the bright suggestions armchair generals have made since that day. But even Robert E. Lee couldn't have gotten his people out, with Napoleon and Alexander advising him. It wouldn't have mattered if the other two troops were with him. It wouldn't have mattered if they'd run for it like some suggest, or made the stand on the hillside as they did. They could have killed an Indian with every bullet they had with them, and they still would have gone down in the end. I've done the mathematics involved. Each trooper had five rounds in his gun, and figuring ten or more Indians rushing every man . . ."

"I'll take your word for it," Longarm cut in. "I know how confusing a *small* gunfight can get. I've rethought a few the next morning, in my time."

"It's those bastards in Washington," Kehoe growled, pouring himself another shot. "Cheap, money-pinching chiselers in Congress who cover up their own crimes at our expense."

Now, *crime* was a subject Longarm was more interested in. So, despite wanting to get back to Penny, he asked, "What crimes are we talking about, Captain?"

Kehoe said, "Hell, we all know Custer would still be alive if they hadn't stolen six million dollars from the Sioux. Custer himself charged the Interior Department with grand theft. Didn't you know that?"

"I knew that. I'm sort of surprised the army knows about it."

Kehoe gulped his drink, poured another, and growled, "Jesus Christ, do you think we *like* policing an area almost as large as Europe with a couple of regiments of underpaid troopers? I haven't a man under me who couldn't make more money punching cows, and half of them don't speak English."

Longarm blew out a large cloud of cigar smoke. "I know the army pays thirteen dollars a month. Get back to the crime stuff. But forget the money Red Cloud never got for the Black Hills. I know Congress thought a war was cheaper than paying for real estate, but that's ancient history. Are you saying somebody is still cheating the Indians?"

Kehoe gazed deeply into his shotglass. "I can't point a finger at anybody directly, but I know they've been screwing *us*. They send us patched uniforms and ammunition left over from the Civil War. We get paid up to three months late, and the quartermaster sends us ration cans of shit a coyote would gag on."

"I've heard all this," Longarm cut in. "Washington is trying to balance the budget or something. But I can't act on soldiers' gripes. I thought you had a charge to make."

"Well, doesn't it stand to reason that somebody is making money on all this new Indian trouble? They always have in the past!"

Longarm pursed his lips and said, "I follow your drift. Money is the root, like the Good Book says, and somebody sure is going to a mess of trouble to get us into a war this summer."

He finished his own drink and put the glass down as he mused, "I don't see how you army men would profit. The Indian bureau seems to be running smoother than usual. Despite your suspicions, the old chiefs don't seem to be looking for trouble this summer."

"What about Wovoka himself? Isn't that crazy Paiute behind this Ghost Dance business?"

"The Ghost Dance is a symptom, not the disease. You just said Wovoka was crazy, and that somebody usually makes money when anything important happens."

"Meaning a white man?"

"Well," Longarm said as he took a final puff on his cheroot and dropped the butt into a cuspidor, "it ain't Indians who're sending you foul rations and patched uniforms, and the white man doesn't figure to let any Indians make any real money if there's money to be made."

Somebody said, "What in the whiz-bang hell is that?" as Longarm led Penny out to Gatewood's buckboard the next morning. The occasion of the excitement was moving up the street toward them, and Longarm was a trifle confused by the sight, too.

Three garishly painted circus wagons were approaching, drawn by snow-white draft horses. Gilt letters on the lead wagon proclaimed it as the property of Colonel Comanche John's Wild West Circus. Longarm assumed that the driver of the wagon had to be Comanche John. This creature had a white beard and mustache, so it was probably male, despite the shoulder-length white hair. It wore a white Texas hat big enough for a modest-sized Indian family to live in. The rest of it was covered with snow-white fringed buckskin, with gilt glass beadwork. As Longarm and Penny got to the buckboard and he helped her up to sit beside the Gatewoods, the circus wagon stopped beside them and the gleaming buckskin-clad apparition said, "Greetings and salutations. We are bound for the Pine Ridge Indian Reservation. Allow me to introduce myself . . ."

"You can introduce yourself, but you're not driving that rig onto *my* agency," Gatewood told him.

Longarm reached out to touch Gatewood's leg as he murmured, "Let the man have his say."

Gatewood looked confused, but nodded. The colonel said, "As you must know, I am the famous, one and only Comanche John. Unlike my miserable rival, Buffalo Bill, I do not use Mexican cowboys to play the part of wild Indians in my productions."

"What *do* you use?" Penny asked with a smile.

"Why, little lady, I use real wild Indians, of course! That is why we are on our way to the Sioux Nation. I intend to sign up a full crew of bloodthirsty savages to attack my helpless pioneers in New York City this fall."

"Do you think the New York police will allow that, sir?"

"Ah, little lady, I see you have a sense of humor. Has anybody ever told you that you'd look pretty in pink tights? The Indians I hire will of course use blanks and rubber-tipped arrows."

Gatewood started to say they'd do no such thing, but Longarm nudged him again and called out, "You just head right up this road and we'll catch up as soon as I fetch my saddle mount, Colonel. We'll show you how to get to Pine Ridge."

The colonel doffed his hat to them, cracked his whip, and drove on. As the other wagons passed, driven by more normal-looking human beings, Gatewood exploded, "Have you gone crazy, Longarm? We've already got a mess of Indians stirred up out there. God knows what the Sioux will make of this traveling freak show!"

Longarm pointed with his chin at the last wagon as it passed. It was driven by a sort of gypsy-looking gal who cracked a mean whip. The wagon was fire-engine red. Longarm said, "I ain't sure some Indians ain't already excited about at least *one* of those wagons."

Gatewood's mouth fell open as his head swiveled to follow the passing wagon.

"That gal driving it is dark enough to pass for Indian, too," the lawman pointed out.

Penny still looked blank, but Mrs. Gatewood gasped, "Surely that Paiute medicine man isn't traveling with a circus, and even if he is, that was a *girl*, just now."

"That hadn't escaped my notice, ma'am. I'll get my pony. You folks drive on and I'll catch up."

As he crossed to the livery in the cloud of dust stirred up by all the wheels, Longarm was already having second thoughts about his suspicions. That gypsy-looking gal driving a big red wagon fit the description of Wovoka's missionary, Kamono, if you swapped the skirts for a breechclout. But Mrs. Gatewood was right, it made no sense. Why hide out with all sorts of medicine tricks and then ride smack into the bear trap in broad daylight? On the other hand, how many folks with dark hide and long black hair could be traipsing about in big red wagons?

He tipped the stable boy a nickel, mounted up, and lit out after the caravan up the road. He saw that Gatewood had driven wide to take the lead, so he fell in beside the red wagon, smiled over at the dark female driver, and said, "Howdy. My name is Custis Long."

The girl on the wagon seat said, "They call me Princess Silver Moon. Are you the law, or just a lonesome cowboy?"

He saw that she wasn't very neighborly, so he said, "I'm a deputy U.S. marshal. You folks are driving onto federal property, so let's not get off on the wrong foot, ma'am."

Princess Silver Moon nodded after a moment and said, "I didn't think you looked hard-up. All right, I've got nothing to hide. My right name is Kathy O'Shea, I was born somewhere in New England by the side of the road, and I'm not wanted anywhere." She cracked her whip and added, almost to herself, "That's for damned sure."

Longarm looked her over as he digested her words. She wasn't an ugly woman, but she wasn't all that exciting, either. The dusty, unkempt black hair and jingle-jangle brass earrings made her look sort of slatternly, and few well-bred white gals let the sun tan their faces that dark. Her trail-dusted gypsy-dancer outfit probably wasn't her best dress, so he allowed that she wasn't at her finest this morning. But even polished up and curry-combed, she'd have looked sort of wild.

"Kathy O'Shea ain't a very gypsy name," he pointed out.

"My people were tinker, not Rom," she replied wearily.

He nodded, and she shot him a look before she said, "Most folks ask me what that means."

"I know," he said. "I surprise folks too, when they find out I can read. I've never been to Ireland, but I know about the Irish folks who took up the gypsy life when the potato crop went bad. What happened to your kin on this side of the pond?"

"My mother died giving birth to me in a ditch, after the good people of Boston ran them out of town. My father was knifed a couple of years ago in Frisco. So you might say he raised me coast-to-coast."

"In that wagon?"

"No. We wandered mostly in gypsy carts. This one belongs to the colonel. He liked my magic act when he caught it at the Omaha State Fair, and before you ask, I'm not sleeping with him."

"I don't ask a lady things like that," Longarm said. "It ain't my business. But I can see at least some other lawmen have been rough on you."

101

She shrugged and said, "Oh, you get used to it on the road. I've only been raped in two jails, so far. It's those small-town deputies stealing all my valuables that riles me. It's hard as hell to put together a medicine show from scratch."

"Medicine show, ma'am?"

"Oh, come on, you've seen my act, or one like it. The colonel says I don't have to peddle Genuine Seneca Snake Oil at the end of my act, now that I'm with the circus. But the show I put on is the same old stuff. Where were you brought up? Every hick in the country must have seen a medicine show by now."

Longarm nodded and said, "I was thinking on another track. Medicine shows used to come through town where I grew up, in West-by-God-Virginia. Out here we use the word 'medicine' a mite different."

Longarm smiled to himself as he remembered a night in his boyhood when the world was younger and the crickets chirped on a soft summer evening. He and his folks had driven into town and he'd followed the drumbeats through the warm night air to a torchlit gathering where a traveling patent-medicine man had set up his wagon. The big tailgate had been folded down as a stage, and a colored man wearing an Indian headdress was beating a large tomtom. The Negro had smiled and winked at him while the "professor" whipped colored silk kerchiefs out of a hat and did crazy tricks with big brass rings. The boy Custis Long had enjoyed the show immensely and would have bought one of the bottles they sold at the end of the pitch if he'd had a dime, but later his dad had told him the professor wasn't really a magician and the bottles were just filled with colored water and might not cure baldness and such after all.

Longarm remembered something he'd learned later about cure-alls, and he asked the tinker gal, "Are you carrying and distributing distilled spirits, ma'am?"

Kathy said, "I have a jug of corn squeezings for my own use in the back, but I told you I'm not peddling anything but sleight-of-hand these days. The colonel said it was illegal even to *give* an Indian alcohol, mixed with branch water and coloring or not."

"Hmm, I see the colonel has more sense than you'd know from just looking at him. This ain't a very big circus you have here. How many wild Indians do you figure he has in mind to take on the road?"

"This ain't the main show," Kathy told him. "We left our big top and the elephant in the Scotts Bluff railroad yards with most of the crew. What you see here is the advance act. He thought we ought to give the Indians at least a hint of what they'll be joining. The colonel's wagon is his ticket office and quarters. That green wagon just ahead carries the steam organ and the gent who plays it. He asked me to tag along and do my magic act."

"Are you a good magician, ma'am?"

"Would a good magician be traveling with one elephant and an old drunk? I'm good enough for a one-ring show, I guess. I can saw you in half or pull an egg out of your ear, if you haven't a better way to spend an evening. My props are the usual magic-shop stuff. My hands are too small to palm anything bigger than a deck of cards or a few yards of silk. You should have seen my father when he was alive and sober. He could materialize live birds and pull real snakes out of girls' hair. They used to scream like hell. The moron who killed him said he was in league with the devil."

"I'm sorry to hear that, ma'am. It's only fair to warn you that the folks up the road ahead tend to take magic serious too. As a matter of fact, I'm looking for a Paiute who's said to be a wizard. How do you feel about cooperating with your Uncle Sam?"

"Do I have any choice?"

"You weren't invited to drive onto federal land. Once you folks are on the reservation, I might order you about and I might not, depending. I'll have to make you stop if I think you're getting the Sioux too excited. I might want you to study even *more* magic, if I can see a way to disenchant them with that other wizard. I know a mite about the way most magic works. This book I found in a library said it's all something called misdirection."

"Of course. Everyone knows that."

"Not many Indians do. They're handicapped by this notion that what a medicine man tells them is true. They don't lie as good as us. Can I ask you how to do one trick?"

"Sure. What do you want me to teach you, the linked rings, the sponge-rubber eggs, or colored-water tricks? Colored-water tricks are the easiest to learn. It's all simple chemistry."

"How would you make a big red wagon like the one you're driving vanish into thin air?" he asked, smiling.

"That's heavy stage stuff," she replied. "I've never worked theaters, but I suppose if I had black velvet drapes and smoke effects with black ropes running up into the flies . . ."

"I'm talking about doing it on open prairie. No trapdoors. No curtains or overhead pulleys."

She glanced at him as though she thought he was crazy. "Find something easier. There's no way to dematerialize anything you can't slide up a sleeve, out in the open."

"That's where you're wrong. An Indian medicine man keeps doing it. It's just come to me that the man I'm looking for might have been with a snake-oil show, one time."

"You say this breed or whatever can make something the size of a wagon vanish in thin air, under an open sky?"

"It sure looks like he can."

She shook her head and whistled softly. "If I could do that, I'd be rich and famous. What on earth is a magician like that doing out here in the sticks?"

"Stirring up trouble. You've likely read about the new Ghost Dance religion. The idea seems to be that if enough people here on earth raise enough hell with the white man, all the dead Indians and buffalo will come back to drive the white folks off and live happily forever after. But even a disgruntled Sioux takes some convincing. So they have these road shows out, making Heap Big Medicine and selling magic shirts."

An appreciative gleam appeared in the girl's eyes.

"A medicine-show sales pitch, eh? How much do they get for these cure-all shirts?"

"I don't know. Not much, I reckon. Their customers don't have much income."

"Then that makes even less sense, Marshal. Why would a really good magician waste his talent like that? Don't you know what Barnum would pay a Heap Big Injun who could even saw his squaw in half?"

"Hmm, I follow your drift. This jasper I'm talking about might be sincere about his religion, but a sincere preacher wouldn't think he had to resort to mummery, so we do have us a puzzle, don't we?"

"*You* have, you mean. It's not my problem."

"You're wrong, ma'am. I'll be calling on you this evening for some magic lessons. You're going to teach me the basics any wizard would start out knowing."

She shook her head emphatically. "That's impossible. It would take you weeks just to learn enough sleight-of-hand to be the life of the party."

"Shucks, I don't have to know how to do the tricks. I just want to know how they're done. You're just going to show me where the stuff goes when you say 'presto chango.' I don't aim to magic any Indians. I just want to *un*-magic one pesky wizard, if I ever catch up with him."

The three circus wagons rolling in behind Gatewood's buckboard caused about as much excitement at the agency as one would have expected. Sioux didn't get to see much gilt and glitter. The older folks hung back, watching from a safe distance, but the kids crowded in, patting the big horses and laughing fit to bust. Olga Swensen ran out of the house, sobbing that she'd thought they'd all been murdered and scalped, and for a minute Longarm was afraid she'd leap on him, but Olga noticed Penny in the buckboard. Longarm rode over to the colonel and told him not to set up or do anything just yet.

As Mrs. Gatewood invited everyone inside, Longarm spotted young Joseph and said, "Joe, make sure none of these kids count coup on these draft critters. They may let you feed and water them if you all behave. Where's Simon Peter?"

"I don't know," Joseph said. "He rode out to the east last night and hasn't returned. His woman is worried."

Longarm glanced up at the sun and said, "It's early yet. I'll see if I can cut his trail if he ain't back by this afternoon."

He rode to the corral and dismounted, leaving his pony saddled, before he headed for the back door. Before he got there, the door flew open and he saw Penny and Olga come rolling out and down the steps, clawing and yowling like alley cats!

They landed in the dust at his feet, with Olga on top for the moment. Then Penny threw a leg up, exposing her bare behind as she hooked a high-buttoned shoe around Olga's neck, shoved, and put the bigger gal on her back as they reversed positions. Olga's big naked thighs were waving in the air as Penny tried to hammer her brains out against the earth with a firm grip on the rolled braids of blonde hair over each of Olga's ears.

Olga screamed like a banshee and bucked Penny off, and as they went on rolling all around the yard they sure were getting ragged and dusty-looking, so Longarm stepped over to a washtub on the porch and poured it over them. Olga was on top at the moment, so she caught most of it, and her nipples showed pinkly through her wet white bodice as she sputtered and cussed.

By now Gatewood and the others were staring open-mouthed from the door. The agent yelled, "Stop that, damn it! That's no example to set my Indians!"

The Indians were enjoying the show just fine. Even some of the usually solemn older men were grinning ear to ear as they circled the contestants to watch. A brave near Longarm said, "I bet on little squaw. She fight good!"

Longarm saw that the fight was getting uncivilized, so he reached down and got a hold on both of them to haul them to their feet and get their skirts down proper. It was something like reaching into a sack of wildcats.

Penny kicked him in the shin and Olga slapped his hat off as they both started cussing him.

He hung on and shook them like wet rats as he growled, "That's enough, damn it. I ain't worth it. Are you two fixing to behave or do I have to bang your fool heads together?"

Olga started to cry, and for some reason this made Penny start bawling too. Mrs. Gatewood and the tinker girl came down the steps, and the agent's wife said, "Leave these two sweet girls alone, you brute! Haven't you caused enough pain and anguish already?"

Longarm let go and they both fell into Mrs. Gatewood's motherly grasp, sobbing and all tangled up together as she soothed, "There, there, you poor, mistreated things. Just come inside and tell me all about it."

As the three of them staggered off together, Gatewood asked Longarm, "What in blue blazes was that all about?"

Longarm noticed that Princess Silver Moon was smirking strangely as he shrugged and said, "Beats me. I never have been able to understand the critters. It was likely something they et."

Colonel Comanche John stepped gingerly to join them, avoiding the mud puddle that was left as a silent witness to the brawl. He said, "All's well that ends well. When can I powwow with these Indians about joining my show?"

Gatewood looked at Longarm, who said, "Just simmer down a spell, Colonel. Between a funeral and a Ghost Dance raid in the last twenty-four hours, I aim to palaver with them myself before I let anybody else at 'em." He turned to Gatewood and said, "Your policeman, Simon Peter, seems to be missing. Any ideas on that?"

Gatewood frowned and said, "No. I didn't know he was gone. I didn't send him after anyone, if that's what you mean."

"That's what I mean, right enough. He said something about riding off to check something out last night. If you don't know what it might have been, I don't know where to begin looking, and it's one big reservation."

He saw that the circus folk were confused, so he told them, "We had Indian trouble at Whiteclay last night. Since you were on the road to the south, we know they didn't run off with our cows in that direction. But they could be most anywhere, and that's why I want you to just sit tight until we get some answers."

Joseph came over and Longarm told the colonel, "This here is my Dog Soldier, Joe. If I were you I'd hire him to tend to your teams and keep the other kids from stealing from you."

Colonel Comanche John smiled and held his hand up to Joseph. "How, straight-shooter. For many moons I have dwelt among the lodges of your people in peace."

Joseph turned to Longarm, and jerked a thumb in the colonel's direction. "What's he talking about? Is he a crazy person?"

"No, just a white man. You do what he says and I won't let the princess, here, turn you into a frog."

Joseph shrugged and left with the colonel to see about parking the wagons and rubbing down the teams. Longarm found himself alone with Princess Silver Moon, alias Kathy. She said, "You'll get killed if you go in that house right now. Help me with my wagon and we'll talk about some tricks. Magic tricks, I mean. I can see I don't have to teach you any other kind."

He fell in beside her as they walked back to her red wagon. He'd deliberately not asked Joseph or the others if they'd seen it before, so he knew that only the colors matched. Kamono apparently was driving another red rig, too different to be confused with Kathy's. That was both good and bad. He knew he didn't have grounds to arrest her, but now he was stuck with a mess of circus folk in addition to all the other complications of this case.

Longarm said the wagon was all right where it was, parked near the road in front of the house. The colonel and his organist had all the help they needed with the teams, so he followed Kathy up into the wagon when she opened the rear door.

The inside was fixed up like a gypsy tent, with paisley-print draperies and a cot that doubled as a settee. She had trunks and boxes all over the wagon bed and it was sort of crowded for two people, so they had to sit close together as she leaned forward, opened a trunk, and started piling junk on the settee with them. He spotted a dusty battery jar in a corner and asked about it.

Kathy said, "It's dead. My dad used to use an electromagnet for some of his tricks, and I've never gotten around to throwing it out."

She suddenly made a yard of pink silk appear in front of them and said, "This is beginner's stuff, but you're a beginner. Most people don't know how many yards of thin silk you can wad up in the space between your fingers. You'll notice I wear lots of junk jewelry. The glitter and jangle distracts the eye from the sometimes awkward way I'm holding my hands."

"I know a little sleight of hand," he said. "I've played cards in Dodge City. Tell me some more about that electric stuff."

"I told you I don't use it in my act these days. Refilling the batteries is expensive, and I'm not a main attraction. I just slip on a fringed deerskin outfit with a lot of ankle showing, and the colonel gives a spiel about my being a genuine Comanche Princess he adopted to save from sacrifice."

"The Comanche don't sacrifice maidens, and if they did, they still don't have princesses. No Plains tribe has any hereditary royalty."

"Who cares? The yokels who come to our show are confused enough by swishing silk and rubber snakes. Do you want to see me pull a live and hissing cobra from my mouth?"

"Not hardly. Don't you *know* any fancy electric stuff?"

She shrugged and said, "Sure, but I can't show it to you."

"I'll take your word for it. What could a spooky gent do with a live electric battery?"

"Well, he could make artificial lightning with a Jacob's Ladder. He could give a rube a shock with his

109

magic wand. If you had a bank of batteries, you could always do the strong-man trick."

"The what?"

"Oh, surely you've seen the shows where the strong man challenges anyone in the crowd to lift a weight? There's a husky farmer in every town who's willing to bet a dollar on that scam. He gets up on the platform and busts a gut trying to lift the weight. Then, when he gives up, the strong man picks it up with one hand. Sometimes, for a laugh, they have a circus midget do it. But that can be dangerous if the local hero is not a good sport."

Longarm nodded and said, "I've seen that act. I always figured the strong man was just strong."

"Hell, when you're betting the crowd, you don't take the risk of a local who's been forking manure since he was two. Don't you see how it works? There's an electromagnet under the weight."

Longarm said, "I see it now. It ain't the weight that's heavy. The magnet holds it pinned to the floor until the strong man's pretty assistant switches it off with maybe her foot."

"If she's good, she swishes her skirt and lets them see the ankle she's not using."

"All that smiling and bouncing around behind the magician is to draw folks' eyes, right?"

"Of course. One famous magician was so brazen that he simply put things in his hat in full view of the audience while they were watching his assistant trip, almost drop a tray of glass bowls, and recover with a pretty blush."

"What did they do with the glass bowls?"

"Nothing. They were glued to the tray and everybody kept watching for one of them to fall and smash as the poor, pretty, clumsy girl wiggled all over the stage. When the magician wanted to do something astounding, she'd stop fiddling and point at him, and everyone would be struck dumb as he pulled the rabbit from the hat."

"But they never noticed him putting the rabbit *in* the hat! Hmm, this talk is giving me some interesting ideas, Kathy."

"Just so you keep your ideas clean. Does this Indian medicine man have a pretty assistant?"

"I don't know. He might *be* the pretty assistant."

He would have explained, but Kathy was a pro. "Right," she said. "While everyone is watching the left hand, the right hand does something else. How big a tip does this crowd have?"

"How's that? I don't talk circus."

"How much money can anyone make selling their spiel to these Indians? They do have *some* money, don't they?"

"Not much. Each family gets a small cash allowance in addition to free food, surplus army boots and such. They keep saying we don't give them enough. I tend to agree with them, considering how much gold has been dug out of the Black Hills."

"Is it possible that any Indians still have some partial claim on gold-mining property?"

Longarm was as startled and impressed as if she'd materialized Custer's ghost. "You *do* think into all the dusty corners, don't you? I never thought of that. The Lakota Confederacy was promised cash for the Black Hills, but they've never been paid in full. The government said the deal was off when they acted rude to Custer that time. But the tribal council had been legally recognized at the time they signed the last treaty. I'm not certain all the ifs, ands, and maybes have been settled, and the statute of limitations on just debts ain't run out yet."

"Then a recognized chief could sue in federal court for more money, right?"

"I doubt it. The Declaration of Independence didn't have Indians in mind when it said all men were equal. They're officially wards of the state."

"Can't a ward's legal guardian sue for him, if he's getting diddled out of his just deserts?" she asked.

"He can, but the Indian's legal guardian is Uncle Sam, who diddled him in the first damned place. I mean to check your notion out, but it's a long shot."

"*My* notion, Custis? I'm not sure what we're talking about."

"That's all right. Neither am I. Show me some more magic while I chaw on Indian policy awhile."

So she showed him linked rings and had him pick a card, and then he pointed out which shell the pea was under and Kathy said, "Damn! You're good! Are you teasing about not knowing these tricks, or do you just have an eagle eye?"

"I generally see what I'm aiming to notice. I've hunted some, and critters don't advertise their sly moves much, either. You *told* me to watch your hands instead of the rhinestones you keep flashing, didn't you?"

She laughed and said, "I can see that a girl has to be careful what she says around you. And speaking of girls, what did you do to those two, back there by the corral?"

He met her eyes calmly and suggested, "Why don't you ask them?"

"And get myself slapped skinny? I'll pass on that. My gypsy fortune cards will do me nicely, thank you. I can read all but the fine details without even dealing the deck."

"Well, I'd say the fine details are the business of them who know them firsthand. I thank you for the magic lessons. I'd better see if I can locate a vanished red man. We'll talk some more another time."

He got up and squeezed out as Kathy followed. As his boots hit the ground, Kathy leaned out the door and observed, "Well, I'll admit you're nice-looking and those shoulders are sort of exciting, but no fooling, what on earth could you have done to make them act like that?"

"There's things a gent don't say about any lady, ma'am."

"Don't go formal on me, Marshal. I'm not asking if you slept with them. I don't need a crystal ball to answer *simple* questions."

"I don't get tricked into admissions much, either," Longarm said.

"Well, you must have done something above and beyond the usual. But I see I'll never find out what it was, unless . . ." She blushed and said, "You're right.

112

There are some things only a fool would want to delve into."

She ducked back inside as Longarm shrugged and turned away. He caught himself starting to grin, and he made himself stop. He had enough on his plate as it was, and if he was any sort of a man he'd march right in that house and face the music.

But what the hell, it wasn't suppertime yet, and it was his simple duty to ride out and look for that missing Indian.

Chapter 6

The trouble with reservations was that folks stayed put. It had been easier to track Indians in the Shining Times. It wasn't that there were no tracks around the agency; there were too damned many of them. The bands no longer roamed about the prairie, and a hoof-print here and some grazed stubble there didn't tell a man much. There were beaten paths between the various sub-agencies and campgrounds now.

Pine Ridge covered a lot less ground than the Sioux had been promised when they laid down their arms, but it was still bigger than most white counties, and Longarm knew it would take a couple of days to ride across it in a beeline. He could circle for a month without really covering it all, and he couldn't say for sure that Simon Peter was even *on* the reservation!

Simon Peter could have ridden south into Bennett County, where the Seventh Cav was already running around in circles. He could have headed over to the neighboring Rosebud Reservation. He might have gone anywhere. So Longarm headed for the camp of Tipisota, hoping that if they knew anything, they *might* not lie to a white man about it.

He called out from the slope above the wooded creek, and waited past the requirements of common courtesy for an answer. Then he rode in. The tents were still there, but the Indians weren't. Tipisota's camp was deserted and the fires were all out.

Longarm put a cheroot between his teeth, lit it, and started to circle. He rode across the shallow creek and cut their trail on the far slope. They hadn't even tried to hide the passage of that many ponies, so the trail was easy to follow. But they had a good deal of lead-time on him, for he knew he was riding faster than they'd have moved out with even the kids and old folks riding. He crossed a sandy draw where the pony tracks told him that many of the animals were carrying two or more. But as he squinted ahead from each rise he topped, he couldn't see their dust. They'd lit out a good while back, and since they'd even packed the grandmas and kids, they'd figured on heading somewhere important.

The trailing got easier as the sun sank lower, side-lighting the trampled grass. There were no other stray hoofmarks now, and he was on ungrazed virgin prairie. The grass was rank as well as summer-browned. Now that the buffalo were gone, if they weren't replaced with cows right soon, there was going to be a really dangerous fire hazard out here. He knew the Indians weren't allowed to fire the prairie anymore. Folks who'd never seen an uncontrolled prairie fire couldn't see much sense in setting the grass alight on purpose. But the old buffalo hunters, white as well as red, had kept the range in a safer condition by torching off the thatch every few autumns when the wind and escape routes were right. He wondered if Gatewood could bend the rules if a fellow white man and old cowhand advised some burn-offs. None of the kids had ever seen the blue hazes of an old-fashioned Indian summer. Longarm smiled sort of wistful as he thought back to his boyhood and the red, hazy sunsets in the fall. As far east as New England the old folks told the kids that the Indian-summer skies were caused by "Indians burning leaves." It hadn't been until he came west, after the War, that he'd found out it wasn't a myth like Santa Claus.

He spotted wagon tracks cutting in at an angle, and dismounted for a closer look-see. He found some ants, mad as hell, repairing their ruined city. He dropped to one knee and found where a wagon wheel had run over a split hoofprint he remembered seeing before. So the wagon had passed this way after Tipisota's folks had. An angry red bulldog-ant charged up his thigh, snapping her jaws, and he flicked her off with his fingernail,

115

saying, "Simmer down, ma'am. It wasn't me. Your village was attacked by Indians."

He stood up, remounted, and rode on. He and the pony cast a long shadow as the sun sank lower behind them; he knew he faced a night ride back to the agency now. But he was used to spreading his roll on the prairie, and sleeping on an ant pile might be more comfortable than facing the music with two pissed-off women.

"Damn that Olga," he sighed to his shadow. He'd known there was only a fifty-fifty chance of her being a good sport. Women whooped and hollered about a fate worse than death and made a man promise he'd never tell, but he'd met few who didn't brag more about getting "ruined" than a fourteen-year-old boy did about his first piece.

He knew she'd have been just as likely to make trouble if he'd resisted her advances, so what the hell. He'd have been in trouble with Penny anyway, and still wondering if he'd missed anything with Olga. Now that they were both mad at him, he could concentrate on his job, which was getting more tedious by the minute. He was miles from Tipisota's now, and all there was to see was grass. Another wagon track joined the parade to wherever the Indians were headed, to the east.

The sky was a deeper shade of blue over that way now, and sunset was sneaking up on him. The trail led up another rise to vanish over the near horizon. Longarm hoped to have a better view from up above, so he heeled his pony into a trot upslope. He reined in on the crest, looked down into the next draw, and suddenly knew just what George Armstrong Custer must have said on an occasion like this, not so long ago or very far away. Longarm said the same thing.

"Goddamn! Let's get out of here!"

He spun his pony around and started moving the other way at a flat downhill run.

There'd been a big red wagon and some others parked by the winding stream in the draw he was now leaving behind him. There'd been one hell of a crowd of male, female, and kid Indians gathered down there too. The ones on horseback had started right up at him the moment he topped the rise to be outlined like a big-ass bird against the sky!

His tired pony ran as disappointingly as hell, considering that they were going downhill and he was whipping it with the rein-ends. Behind him, somebody yelled out, "Hey-yo-ha-yahahhh!"

Since that wasn't his name, Longarm didn't stop to ask what they wanted. A bullet dug up dust and grass stems to his right, and he said, "Come on horse, *move!* I know you don't have to take this as serious as me, but you're going to have to run faster anyway!"

It got worse going up the next rise. Like other Indian ponies, his borrowed mount didn't have the reserves of the slower grain-fed horses white men usually rode. It could move like spit on a hot stove for the first mile or so, but it had no second wind. The Indians chasing him were riding fresh mounts. They didn't need any second wind; at the rate they were gaining, they'd have his hair before their mounts began to fold.

He swung around in the saddle and took a potshot with the rifle to show them he didn't like to be crowded. Not one of them took the hint. They were wearing those damned medicine shirts and were spreading out as they came, meaning to hit him from both sides as they overtook him. He made it an even dozen. He tore over the crest and down the next slope, gaining a few yards and then losing them again as the Indians boiled over the ridge in a long skirmish line. He knew it couldn't go on like this much longer, so as he got to the next crest he reined in, dumped his pony on its side, and dropped down in the tall dry grass to make his stand. The Indians just downslope, out of range to the east, reined in to powwow about the best way to finish the fight. If they had any sense, they'd circle him and close in, throwing lead from the far side of their mounts. He wondered if he could drop a dozen ponies with the thirteen or fourteen rounds he had in his magazine, then still be able to stop one dozen pissed-off Indians with the five in his Colt and the two in his derringer. He reached down for the bowie in his boot sheath, and stuck the knife in the sod where it would be handy. They were taking their time in planning his demise, since they could see he wasn't going anywhere, so Longarm fished out a cheroot and started to light up. Then he considered the tinder-dry straw he was lying in, and hesitated. He stuck a finger in his mouth, then held it up to test the wind. He grinned like a coyote in a sheepfold, and struck the match. He didn't set fire to the grass he lay in. That would have been foolish. He pulled up a big clump of grama, roots and all, set fire to it, and heaved it out between his pony and the Ghost Dancers. Without waiting to observe the results, he repeated the action with another clump, and another, and when the first match burned down, he lit another one. He had plenty of matches.

The results were spectacular. Each firebomb he threw splashed flame and blue smoke as though the prairie were a pool of coal oil. The Indians on the far side were hazed by smoke and yelling dreadful things about his lack of responsibility. They were likely thinking of their wives and kids in the path of the prairie fire. Longarm nodded and said, "You just go on along and get all those folks on the far side of that creek and we'll say no more about it."

One of the Indians came tearing upslope at him through the smoke, shaking his rifle like a fist. Longarm decided to see how good those medicine shirts were. He braced his Winchester across the pony's side, fired, and showed one Ghost Dancer that there were limitations to his faith. The man went down with a surprised look on his face and one lung blown out the back of his fancy buckskin shirt.

There were no other takers. The one he'd shot rolled down the slope into the flames, screaming pretty loudly for a man with only one lung. Longarm couldn't see the others. They were likely riding fast to warn the others. If they rode as fast as hell, there was a chance they'd make it. He figured the wildfire he'd just set was racing east at about twenty miles an hour.

It was a spooky sight, even from the safe side. The

billowing blue wall of smoke towered like marching thunderheads, sucking red confetti sparks a mile high. He knew each and every one of those burning grass stems promised to explode like a bomb in any clump of wind-dried grass it landed in. If the Indians to the east were smart, they'd stand in the creek, fire the far slope, and walk up into the char and ash of their own backfire. If they just ran, Billy Vail was going to give Longarm pure Ned for *this* solution to the Indian problem! He was glad, at least, that Tipisota would be over there on the other side of that hell to show them how things were done in the Shining Times. Longarm didn't want to wipe the Indians out, he just wanted to civilize them a mite.

He rose and hauled the bewildered pony to its feet, saying, "Well, you've had your beauty rest, you lazy son of a bitch. We'd best get on before some wiseacre thinks about cutting around that fire for another try at us."

He mounted up and rode down toward the Indians and into the black, smoldering sod of the first burn. The pony didn't think much of the idea until Longarm had whipped his hat across its face a few times. "I'm not trying to cremate you, old son," he said. "We won't leave a trail worth mention in this char, since the wind is still blowing ashes every which way."

He walked the pony south through the fetlock-deep ash. The sky was red on both sides, since the sun was going down to the west while the prairie burned to the east. They ran out of burn in a little over a mile, but he knew they'd have trouble tracking him far in the dark, so he cut toward the agency over untouched grass. The pony perked up, knowing it was headed home. But Longarm held it to a trot. He had a long ride ahead, and a man never knew when he'd need that last burst of speed from his mount.

As he spotted a line of dots to his right against the sunset, Longarm thought for a moment that the time was about to arrive. Then he saw that it was a column of mounted troopers, so he headed to meet them, waving his hat until they spotted him and reined in. He put his hat back on, raised his rifle over his head, and pumped it up and down three times. They recognized the "enemy ahead" signal and started to form a defense. As he rode into the line of dismounted troopers with their horses to the rear, he saw that it was Captain Kehoe's outfit. The captain called out, "What's up? Who started that fire over there?"

Longarm reined in and dismounted before he said, "I did. Did you tell Gatewood you were on the reservation?"

Kehoe looked surprised. "I didn't know we were on the reservation, but I'm not surprised. We've been trailing those stolen cattle." He pointed with his chin.

Longarm spotted the fresh cow pat in the grass and said, "So I see. Those raiders took the cows over thataway for a big barbecue and medicine show. I stumbled in on it uninvited and they just made me a believer in George Armstrong Custer."

"Jesus Christ! How far are they, and how many?"

Longarm hesitated before he replied, "You strike me as a sensible gent, Captain. Before we get all hot and bothered, how good are you at separating the sheep from the goats? I'd say ninety percent of the crowd ahead are innocent bystanders, and a mess of them are women and children."

"You call people who steal cows and attack you twice 'innocent bystanders'? I'm a Christian man myself, Longarm, but you carry it beyond the call of duty!"

"Now don't get your bowels in an uproar. You and your boys trailed the right cow thieves, and my hat's off to you for the slight lead they have on you after an early start. I'm not really fond of the ones who keep trying to lift my hair, and I just proved it by putting one of the bastards on the ground."

"Then what are we waiting for? Let's charge in and get the rascals!"

"Let's *walk* in and make sure we get the right ones," Longarm amended. "Only a dozen in the whole crowd saw fit to chase me. The rest were as surprised as I was. The way I put her together, Kamono has called a powwow with free eats to convince the Sioux on this reservation that he has Heap Strong Medicine."

"*This* reservation, Longarm? Are you saying the Ghost Dancers we tangled with last night weren't from Pine Ridge?"

"It's a safe bet, since the one I shot at close range was a Cheyenne, if I still know my warpaint. I know that red wagon was down there in the draw too, because I saw it just before my business called me suddenly away. There's only one other red wagon I know of on this reservation, so why don't we set and rest a spell? The moon will be up early. How far can anyone drive a wagon in a few hours, red or not?"

Kehoe started to object, but then he turned to his lieutenant, who'd been listening at attention down the line, and said, "You heard the man, Lieutenant. Field rations with no fire. Water the mounts and post the perimeter pickets first."

"Permission to make a suggestion, sir?"

"Permission granted."

"I'd like to post a lookout on that rise over there to the north. It dominates the terrain all around."

"Good thinking. Carry on, Lieutenant."

The boy saluted and spun on one heel to start barking orders. Kehoe chuckled and said, "In a month or so he'll know enough to let the NCOs do that. As I see your plan, the party should be breaking up about now."

Longarm nodded and said, "Yeah, a lot of smoked-up folks are going home to eat sensible government rations, now that they know that at least one white man knows the address. Kamono and his Ghost Dancers will be lighting out for parts unknown. Anyone can shuck a shirt and wipe his face clean, but that red wagon sort of stands out. If we ride in a firm but fair sweep, we ought to nail the bastard this time. He can't have gone far and there's no place to hole up."

"I said I understood your plan. What do we do with the Paiute troublemaker when we catch him? Hang him from his own wagon tongue?"

"I wish you wouldn't. I've got a warrant for his

121

arrest. Throwing in that gent they killed in Whiteclay, there's enough of a charge to hang him."

"That's what I just suggested, damn it."

"I know, but they're stuffed with martyrs killed by the U.S. Cavalry. I don't want to make a Messiah out of Kamono, I want to see him end his career as a convicted felon. Indians are used to dying, but jails and court proceedings scare the piss out of them. Besides that, the old chiefs mostly read. They say Sitting Bull has a subscription to the *Washington Post*."

"You're joshing."

"No, I ain't. How do you think a wise man persuades folks to think he's wise? Anyway, the chiefs and medicine men keep posted better than a lot of folks give them credit for. I want them to read the charges in the papers. I want Kamono and his head spook, Wovoka, shown up as cow thieves and scamps. I want folks cooled off and thinking clear when Kamono goes to the gallows, six months or so from now." Longarm lit a cheroot before he added, "We might get some information out of Kamono too. If he wants to tell us where Wovoka and the other ringleaders are, I'd be willing to settle for just locking him up."

"You've made your point," Kehoe agreed. "I'll handle anyone we catch with kid gloves. Or I will until one of my men or horses gets hurt. After that, the gloves come off."

The moon was blue as it shone down brightly through the haze, so Longarm could see a country mile across the blackened prairie sod as he rode at the head of the column with Captain Kehoe. They'd agreed not to spread out in diamond patrols until they reached the far side of the creek, where Longarm had spotted the medicine man's wagon.

They'd already seen other wagons. They kept meeting, or almost meeting, scattered parties of worried-looking Indians. But each time, Longarm shook his head and the troopers rode on, pretending they hadn't noticed the Indian families, either.

They rode down into the draw, dismounted, and

scouted for sign. A trooper called out, and when Longarm joined him he pointed to wagon tracks running upslope to the southeast in the charred sod. Longarm congratulated the trooper, and as Kehoe came over, he said, "They built a backfire like I figured they would. They moved up there and waited for the main fire to die out and cool off before they headed home. See that rattle some baby dropped?"

Kehoe nodded and said, "That one set of tracks runs right up over the crest. The driver wasn't headed for the agency."

"Right. We can't say for sure whether he was coming or going, but either way, I'd say Kamono left those wheel ruts. He either lit out for the Rosebud Reservation or Bennett County, smack between here and Rosebud. Sort of a funny place for whites to want to live, but I don't make the rules."

Kehoe looked skeptical. "He'd be taking a chance driving through Bennett, wouldn't he?"

"I don't see how it would be a bigger risk than that other reservation. They're both patrolled by lawmen."

"Yeah, but the lawmen in Bennett County are white," Kehoe pointed out.

"I know. They'd be easier for a sly Indian to fool than Indian officers might be. Driving a wagon and dressed right, he could pass for a breed or a Mexican. But let's not jaw about it. Let's mount up and find out."

So they did. Longarm had to admit that wherever Kehoe had gotten his troopers, he'd trained them well. They fanned out in a line of half-squad patrols, each led by a corporal or a lance corporal and keeping in contact with little fuss as they swept a swath that reached out of sight over either horizon on the flanks. They moved at a mile-eating if uncomfortable trot, and Longarm knew they were gaining by the hour on any mortal wagon team that might be ahead.

Kehoe did things by the numbers, with more fancy shouts than cowhands driving a herd would have needed, but he called his breaks at the right times and kept his sweep in good order. The only problem was that after a night in the saddle, they hadn't caught up with anybody.

Kehoe ordered a dawn mess break as the sun peeked over the rim of the world at them again, and as Longarm stared morosely down at the dew-wet grass, the captain asked, "Well?"

Longarm said, "The stems are long sprung back. It's sure starting to look like we lost that wagon."

"I can see that," Kehoe admitted. "But where in hell could he have gone? How fast can you drive a wagon?"

"Not that fast. I only got one look at it, but it was a big, heavy bastard with solid side panels, like an ice wagon. He probably uses it as his quarters as well as a pulpit."

"We let a couple of wagons through, last night. Colors are sort of hard to read by moonlight."

"I know. But I looked anyway. None of those Indians were headed home in a red wagon, and none of the ones I saw were built like an ice or circus wagon."

"Isn't there some way he could have disguised his rig? Some of those we let through were prairie schooners. What if he threw a tarp over its solid sides?"

"He'd wind up with a square-topped prairie schooner, which I was careful to keep in mind. We only passed a couple, and I swung in to make sure. One had a blue bed and the other was unpainted wood. They both had regular wagon bows under their canvas too."

"Could you, well, *repaint* a wagon on short notice?"

Longarm smiled. The captain was really reaching. "Have you smelled any paint lately, Captain? Hell, if he has time to stop and repaint his fool wagon, he has no need of it. He's so damned far off that it doesn't matter what color it might be!"

"What do we do now?" Kehoe asked.

It was a good question.

Longarm sure wished he had an answer.

The map said they were off the reservation, and Captain Kehoe said the army didn't allow him to just fool around. He was supposed to bring his soldiers back when they weren't doing anything important. So Longarm said goodbye as they rode off to go home and paint rocks white or polish their brass.

Longarm decided that, as long as he seemed to be on a fool's errand himself, he'd ride on to the county seat and see if Kamono had been picked up for loitering.

The town of Martin was a mite larger than Whiteclay to the west, but that didn't mean it was big. The county sheriff was a red-faced, friendly old cuss who hadn't heard about the man killed in Whiteclay, but he said he wasn't surprised. He offered Longarm a seat in his office, got out a bottle, and poured as he explained, "We don't work tight with the law on the wrong side of the territorial line, but it's too bad they killed that gent, even if he was a Nebraskan. Them damn Sioux have been killing folks as long as I can remember."

"The war party was painted Cheyenne," Longarm pointed out.

"Whatever. Cheyenne are no damned good, neither. If they make the mistake of trying for a scalp over here, we'll tame the shit out of them, whoever they may be."

Longarm sipped his drink. The bottle may have said it was bourbon, but the taste was white lightning. He asked, "Doesn't it make you folks a mite nervous, living here sort of cut off from the rest of the country by two Indian reservations?"

"Hell," the sheriff said, "we was here first. The Indians were up in the Black Hills when this country was settled. All but a few, at least. The old boys who trailed the first cows up from Texas a few years back shot off such redskins as were here. Then the damned old government carved reservations out of open range all around us. We had too many voters registered for 'em to grab this part, but some ranchers was evicted and they're still sore as hell. That's why if them Sioux know what's good for 'em, they'll stay the hell out of Bennett County!"

Longarm took another experimental sip and said, "You ain't *all* mad at them. The BIA tells me there was a white man selling corn squeezings to the Indians not too long ago."

The sheriff nodded. "The Carson Brothers. They have a still on their spread over near Black Pipe. But they've quit selling redeye to the Indians. Uncle Sam raised hell in the first place, and they found other customers with more money to spend in the second."

"I noticed. I don't reckon they ever got around to filing for a distillery permit, huh?"

The sheriff leaned back in his chair and rubbed his considerable paunch. "Don't know. I never thought to ask. I ain't a revenue agent. Are you?"

"No. I told you I worked for Justice when I showed you my badge. If you say the Carson brothers ain't selling firewater to the Indians, I'll take your word for it."

The sheriff looked mollified. "It's just as well for all concerned. The Carson boys are ornery, even for Bennett County. What else is there that I can maybe fill you in on?"

"Would you have a list of folks who filed on any land the Indians might otherwise have wound up with?"

"No, but the county clerk would likely let you look at his records. Are you hinting at a land grab, Marshal?"

"Don't know. The last time there was spooky doings on a reservation, I caught a crooked white man at the bottom of it all."

The sheriff snorted, "Hell, everybody knows this Ghost Dance bullshit was thought up by that crazy Paiute, Wovoka."

"Oh, I'll allow there are crazy Indians, Sheriff. But even in the Black Hills mess, there was money at the root. Folks are always climbing on a soapbox to preach, but I've found that damned few take them serious unless they've got money backing them. This jasper Kamono didn't build his circus wagon out of willow twigs and rawhide. He has to park the fool thing somewhere between appearances, too. You say these Carson brothers can be found near Black Pipe?"

"I did, but take my advice and stay the hell away from them. I already told you nobody in these parts ever mentioned a stranger passing through in a big

126

red wagon, and the Carsons won't take it neighborly if you go accusing them of being renegade whites."

"I won't accuse anyone of anything until I catch them at it," said Longarm, putting down his half-filled glass as he stood up. If the Carson brothers were responsible for its contents, they deserved twenty years at hard labor, but the sheriff was right: it wasn't his job to pass judgement on the stuff they made, as long as they weren't running it to the Indians. He wasn't even worried about that, as a matter of fact, unless their delivery cart was a big red wagon.

After he left the sheriff's, Longarm went to the Western Union office. He sent a mess of inquiries to various government agencies on just about everyone he'd met recently. When he billed it all to his Denver office the telegraph clerk said, "We sure are getting a lot of Uncle Sam's business lately."

"Do tell?" Longarm said, perplexed. "I thought I was the only federal man in town."

"You are now, I reckon. Yesterday a reservation lawman was in here sending wires fit to bust."

"Was he an Indian named Simon Peter?"

"He was. I thought it was sort of peculiar, but what the hell, he knew how to write, and he sent the messages collect."

"Who did he wire, and about what?"

The clerk looked uncertain as to whether he should answer, so Longarm took out his wallet and flipped it open to display his badge. "I'm the senior federal lawman hereabouts and Simon Peter is working under me."

The clerk smiled thinly. "I don't doubt that, but he allowed the wires he sent were sort of secret."

"Let me put it this way. Western Union's lines run across a lot of federal land. You likely know I can't pull enough rank to put Western Union out of business, but I can raise enough hell to get an uncooperative jasper called on the carpet for making a company vice-president late getting home to supper."

The clerk's sickly smile vanished abruptly. "Whoa up there, mister," he said, holding up a hand. "You know so much about Western Union, you sure ought to know the rules I got to follow, so don't go taking it personal. I don't aim to get in hot water over an Indian, so I'll tell you. Just don't tell anybody else what I told you. Deal?"

"Deal," Longarm said, nodding, and the clerk went on, "He wired the Rosebud Reservation to ask if they were missing any Cheyenne, and they sent back that they weren't. Then he wired the Interior Department that he didn't have anything new on some gate, and that he was checking out the seas."

Longarm frowned and said, "Let's study on that some more. Was it 'gate' or 'Gatewood,' and did he say 'seas,' like the ocean, or did he mean something else?"

The clerk scratched his head vigorously. "I don't have the best memory in the world, but I'd have remembered if he'd spelled out Gatewood. He's the Indian agent over to Pine Ridge, right?"

"Right. So 'gate' is a code word. What about the 'seas'?"

"I'm sure he said 'seas,' like the ocean. He said to tell the Treasury men to hold off until he'd had another look at the seas."

Longarm thanked the clerk and left, scowling. The damned fool Indian might have *told* him he'd been authorized to do investigative work by the Indian agency. These interdepartmental feuds were a pain in the ass. But if the BIA had a man they trusted that much on the job, why had they asked for help from Justice? Were they *using* him and Billy Vail? He knew an extra pea under the shells made for one razzle-dazzle game. But who in thunder were they out to razzle-dazzle? Kamono was a trickier-than-usual Indian, but the trouble he'd been trying to stir up hardly called for anything this convoluted. He knew better than to demand an explanation from the Interior Department. They were already holding back when they'd sent for him.

Simon Peter's code wasn't all that complicated to figure out. 'Gate' stood for 'Gatewood,' so the BIA was double-checking their new agent through an older, trusted Indian employee. It wasn't even a mystery what they wanted Simon Peter to check. Crooked agents followed a pattern that was downright tedious. A white patronage appointee could get cocky, lording it over folks he felt superior to. Nobody listened when an Indian complained that he was getting robbed, so many an agent figured he could get away with dipping his hand in the till. That reptile he'd arrested on the Ute reservation had been banking a thousand a month in Salt Lake City, without letting any Utes really starve to death. When a man buys for a couple thousand families, a little short weight here and a late ration there can add up.

But if Simon Peter said he had nothing to report on 'gate,' it was a safe bet that Gatewood was behaving himself. Simon Peter wasn't given to blind admiration for any white man. 'Seas' likely meant the Carson brothers, since the BIA already had them down as firewater traders, and Black Pipe was only a day's ride from here. Simon Peter had asked Rosebud for information because his ride to the 'C's' would put him near the Rosebud line and he didn't want to ride back to Pine Ridge through a reservation jump. He couldn't have known when he sent his wires that Kamono and his Ghost Dancers were having a barbecue on his own beat.

The county clerk wasn't in his office, but his female file clerk said she'd be happy to help Longarm any way she could. She was a pretty little strawberry blonde, despite her cheaters and a yellow pencil stuck in her bun, but Longarm figured she just meant she'd help him study the county records.

She got out a big dusty ledger and showed him to a seat at a desk behind the counter. He blew the dust off and asked if he could smoke while he went over the sheets. She said he could, and offered him a cup of tea, but he said he was in a hurry. She looked sort of disappointed.

Longarm was disappointed too. He couldn't even find a recent request for a grazing permit on the Indian lands. He ran his finger down the list of registered brands and saw why. Bennett County was still mostly open range. Why pay a grazing fee you didn't have to? He found the Carson brothers' brand. It was the Double C. They didn't show much more imagination than Simon Peter. According to the records, their folks had staked the usual homestead claim of a quarter-section, just after the War when folks still thought a quarter-section was enough land to live on out here. He knew they'd have water and a herd out grazing the surrounding range. He'd know when he tallied their herd if they were still selling firewater wholesale, or if it was just a sideline to accommodate the neighbors.

He closed the ledger and asked the strawberry blonde if she had the files on any recent or pending lawsuits, and she wagged her tail and fetched him a pasteboard box of process papers. He was almost sorry he'd passed on her tea as he chewed his cheroot and pawed through them. The folks around Martin were litigious as hell. They sued each other over chickens scratching in the flowers out back, or a hound that barked all night. Some woman had asked for a peace bond on a neighbor who fussed at her over the fence. Another lady was suing a whorehouse over her husband coming home with the clap. But he couldn't find any land disputes or a claim against the government. It was all just the usual small-town stuff. He left the records office grateful that he wasn't the judge who had to pass on all this chickenshit.

His throat felt raspy from the dust that legal records seemed to produce all by themselves, so he headed for the saloon, figuring to buy a bottle of Maryland rye to take with him as he rode over to Black Pipe.

Chapter 7

It was a hot, dry day on the High Plains, but the pinto didn't sweat much. An Indian pony could trot forever, even if it couldn't run much after one burst of speed. Longarm kept an eye peeled as he rode. He didn't expect to run into a war party in such settled country, but he'd learned that the Ghost Dancers didn't know the rules. He hadn't gotten much of a look at any of them, close up, but they had to be mostly kids. He knew there was many an unreconstructed old warrior who'd be only too anxious for another round with the Great White Father's paler kids, but so far they'd acted too wild to have an experienced leader. Wovoka, Kamono, and the other known leaders of the Ghost Dance movement were either too young to remember the Shining Times, or they were from tribes who'd never really fought the army. That was likely why they talked so brave. He'd been brave to the point of stupidity in his first war, too.

He cleared his mind of questions he couldn't answer. He'd told the folks he'd wired to reply via the office in Whiteclay; maybe he'd have some answers when he got back there. His chances of getting back there would be better if he concentrated on the here and now. He'd already figured out what he'd say if Gatewood asked why he hadn't had his replies sent directly to the agency. He knew there was nothing he could say to Olga, Penny, or Mrs. Gatewood, so he decided Pine Ridge didn't exist until he was through in Black Pipe. He had no idea what he'd find there, he just had to make sure no more folks came popping over a ridge singing death songs at him.

So, while most other white men might not have been

131

interested in the distant dispute of a raven and some carrion crows, Longarm took notice, and swung off the trail to see what all the fuss was about. The big black birds saw him headed their way and forgot their quarrel as they circled and cussed him. As he rode up the slope of the rise they'd been disputing, one of the crows spooked his pony by diving at them like a hawk. Longarm steadied his mount and said, "Hell, can't you read a bluff, horse? I thought you grew up out here."

The pony balked and dug in his hooves, trying to throw the bit as he shook his head from side to side. "I smell it too," Longarm said, "but we're going anyway."

He dismounted and led the pony by the reins, holding his rifle in his free hand. The pony complained and had to be half-dragged, like a stubborn pup on a leash, but they made it to the top of the rise. Longarm stared down at the corpse on the far side and slowly took off his Stetson.

It was Simon Peter. The Sioux policeman had been worked on by the carrion crows, but Longarm could see that he still had his hair and hands. If he hadn't been gunned by a white man, it had been Indians who aimed to show contempt. Longarm knew the worse thing a warrior could say about a fallen enemy was that he'd fought so badly he wasn't worth counting coup on, but he hadn't figured Simon Peter for a bad fighter.

He said, "I'm sorry, horse, but I mean to have a closer look and I know better than to let you loose."

He tried to drag the pinto closer, and when it reared and tried to kick him, Longarm slapped it hard on the side of the head with his Stetson.

The pinto got the message and only shivered and nickered as Longarm dragged it over by the dead Indian. Simon Peter's pistol was still in its holster. Any saddle gun he might have had was long gone, with his mount. Longarm could see now that he'd been shot between the shoulder blades. The ground on the wind-swept ridge was as hard as cement and covered with short stubble, so there wasn't much other sign to read. It looked like the Indian had either been blown off his own pony as he ran from someone, or simply bush-whacked from behind and never knew what hit him.

Longarm dropped to one knee, placed the rifle on the sod, and went gingerly through Simon Peter's pockets with his free hand. He put the Indian's wallet, pocket knife, and loose change in his own coat pocket. Then he took a deep breath and turned the cadaver over. It was stiff and flat on the bottom, like a dead cat. The badge pinned to Simon Peter's vest was U.S. Government property. Simon Peter's kin could have everything else, but Longarm removed the badge and pocketed it.

He told the dead man, "I'll send someone back from Black Pipe with a buckboard for you, old son. I'm sorry about the way those birds are treating you, but I know you'd want to be buried among your own, so there's nothing either of us can do about it."

He led the pony away, upwind, and a big black crow flew down to stake a claim on Simon Peter's head. The other crows landed all around and started edging in. Longarm knew he was being foolishly sentimental, but he raised the muzzle of the Winchester and blew the crow on the corpse's head to feathers anyway. The remaining crows took off in every direction. Longarm mounted up and rode on. There was nothing else he could do except take a good slug from the bottle in his saddlebag, so he did.

He used up most of the day getting as far as Black Pipe. The Carson spread was closer, but he swung wide and bored on in to tend to his first chores first. He found the local coroner, identified himself, and got the coroner to agree to gather up what was left of Simon Peter in the morning and send it to Pine Ridge in a closed casket. When the coroner opined that some quicklime and pine oil might not be a bad idea, Long-arm said he'd pay for that too. He figured he'd get to Pine Ridge before the body and have time to break the news gently to Simon Peter's window and orphans.

Leaving the coroner's office, Longarm went looking for the town law to make a courtesy call. A deputy said he'd find the constable in the saloon, so Longarm went there.

The Black Pipe law was middle-aged, dressed in baggy wool trousers and a balbriggan shirt with a rusty badge pinned to it. He had squinty but friendly eyes, and his nose and cheeks were puffy and decorated liberally with grogblossoms. Longarm told him about the killing and asked if they'd had any Indian trouble. The constable said, "Well, we *see* a mess of redskins riding past, but I can't say we have much trouble with them. They know better."

A gruff-looking man at a table in a corner chimed in, "Damned right. We don't take no shit off Injuns in Black Pipe."

Longarm saw that the loudmouth was dealing solitaire, and tried to ignore him as he asked the town law, "Are you saying they move back and forth between reservations?"

"Yep. They ain't supposed to, but they do it anyhow. Uncle Sam was dumb to put reservations right next door to one another if he wanted his Injuns to stay put."

"I know. Tell me, have you ever seen an Indian, or maybe a breed, in a big red wagon?"

"Big red wagon? I can't say I have. How about you, Willy?"

The man in the corner shook his head and said, "Nope. Ain't seen one in a hansom cab or coach-and-four, for that matter. The raggedy-ass bastards are lucky to have ponies. If it was up to me, I'd shoot all their ponies, like Custer did at Washita. Maybe then the rascals would stay home nights."

Longarm nodded and said, "I didn't expect to get lucky with that medicine wagon, anyway. Can you gents tell me how I find the Carson spread?"

The constable didn't answer. Longarm noticed that he was edging down the bar as the man in the corner asked, "Who wants to know?"

Longarm said, "I do. I'm a deputy U.S. marshal and—"

The other was rising and going for his gun as he roared, "I *knew* it!"

Longarm crabbed to the side as he reached across

134

his belly for his own .44 and yelled, "Hold your fire! I'm not a revenuer!" But the other answered by hauling out a Walker-Colt conversion, so Longarm sighed and shot him.

He only shot the fool once, but once was enough when it took a man just over the heart and bounced him off the wall. The man he'd shot died on the way to the floor.

There was a long, pregnant pause. Then the constable said, "Jesus. You'd better start riding, friend."

"Who was he?" Longarm asked, and the town law said, "Willy Carson. Like I said, you'd better ride."

"You saw him draw on me, didn't you?"

"Sure I saw it. It was pure self-defense and we'll say no more about it. But for God's sake, get out of town before his brothers hear about it!"

"Brothers? More than one? I thought there were just two Carson brothers, Constable."

"You thought wrong. There were four, until just now. That means you have three more Carsons and maybe a five-minute head start."

"Damn it, I rode all this way just to talk to the Carson brothers."

"I know, and you just found out how conversational they are. Willy, there, was the runt of the litter and not as ornery as the others."

Some townies had come to the open door, attracted by the sounds of gunplay. Someone in the crowd who couldn't see asked what had happened, and a man with a better view called back, "That long drink of water just gunned Willy Carson, ain't that a bitch?"

The bartender came back into the room and said, "I sure wish you'd take your trade elsewhere, mister. That drink is on the house, but my pier glass came all the way from Chicago!"

Longarm looked at the town law and said, "I know this is a foolish question, but are you up to backing another lawman's play?"

"Not hardly. It was your notion to shoot him. I done my duty in warning you to run like hell. By now some fool with a love of excitement will be on his way to tell the Carson brothers what just happened to their baby brother. So it's been nice meeting you, but my old woman will be expecting me home for supper."

Longarm nodded and walked out as the crowd parted like the Red Sea had for Moses. He reloaded his revolver thoughtfully in the soft late-afternoon light, and folks kept crawfishing away until he had a hundred feet of boardwalk all to himself. Longarm walked to the pony he'd tethered at the rail in front of the saloon, and holstered his revolver again as he slid the Winchester out of its saddle boot. Someone down the street marveled, "Jesus! He must be aiming to stay!"

Longarm levered a round into the rifle's chamber, got away from his innocent pony, and moved along the storefronts until he found a blank wall for his back and a rocking chair for his rump. He drew the chair up near a post and sat down with the Winchester in his lap. He braced one boot against the post and began to rock, gently. He thumbnailed a sulfur match into flame and touched it to the cheroot between his teeth. Waiting like this was tedious, but he didn't see what else he could do. Riding out to the Carson spread now would be pure suicide.

A million years went by, but the sun was still sitting there near the western horizon when somebody called out, "They're riding in. I don't know about you boys, but I got a cow to milk."

Longarm stared down the street. The dust was the color of rose petals under the blood-red sky. Three riders reined in near a dry-goods store a hundred yards away, dismounted, and tethered their ponies to walk the rest of the way in. They walked like pit dogs sniffing unfamiliar surroundings, spread out and sort of stiff-legged. Longarm knew they were familiar with Black Pipe; they had the town bullied something pitiful. It was the idea that someone had stood up to a member of the clan that had them a mite confused.

They saw Longarm sitting there. They swung wide to the far side and then crossed slowly to where he sat, with the sunset at their backs. Longarm had figured that giving them that advantage might put them in a more talkative mood. They faced him as three ominous black shadows, outlined in red. They stopped in the center of the street and waited for a moment before one of them said, "Howdy."

Longarm nodded and said, "Howdy your own self. Can we talk some, first?"

The apparent spokesman of the group said, "We just have a couple of questions. What happened to Willy, and are you the one who done it?"

Longarm said, "Willy got himself hurt by slapping leather instead of listening."

"We're listening, mister."

"Number one, I am not a revenue agent, but your brother must have mistaken me for one."

"We don't need no number two, mister. It don't matter who you are if you gunned Willy. So tell us true. Was it you?"

Longarm said, "I'm afraid so." And then, since all three of them were slapping leather at the same time, he kicked away from the post and rocked himself over backwards to hit the planks rolling, as he opened up with his own gun. It was confusing, even to Longarm, but he had the advantage of knowing where he was, as he kept rolling and firing.

The Carson brothers shot the hell out of the chair bottom, and would have done the same for Longarm if he'd let them, but a bullet dropped one, and then another, before the last one on his feet gauged where Longarm was rolling to and put a bullet there. Longarm had expected that too, and returned the fire, prone, with his elbows braced on the walk. The Carson brother spun around, sort of dancing a jig, and fell facedown in a watering trough to die.

Longarm muttered, "Shit," and got to his feet. Folks were edging gingerly from the shadows as he walked over to the nearest one, turned him over with a boot, and said, "Double shit."

The one in the middle of the street was still breathing, just barely. Longarm was surprised at how young and clean-cut he looked. He smiled down and said,

"I got a couple of questions to ask before I send for a doc."

The boy grimaced and said, "Fuck yourself."

Longarm said, "I'd sure save a lot of time and trouble if I knew how to do that, old son. But let's talk about the firewater you've been known to sell to Indians."

"Go to hell, you motherfucker."

Longarm kicked him gently, and said, "Somebody with a nasty temper gunned an Indian lawman named Simon Peter. I'm trying to find out if it was before he came to see you boys, or after."

The man at his feet didn't answer. He couldn't. Longarm said, "Well, since you were impolite enough to die on me, we'll just say no more about it."

The town law came over and surveyed the carnage, saying, "Jesus H. Christ! I'd have said it was impossible for one lawman to take on the Carson brothers!"

"I noticed as much. Is this the last of them, or do you have any more dismal surprises for me?"

"Marshal, there is not a man in this county who would squat to shit before you said he could! I have never seen gunplay like that, and I used to work in Dodge."

"I like you, too. The point is that I'll be riding out to their spread now. Is there anybody out there I should know about?"

"Nope. They lived alone. Nobody with any sense ever went near the place."

A townie in a dusty business suit came up to say, "You've done this community a service, sir. I am Mayor Klingman and this occasion calls for a celebration."

"You celebrate all you want," Longarm said. "I've got more important places to be."

The evening breeze carried the stink of sour mash a mile, so Longarm knew they'd given him the right directions as he crossed the cattle guard in the fence around the Carson spread.

The sod house was dark and silent, but as he dismounted in front of it, a mangy yellow dog came around the corner and headed for him, fangs bared silently. Longarm had met up with dogs like that before, so he shot it. As the sound echoed away, it seemed he heard someone moaning on the wind, somewhere. He didn't think it was the dog; a dog doesn't moan much with its head blown to hash.

He tethered the nervous pony, then circled in and rapped on the door with his pistol barrel. Then he kicked the door in and dove inside, crabbing to one side to avoid being outlined. As he waited on one knee, he heard someone sobbing. It sounded like a girl. He called out, "Ma'am?"

Someone answered in what sounded like Lakota. He saw that there were limitations to the conversation, so he lit a match with his left hand, holding it well away from the rest of him as he rose, his gun in his right fist.

She was Lakota, all right. Naked as a jay and tied to a brass bedstead with rawhide thongs at the wrists and ankles. She was staring at him like a frightened deer. He walked over to a coal-oil lamp and lit it with the match as he put the gun away and said, "Everybody kept telling me they were ornery, but this is ridiculous."

He took out his jackknife as he stepped over to the bed, and the bound Indian girl screamed in terror. "Simmer down, honey," he told her. "My name ain't Carson." As he started cutting her free, he said, "They call me Longarm. Who might you be?"

She stopped screaming, but she was shivering like a half-drowned kitten and kept staring at him, frightened, as she said something else he couldn't translate in her singsong language.

"Save your breath. I can see what happened here. Raping a ward of the U.S. Government is a federal offense, but you'll be glad to know there's no need for you to testify."

He knew she didn't understand, but as he'd hoped, the gentle words calmed her some. As soon as she was free, she scooped up a filthy sheet and tried to cover her nakedness. Longarm said, "You just go ahead and get dressed, if you can find your duds. I'll mosey around out back for a spell."

He left the captive to her own devices as he ducked out to explore the premises. There wasn't a hell of a lot to see. The Carson boys had lived in squalor and the only livestock they'd had, besides the cur dog, were the ponies they'd ridden to town. He found the mash tubs and the still, and since there was an ax handy near the woodpile, he busted things up. He didn't care what folks drank, but it gave him a chore while that Indian gal put herself back together.

When he went back in, he saw that she'd found a print dress and some moccasins. She'd been braiding her hair, sitting on her heels in the middle of the floor, but when she saw him she leaped up and ran over to grab his hand and kiss it. He tapped himself on the chest and said, "Me Longarm, savvy?"

The girl touched her own breast and said, "Shewelah," which was either her name or Lakota for "tits." He figured it was more likely her name.

Longarm thought for a moment, then pointed at Shewelah, and made the sign for "Cheyenne" by drawing a finger across his open palm. The girl shook her head and put a finger to her eye to draw it down her cheek as she said, "Hunkpapa. Shewelah Hunkpapa."

"Me savvy. You . . . Pine Ridge?"

That seemed to jar something loose and she nodded and said, "No savvy American beautiful. Shewelah come Pine Ridge belong?"

"That's good enough. We'll find out later how you got here, now that I know where you belong."

Either she understood or else she was feeling friendly. She came over and took his hand as if she were a child. Then she started to cry. He patted her shoulder and said, "It's all right. You're going home. I'm just studying on how."

He led her out and put her up on his pony. Then he started leading it as the Indian gal began to sing for some reason. They were all right until she saw that he was leading her toward Black Pipe. Then she started yelling and pointing at a star to the west. He said, "Simmer down. I know what I'm doing. It's romantic as anything to ride double, but it's nearly sixty miles to Pine Ridge, and your cousins keep chasing me. If it's all the same to you, we'll pick up some ponies before we light out."

She didn't understand, but she gave up and just sat there, scared, as he led her into town. Some townies greeted them joyfully and asked him what he had there. Longarm said, "What I have here is one reason we need an army in peacetime. What happened to those ponies the Carson brothers rode in on?"

"Oh, they'd be over in the livery," one townsman volunteered. "Mayor Klingman impounded them for the city to pay for the Carsons' funerals."

"He did, huh?" growled Longarm, leading the girl and his pony to the livery as the citizens tagged along to watch the fun. But there wasn't much excitement. The constable was there and said the horses were municipal property, but Longarm told him to saddle one up anyway. He said the other three belonged to the Indian gal too, as spoils of war. When they asked him what war he was talking about, he said, "The one I'm trying to prevent."

Then he put Shewelah in the saddle, gathered up the leads, and mounted his own pinto to ride out.

Nobody argued.

They almost made it. With fresh horses to relay, Longarm didn't need to call many rest stops, and while Shewelah was a poor conversationalist, she rode as well as he might have expected a born horse-Indian to ride. She couldn't tell him how much sleep she'd been getting between rapes at the Carson spread, but it figured to be more than he'd gotten lately. Longarm could last as long as seventy-two hours without sleep, but the ponies weren't that tough. By the time they'd carried Longarm and the girl through the night and halfway through the morning, they were so bushed that not one of the five could have run ten paces, carrying a load or otherwise. So when Longarm spied a cluster of cabins on a nearby rise, he consulted his map. He knew they were somewhere on the reservation now, but still at least fifteen miles from the agency. The map said those cabins ahead and to the right were a substation and trading post. Or at least they were going to be, when and if they were ever finished. He remembered Gatewood saying that all new construction had been halted until this Ghost Dance craze died down. He led the girl and their five ponies over to the cabins and saw that they were still raw wood, with no window glass or other hardware. They were set above a winding creek. The map said the creek was called the Wounded Knee.

As he called a halt in the lee of a cabin, Shewelah gestured that they ought to go on. She rolled her eyes and made all sorts of signs with her hands. Longarm only understood enough to see that she was anxious.

He said, "Me savvy. You want go home. But these ponies are about to founder and I don't feel so spry myself right now." He hauled her out of the saddle and pointed at the cabin door as he continued, "We'll hobble them and let them graze or doze or whatever for a couple of hours. You and me will hunker down and let the noon sun fry somebody else for a spell. Then we'll all ride in this afternoon, fit as fiddles and in plenty of time for supper."

She went inside, shaking her head and cussing in Lakota, and Longarm unsaddled the pony he'd just dismounted from. It dropped its head and was asleep before he'd finished hobbling it.

He dragged the saddles into the cabin. Shewelah had spread her print dress on the dirt floor and was sitting there naked, with a resigned look on her pretty face. Longarm put the saddles in a corner, propped his Winchester near the doorway, and tried to make his hands follow his words as he said, "I don't aim to take advantage of you, honey. Put your dress back on."

It took her a while to grasp his meaning. When she did, she clouded up and started to cry some more. She put on her dress, smiled timidly, and kissed his hand again. White folks had sure treated her mean for a spell, but she was getting the message that he was different, it seemed.

Longarm pointed at her and made the sign for sleep. Then he went over by the door, hunkered down with the rifle across his thighs, and repeated the gesture.

Shewelah pointed at him and made the sleep sign. He said, "I can get by with a nap now and again. You just stretch out, honey. I'll be all right."

The Indian girl curled up like a cat on the floor and dozed right off. Longarm listened to her breathing as the day got lazy and his own eyelids drooped uncontrollably.

He slept for maybe two hours before he was awakened rudely.

He fought his way up from the nightmare he'd just been having, and then, as his head cleared, he saw it hadn't been a nightmare after all. He was spread-eagled on his back, with an Indian sitting on his chest. Four more had his wrists and ankles pinned. Shewelah was fussing at them and the eight or ten others crowded all around. The Indians wore blue warpaint and medicine shirts. Longarm stared up at the one aboard his chest and said, "Howdy. You boys are likely to get in trouble, carrying on like this."

Shewelah came over and started pounding on the man on Longarm's chest, yelling at him in Lakota. His friends hauled her off, telling her to be still, most likely, but in a different-sounding lingo.

He knew that while the Cheyenne were members of the Lakota Confederacy, or Sioux Nation, they spoke an entirely different tongue.

Longarm tried saying something friendly in the little Algonquin he knew. The man sitting on his chest replied by grinning like a shit-eating dog and raising his war club. But before he could swing it, a voice yelled in English, "Stop! Shewelah says he is a good person!"

The man who'd shouted from the doorway was another Indian, wearing army pants and an ordinary-looking buckskin shirt. The Ghost Dancer who'd been about to brain him growled, in English, "There *are* no good Americans." Longarm knew they weren't speaking

143

it to be polite to a guest. English and sign were the lingua franca of the Plains tribes.

The Sioux in the doorway said, "We don't have to be told how bad the Americans are. But I think we should take this one to the old men anyway. The woman says he saved her from other bad Americans."

"I think she speaks with a woman's tongue. He's probably been fucking her."

"I think if you say that again, I'll have to kill you. We are talking about a Hunkpapa woman. We are talking about a granddaughter of the great Tatanka Iyotake!"

The Indians holding him had a chat about that in their own guttural language. Then they hauled him to his feet and frog-marched him outside while the girl kept shouting in Lakota. There were a mess of Indians all around, and most of them wore natural clothes instead of the paint and medicine shirts of the Ghost Dancers. But he could tell that some of the others thought he deserved rough treatment by the way they gestured at him.

The brave who'd saved him held up a hand for silence and shouted, "Hear me! I fought at Greasy Grass. I count coup on eight Americans and sixteen Crow. I am not a friend of the Great White Father. But justice is justice. I know Shewelah is a good woman. She says this man killed four men who were holding her captive. She says he gave her their horses. She says that though he has had her at his mercy, and has seen her naked, he has not touched her shamefully. *I* say that I will speak for him before the old men. If anyone hurts him before the old men tell us to, I will fight them. I have spoken."

He stepped over to Longarm and said, "They have taken your guns. Will you behave if we let you walk?"

"I don't seem to have much choice. They call me Longarm. Who might you be, friend?"

The Indian said, "You can translate my name as American Scalps, but I don't think I want you to call me a friend. Come, the others are just down the creek."

They let him walk, but a Ghost Dancer hung onto

144

each of his arms as they all set out. They went around a couple of bends and through some crack-willow, and then, under a grove of cottonwood, Longarm saw a semicircle of tipis, set up to face a big red circus wagon.

Most of the Indians from the camp were walking with him, but as they approached, he saw some others waiting, sort of poker-faced. There were older Lakota wrapped in blankets. The tailgate of the wagon had been folded down to form a stage with shabby buffalo robes draped all over it and a whitewashed buffalo skull with gilded horns on a pole above. The Indian standing on the stage was wearing a Ghost Dancer's shirt and the damnedest paint job Longarm could remember. His face was painted white and black to look like a grinning human skull. His long hair had been pomaded with bear grease and vermilion clay. A sort of halo of eagle feathers had been pinned to the back of his head. He raised a rattle and pointed it at Longarm as they led him closer. The medicine man knew half of his audience didn't speak Paiute either, so he used English as he shouted, "The Great Spirit smiles on us today. I can show my hesitant brothers how easy it is to kill an American."

Longarm noticed little Shewelah running over to wrap herself around a moon-faced old man wrapped in a red blanket. He smiled thinly at the man who was shaking the rattle at him and said, "You must be Kamono. I've been looking high and low for you. I'm a deputy U.S. marshal and I have a warrant for your arrest."

Kamono said, "I know you too, Longarm. You think you are so smart. I heard what you did to my brother on the Blackfoot reservation that time. You will not twist my words the way you did his."

"I did make him look sort of foolish, didn't I? I notice you're sporting a mess of eagle feathers. I didn't know you Paiutes fought that hard in the Shining Times. I've shot it out with your Shoshone cousins, over by South Pass. I'll be switched if I remember a Paiute entitled to that many coups. Who did you kill to get them, a mess of rabbits?"

Kamono sneered and said, "It won't work this time. My wise leader, Wovoka, said men like you would try to divide us by reminding us of ancient history. My message deals with the future, not the past. All Indians share the same shame now. You people have made us all poor and weak. When our dancing brings the Grand-fathers back from the Happy Hunting Ground, to join us in our united front against you, it is *your* kind who will dig for roots in the desert, if any of you are left alive at all."

He called out something to the men holding Long-arm, then he said, "You do not believe me. But it does not matter. You will not live to see the last great up-rising."

But as Longarm tensed to go down swinging, the older man in the red blanket stepped forward and said, "No. We have agreed to listen to your messages from Wovoka. We are waiting to see the strong medicine you say you have. The young men say they want to join you. Maybe we old men will agree and maybe we will not. We have yet to make up our minds. Until we put on our feathers and paint, no blood can be spilled on this reservation."

Kamono sneered, "I know the great Sitting Bull is afraid of his white masters, but as I am a guest, I will listen to his woman-talk."

Tatanka Iyotake's wide face remained impassive as he said, "If you must give me a name in English, I prefer to be called the Buffalo Bull Who Waits. I don't know why they think I sit down all the time. Before you were born, I had my first scalp locks hanging from my shield. I did not get them sitting down."

The painted young Paiute saw that perhaps he'd gone too far and said, "I know my grandfather was a brave fighter once. But he is old and he speaks of caution while the whites go on robbing us."

Tatanka Iyotake snapped, "My council at the Battle of the Greasy Grass was not to give the Paha Sapa to the Great White Father. If people had listened to me then, we would still *have* the Paha Sapa. I told them to offer terms while the Americans were still frightened

146

about Custer. But there were young men like you there. There are always young men like you. You run around acting crazy until the Americans come with Hotchkiss guns and take even more land away from the survivors."

Kamono said, "Red Cloud and Crazy Horse were brave, but they had bad medicine. Hear me, Grandfather, this time things will be different. This time it will not be just a few Indians rising against the Americans and their Indian allies, the Crow and Pawnee. This time we have the spirits and Wovoka's medicine on our side. Would my grandfather counsel peace if he knew the spirits were with him?"

Tatanka Iyotake said, "Of course not. But I haven't seen your strong medicine. You invited us here to show it to us. Where is it? Any child can paint pictures on his shirt."

Kamono pointed at Longarm and said, "I was about to show you, when this enemy came to intrude on our ceremony."

Longarm called out, "I didn't come, I was dragged. But don't let me stop you, old son. You just go right ahead and pull some rabbits out of the hat. Or doesn't your medicine work when a white man's watching?"

Kamono said, "The spirits are offended by your being here."

Longarm laughed and answered, "Do tell? You sure will be in a fix when it's time to fight the cavalry, won't you? The last I heard, the whole Seventh Cav is white. Of course, the Tenth Cav is colored, so maybe you can fight them, if your medicine don't work near white men."

The Paiute looked confused and Tatanka Iyotake said, "This is very upsetting. You tell us we can beat the Americans with your medicine, but then you say it doesn't work near white men. How are we to get at the Americans without strong medicine? They have an annoying habit of shooting back."

Some of the other Lakotas were muttering, and Kamono saw that he was losing his pitch. He nodded and said something to two of his Ghost Dancers. They climbed up on the stage, parted the buffalo robes, and

147

dragged something out of the wagon. It was a common blacksmith's anvil. Longarm figured it weighed about a hundred and fifty pounds. They set it down on the stage, but not before Longarm had noticed the paint mark where it was supposed to go. He sort of looked off in the distance as Kamono went into a little dance around the anvil, yelling his head off. He knew that was the distraction part, so he kept a casual eye on Kamono's assistants, and sure enough, one of them moved over to stand on another painted mark. The plank under his right heel didn't give much, but how far did you need to push an electric button?

It was too good to be true. It was the stale old carnival trick Kathy O'Shea had told him about! He figured everybody who'd ever hung around a traveling show knew it, but of course these reservation Indians were sort of country.

Kamono pointed his rattle at the anvil and said, "My brothers saw that it took two men to pick that block of iron up. Is there anyone here who thinks he can lift it alone?"

The crowd discussed that among themselves in Lakota. Then American Scalps, who looked husky as well as reasonable, spoke up. "I think I can do it."

He climbed up on the stage, got a good two-handed grip on the anvil, and heaved. Naturally, nothing happened. American Scalps' face got dark and the veins of his neck bulged out as he lifted with all his might. He'd have gone on trying, but Kamono said, "Enough. My brother is strong, but no ordinary human can lift such a weight. Let me show him how it is done."

The bigger Indian moved aside, looking puzzled and sheepish. The smaller Kamono bent, braced his legs, and as his assistant released the magnet's switch, he lifted the anvil to waist height, held it for a chorus of amazed approval, and carefully set it back on its mark. Longarm could see that the effort had strained him, since he wasn't all that big, but he'd told them the thing was heavy.

Kamono smiled down and pointed his rattle at Longarm. He said, "I will show you how strong the white

148

man's medicine is. Let the captive come up here and try to lift this iron."

Longarm said, "I've got a better idea. Hand me my gun and let me test your magic shirt with a couple of bullets."

Kamono laughed. "Maybe later. First you lift the iron."

Longarm climbed up to stand beside the Paiute. He knew how the trick worked, but how was he to bend down and grab the anvil while he shoved that son of a bitch off the switch?

He stared down at the audience, then he suddenly grinned and said, "I'm only a guest here. I think we ought to settle once and for all who the greatest medicine man is! I'll just pass for now, and give Tatanka Iyotake my turn."

The other Indians thought it was a hell of a good idea. But as the old Buffalo Bull Who Waits climbed stiffly up to join them, he frowned at Longarm and said, "You must really want to die, you fool."

Longarm said, "Hell, you can do it, Chief. Everybody stand clear and give the man some room!" Then he backed away politely.

He waited until the old warrior had dropped his blanket to reveal a flabby but still muscular torso, and had bent over, resigned, to give it his best shot. Then, as Tantanka Iyotake got a good grip and started to heave, Longarm shoved the Ghost Dancer off the loose plank, saying, "Back up, damn it. You're crowding your elders."

As the electromagnet was switched off under the anvil, the old man's desperately straining strength plucked it from the boards and raised it to the level of his chest. Tatanka Iyotake was so surprised he forgot his poker face, but he grabbed opportunity by the forelock and, as long as he had it that high, kept lifting. Even Longarm was impressed when the proud old man raised it high above his head, grinned like a boy at the confused Kamono, and said, "You're right. It is rather heavy. Can I put it down now?"

Longarm pointed at a spot on the platform and said,

149

"Set her down right there, Chief." He hadn't pointed to the mark above the magnet, so, switched on or not, the anvil was just so much scrap iron now. Longarm moved in before Kamono could think up a mystical objection. He grabbed the anvil, heaved, and raised it high himself, as he grinned at Tatanka Iyotake and said, "You're right. You're a strong old man, ain't you?"

As he set it down politely on the stage, but not on the mark, Tatanka Iyotake frowned down at Kamono and said, "This is very confusing. What is so special about all this? Anyone knows a man can pick up a weight if he is strong."

Longarm saw that American Scalps was still red-faced as he watched from the far side of the stage. So Longarm said, "American Scalps was just being polite. He didn't lift it because he hates to show off, I reckon. Do you want to show us you can do it now, American Scalps?"

The Indian didn't look like he wanted to, but he shrugged, came over, and tried again. This time, of course, the husky Lakota picked it up, grinned, and pumped it over his head a few times as the crowd roared approval. American Scalps put it down after a time, since it really was as heavy as hell.

Longarm nodded at Kamono and asked, "Ain't this fun? Let's see *you* toss it around now. How about putting it over your head, like the rest of us kids?"

"You played a trick on us!" Kamono hissed.

"Well, sure I did. The Seventh Cav is filled with tricky rascals too. If you aim to have a war with us, you'll just have to get used to that. Do we have a deal?"

"A deal? What are you talking about, white man?"

"Well, I could try to explain electricity to these folks, but I'd rather be home alive for supper. I thought you might like to send me on my way."

"But if I let you go, you will come back to arrest me, with many others."

"That's true. I can see you have a right good education. Meanwhile, I've been polite as hell about taking you up on that demonstration of the shirt you're wearing. I know they'd kill me if I killed you, but if I'm done for anyway . . ."

"Hear me!" shouted Kamono. "I have decided to yield to Tatanka Iyotake's good counsel. American Scalps says this white man did a service for a tribeswoman. I agree that we should make an exception in his case. I say we should let him go, this once."

Most, but not all, of the Indians seemed to approve. Tatanka Iyotake muttered something to American Scalps, and as the younger Lakota dropped away, the old man took Longarm's arm and said, "Come. I want you out of here before some young man reaches for the ears of my people."

Together they jumped down and the old man bulled a way through the crowd to where American Scalps was standing with Longarm's guns and pony. The girl Shewelah ran up and started singing with tears running down her cheeks. Tatanka Iyotake nodded and said, "My granddaughter says she never got to thank you properly. She wants to give you all the horses."

Longarm smiled down at the girl and said, "Tell her I only ride one at a time. She can keep the horses to remember me by." Before he mounted up, he turned to the old leader and said, "Listen, if you'd ride in with me and let me introduce you to an army man I know . . ."

Tatanka Iyotake shook his head. "I can't take the chance. You just saw the powder keg I'm sitting on. If I'm not here to counsel peace, many more of my people will die."

"Oh? Can I take it you're not for another war, Chief?"

The old man's eyes were bitter as he said, "I am not a chief, as you people use the word, but as long as I draw breath there will not be another war. I know they say I am a troublemaker. I know it makes them mad in Washington when I speak out against injustice to my people. I know many white men want to see me dead. But hear me, there will be no war as long as I am here to counsel against it. It will be after your kind kills me that you'll see your last great Indian war. Tell the Great White Father to leave me alone. I have spoken."

"Will you help us put an end to this Ghost Dance madness?"

"Don't expect me to betray my own kind to you. The other elders and I are trying to keep our people from being killed. We do not counsel peace because we like you, or because we think you are right."

"Men like Wovoka are enemies of both our kinds, sir."

"His missionary, Kamono, will have you killed if you don't get out of here," said Tatanka Iyotake, turning away to follow his granddaughter.

Longarm mounted, nodded down at American Scalps, and said, "Take care of the old gent, will you?"

American Scalps said, "I will try, but I know someday you will have him killed. When you do, look out for me. I will come after you in my paint, and one of us will die."

Chapter 8

Longarm made it to the agency in time for supper. Gatewood said the army was out looking for him and that everybody thought he'd been scalped, or worse.

Longarm said he couldn't think of anything much worse than being scalped, and as they went inside he filled him in on some of his recent adventures. Some, but not all. Kehoe was all right, but Longarm didn't want a cavalry charge breaking up the powwow until Sitting Bull and the other sensible folks had seen the show and gone home.

Mrs. Gatewood, Olga, and Penny were sort of silent at the table. But Gatewood had invited the Wild West folks to supper too, and while Kathy and the old man who played the steam organ didn't say much, Colonel Comanche John made up for it. Longarm sat down and ate and kept his eyes focused down at his plate while the colonel carried on about being a blood-brother to Quanna Parker, the half-white chief of the Comanche Nation. According to Comanche John, he'd saved Texas, or most of it, by making peace with the Comanche just as they had the Texas Rangers crying and ready to surrender. Longarm didn't argue. He knew that Buffalo Bill Cody was a curious mixture of real and make-believe too. So maybe the man down the table had really seen a Comanche or two in his day. After saving Texas some more, the colonel said that if he couldn't get Sitting Bull to join his show, he'd maybe hire Deadwood Dick.

Longarm asked which Deadwood Dick he aimed to hire, and the older man shot him a puzzled look. "The one and only Deadwood Dick, of course. How many Deadwood Dicks did you think there were?"

"Three," Longarm said, "that I know of. One is a colored cowboy, another is an Englishman who worked in Deadwood for a time. The other's just an old American drunk who knew Jim Hickok. All three of them will sell you a postcard with their picture on it."

"That's ridiculous. One of them must be the real Deadwood Dick."

"Well, I'll agree it's comical, Colonel, but I can't see how one has a better claim than another. All three are named Richard and they all lived or worked in Deadwood one time or another."

"But the legends of Deadwood Dick! Surely one of the three did something to get the name."

Longarm washed some mashed potatoes down with coffee, put the cup down, and wiped his mustache with a napkin. "Nope. I disremember ever hearing that anyone named Deadwood Dick did much of anything. I mean, they all wear fringed buckskins and sign autographs and such, but none of them ever had a famous gunfight or shot anybody worth mention. They say the colored one ropes pretty good. I don't think either of the other two could get a job as a ranch hand. But you can hire them for your Wild West show if you want. All three do look mighty wild."

Kathy laughed and said, "I told you I'd heard the same thing, Colonel. I'll bet those stories about Buffalo Bill are bunkum too. Right, Longarm?"

"Nope. Bill Cody really was a market hunter and he really did kill Yellow Hand that time when he was still an army scout. I'm not sure how he got to be a colonel, since army scouts are civilians, but he's a good shot and handsome on a horse. I'd say he's maybe one-quarter real and three-quarters hot air, like the rest of the stuff they write back East."

The colonel frowned and said, "Are you suggesting the West is not wild, young man?"

Longarm speared another slice of beef onto his plate. "Oh, the one-quarter that's real is wild enough to lift your hair or rob your stage. That's why you have to watch your step out here. You never know if some crazy-looking gent aims to sell you a postcard, peddle you a basket, or murder you because he doesn't admire your hat. I've met some folks recently who were wild enough for me."

Mollified, the colonel said, "After supper I was planing to put on a little show. Mr. Gatewood here says it's all right."

Longarm nodded at Gatewood and said, "Indians like shows. What did you have in mind, Colonel?"

"Oh, the usual stuff. Organ music to draw the crowd, a little trick roping, and some fancy shooting. If there's time enough before it gets too dark, Princess Silver Moon might show 'em some magic."

Longarm regarded the colonel for a moment, then went back to work on his roast beef. "She going to wear that Indian getup?"

The colonel blinked. "Of course. Why not?"

"No reason. They like comedy too. They'll laugh their heads off at a white gal dressed up Indian. You'd impress them more, and help your Uncle Sam, if you showed them that plain old white folks can shoot and show strong medicine."

"You mean, just perform in our regular clothes?"

"Yep. Folks they might be planning to attack wear regular clothes."

"Hmm, I follow your meaning. You want us to show them that ordinary white settlers might have a few tricks up their sleeves, eh?"

"Right. The Ghost Dancers keep saying they have a monopoly on Heap Big Medicine. I know for a fact that one of the tricks Kathy told me about has been impressing a mess of Indians. Where would I pick up a medicine show and all the gear, if I was of a mind to?"

The circus people exchanged glances. Then Kathy said, "I suppose you could buy or steal an outfit from some traveling snake-oil salesman. You could put together a tolerable one-wagon show for a thousand or so. The gear is mostly manufactured in New York, but it's spread all over. There can't be many hock shops that don't have a magic kit gathering dust in the back."

Longarm sighed. "That's what I figured."

He deliberately held off until after dessert on the death of Simon Peter. After everyone had been coffeed and pied, he followed Gatewood outside and said, "You go on and watch the show. I have to go tell Simon Peter's widow and orphans what happened."

Gatewood looked astounded. "Widow and orphans? Are you saying he's dead?"

"Yeah, and I like your reaction. Don't mention it to anyone else just yet. I like to watch folks when I surprise them."

"What happened? How did he die?"

"I ain't sure. He might have been jumped by Ghost Dance raiders on his way to the Carson spread; the Carsons might have bushwhacked him on the way home. I'm guessing the second, for now. He'd wired the BIA that he was checking out 'the seas,' and the Carsons were a plural C. The folks in Black Pipe will be delivering him directly. I'd best prepare his kin before he gets here."

Gatewood said, "I'm going with you."

"Don't you want to watch the colonel's show?"

"I've seen a three-ring circus and the Robert E. Lee. Simon Peter was a good man. Consoling widows is part of my job."

So they went over to the Indian cabins. As it turned out, Simon Peter's woman was mission-educated and spoke good English. It made it harder for Longarm. He had to tell her in detail about her man dying on duty. She stood poker-faced in the doorway, holding one baby on her hip and another in her belly, and she never blinked an eye until Gatewood said, "You are entitled to his pension, of course, ma'am."

That made her cuss him in Lakota and start to cry. As Gatewood stood there looking confused, Longarm said, "Your man died well in a good fight. When his sons are old enough to understand, you must tell them their father was brave."

The squaw sobbed and said, "The others already tease them because their father worked for the Great White Father. How can I tell them he was killed by his own kind for being a toady?"

"I said it was a good fight. Simon Peter did not go down fighting his own people. He died fighting white men, and his spirit counts coup on four of them."

"He killed four white men before he went under?"

"You can say that to his sons. The four bad white men he was after are all dead. I helped him some. Tell his sons he took scalps and captured horses. Tell his sons their father died like a Lakota."

He grabbed Gatewood's arm and led him off as the woman went inside to keen. Gatewood said, "I don't understand what that was all about. Doesn't she want the pension?"

Longarm said, "She doesn't just want it, she needs it. But she needed the speech too. These are proud people, Gatewood. Try to keep that in mind as you're doling out the flour and salt. They take the rations because they have no choice, but it burns like fire in their guts."

"Is that why they're always bitching, no matter what we give them?"

"Sure, if you want to call it that. Wouldn't you bitch if you were dependent on some Indian for every scrap of food on your table?"

"I noticed you didn't care if they gave the credit for the taming of those bootleggers to a bushwhacked Indian," Gatewood observed.

"Hell, she knows what happened, but what good would it do her to brag on a white man? I know the regulations say we're supposed to keep reminding them who's boss. But deep down they know that already. It makes them mad as hell."

They heard a burst of organ music and walked on to catch the colonel's act. As they came around the corner of the main house they saw Comanche John standing on the folded-down stage of his wagon, twirling a big white rope in time to the music. Indians were drifting in to watch, trying not to look curious as the colonel made butterfly and community loops all over the place. Behind him, Kathy O'Shea was whipping yards of bright silk out of thin air. Longarm knew the

Indians found that more mysterious. Most of them knew how to handle a rope.

The colonel still had on his big white hat and buckskin shirt, but Kathy looked like a Spanish gypsy in her fandango skirts and shiny junk jewelry. She waved to Longarm as they moseyed over, and pulled a big wriggly snake out of her left ear and threw it in a basket before any of the Indians could get a good look at it. The Indians laughed like hell. It wasn't clear whether they were amused by the rubber snake or by the idea that a white lady had one in her head.

The colonel saw them and called out, "You're just in time. I need someone to throw my balls around."

Longarm blinked in surprise. Then he saw a pasteboard box full of glass balls on one corner of the stage. He stepped over to the wagon. He saw that most of the Indians at the agency were expecting him to do something marvelous. Mrs. Gatewood, Olga, and Penny were watching from the porch across the way. Longarm asked, "What do you want me to do with your balls, Colonel?"

Comanche John patted the holstered nickel-plated Colt '74 on his hip with his free hand, and went on spinning the rope as he said, "Toss 'em up in the sky, of course. Toss 'em high, for I don't like to hit folks when I shoot."

Longarm picked up a glass ball, hefted it, and stared at the sunset sky as he asked, "Can you really hit anything in this light, Comanche John?"

"Son, I can knock a gnat's eyelashes off if it comes at me in the dark. Throw that thing straight up if you don't believe me."

Longarm shrugged and threw the glass ball up in the sky. The colonel never stopped twirling his rope as he drew with the other hand and fired. The glass ball shattered in a cloud of glittery glass, and the Indians watching said something that would have translated as, "Wow!"

The colonel told him to do it again, so Longarm did. The colonel blasted ball after ball, and then he said it was too easy and asked Longarm to toss two at a time.

Longarm said, "You're stretching your luck," but threw two anyway. The gun in the colonel's fist blazed twice and glass confetti floated down. Longarm said, "That's right fancy shooting, Comanche John."

"I know. It took a lot of practice. Do you want to try it, Longarm?"

"In this light? Not hardly. I might hit a man-sized target at that range. But I don't aim to make a fool of myself in front of God and all these folks. I'll allow you are one shooting son of a gun and we'll say no more about it."

The colonel blew some more glass balls to shards, and then, since even he was having a hard time seeing them in the gathering dusk, he put his gun away and let Kathy show off.

Longarm had thought he'd seen it all. But the stuff with the silk scarves was just a warm-up. Kathy started popping things in and out of thin air while the Indians stared, bug-eyed and openmouthed. Longarm knew it was all stage illusion, but he was damned if he could see where she got half the stuff or where it all went afterwards. She materialized a deck of cards, threw them in the air, and caught them as they cascaded down. Then she put them in her mouth and swallowed them before she winked down at Longarm and asked, "How am I doing?"

He said, "Remind me never to play cards with you." She laughed, called young Joseph over, and bent down to pull the cards out of his astonished mouth.

Naturally, all the other kids wanted to get in on it. So she hunkered down and beckoned them in as their parents watched nervously. Kathy was one of those women that children took to, and she had the Indian kids squealing with delight as she teased them and materialized things out of their laughter. She pointed at a little girl and accused her of having a frog under her skirt. The little girl said Kathy was full of it. Then she screamed like hell when the white lady reached under her skirt and hauled out a big green frog. Longarm knew the critter was sponge rubber, and that Kathy had had it wadded up in a little ball between her fingers, but the way it wriggled and kicked looked real enough.

Longarm wondered if it would be possible to get Kathy in a medicine match with Kamono. He knew that any really good stage magician would make the Paiute look pretty amateurish, and Kathy was a cut above the average. As he watched her, leaning on one elbow against the stage, he said, "You'd better quit while you're ahead. It's getting dark and they'll be talking about this for weeks."

Colonel Comanche John heard him too, and signaled for a last big burst of music as he somehow got his trick rope to coil up like a pet snake around one forearm and called out, "Show's over, folks."

Then, as Kathy started gathering her gear, with the disappointed kids staring wistfully, Comanche John came over to Longarm, hunkered down, and asked, "Do you see Sitting Bull in this crowd, son?"

Longarm said, "No. I doubt like hell that he'll come in to watch you. The last I heard, Buffalo Bill is still trying to hire him too."

"Damn it, Longarm, I'm offering as much as Cody."

"I know. But Sitting Bull used to hunt with Buffalo Bill when they weren't having a war. If he goes on the road with anybody, it figures to be with a man he knows."

"I'm as much a friend to the red man as that imposter Cody. I really am on good terms with Quanna Parker and the Comanche. You just wire Texas and see if I wasn't instrumental in getting Quanna to make peace."

"I'll do that, Colonel. Just what was it you did to tame the Comanche?"

Comanche John pointed at the box of glass balls and said, "You just saw my act. I get along well with Indians. You likely take me for a big overgrown boy. But that's what Quanna Parker was too, so what the hell."

"I can see they don't find you as stuffy as the rest of us," Longarm admitted. "But what have you got in mind, a peace treaty with Sitting Bull, or a chance to take him on the road, like a mermaid or an elephant?"

"Maybe I can do both," the colonel said. "If I can razzle-dazzle the Sioux into renegotiating a firm peace and agreeing to forget this Ghost Dance nonsense, would you and the BIA stand in the way of a career for Sitting Bull?"

"Hell, he's free to go right now. The BIA would be only too happy to have him entertaining folks back East instead of bitching about the money he still claims we owe him."

"Fine. When do I get to meet Sitting Bull?"

"His name is Tatanka Iyotake, and you don't get to meet him at all until I wrap this case up."

They might have had an argument, but Kathy suddenly called out, "Oh, look. Someone's coming."

Longarm looked the way the girl was pointing, down the road to Whiteclay. A big black van, drawn by two black horses, was rolling in fast. It looked like a hearse, and for a minute Longarm thought it might be Simon Peter's body being delivered from Black Pipe. Then, as everyone gathered to watch, the van rolled in and braked. A tall, skinny woman in black widow's weeds was seated at the reins. As they stared at her in wonderment, she dropped a cast-iron ground anchor, stood up in the boot, and demanded loudly, "What is going on here? Where is my father, Tatanka Iyotake?"

Longarm walked over to help her down. He noticed that she wasn't bad-looking, in spite of her height and spidery thinness. Her features were delicate and would have been pleasant but for the vise-like tension of her bearing. She refused his hand as she repeated her question stridently.

"He ain't here, ma'am," Longarm told her. "Did you say Tatanka Iyotake was your father? You sure don't *look* Siouxish."

The black-clad woman snapped, "I'm not. My name is Melody Forsythe and I'm his *adopted* daughter. I came west as soon as I heard he was in trouble again. What have you savages done to him?"

"We ain't all savages, ma'am," Longarm informed

her. "You must be that schoolteacher we heard about, the one the Sioux captured that time."

She nodded grimly, and said, "I am and I was. Tatanka Iyotake adopted me into his lodge and treated me as his daughter. I have never forgotten the kindness he and his wives showed me. After he returned me to my people, I tried to repay him by lecturing on my captivity. Now that you crooks are trying to get him in trouble again, I've come to see that you don't do it. Anyone who means to start another war with my Lakota will have to deal with Melody Forsythe, and I assure you I know how to fight, in court or elsewhere."

Longarm sighed, "Aw, shit."

The formidable-looking woman bristled and said, "What was that, young man?"

"I was just saying that you're a mite late for supper, ma'am. But if you simmer down, I might be able to get you some coffee and apple pie."

It was crowded in the house, even if Penny and Olga hadn't been exchanging glances and staring hard at him all evening. So Longarm bedded down in the hayloft over the stable.

He spread his bedroll and crawled in naked, feeling like he'd been dragged through the keyhole backwards. After all he'd been through, he was sound asleep in no time.

But he woke up instantly when he realized he was not alone. Somebody giggled and he felt naked flesh against his own. He shook his head to clear it. Then, as somebody started to fondle him in the dark, he whispered, "Excuse me, ma'am. Who in thunder are you?"

Penny's voice was condescending as she asked, "Isn't he just awful? He's already hard."

On the other side of him, Olga's voice replied, "I told you he practically raped me, dear."

"Great balls of fire!" Longarm gasped. "*Both* of you?"

Penny said, "We decided to make up. There's no use fighting the forces of nature, and the Lord knows there's enough of you to share, you big, weak, wicked thing."

He felt sort of like a slab of sandwich meat between two hot buns as Olga cuddled in from the other side and agreed, "I think a force of nature is just what he is. He has no character at all. But, Lordy, doesn't he do it nice?"

Penny didn't answer. Her mouth was full. As Olga rolled half on top of him, Longarm murmured, "We thank Thee, Lord, for such blessings as we are about to receive."

Chapter 9

Longarm woke up alone in the hayloft the next morning, and limped over to the main house for breakfast. The clanging of Mrs. Gatewood's dinner bell was what had awakened him, and he felt a mite sheepish. The taxpayers didn't pay a lawman to lie slugabed on a working day.

Mrs. Gatewood acted friendly as she set a rasher of bacon and some eggs before him. Agent Gatewood and the circus folk were already finished and were enjoying smokes and coffee by the time he got there, so he assumed at first that the two women were just out sticking needles in the local populace. He noticed that Kathy O'Shea was looking at him thoughtfully. He didn't think that noisy session in the hayloft could have carried as far as her wagon, but women were so sneaky that a man never knew what they might know.

Gatewood was the one who mentioned the three missing women. Longarm had forgotten Sitting Bull's daughter until Gatewood said she'd followed Olga's ambulance in her funeral wagon.

Longarm stopped eating and asked, "You let them go out onto the reservation?"

Gatewood said, "No. I told them I forbade it flatly. But I can't even get the Indians to obey me around here."

Colonel Comanche John said, "I attempted to dissuade the ladies too. I still haven't decided which of the three is the more stubborn. But I wouldn't worry if I were you. They should frighten the average Indian out of his wits."

Longarm rose from the table as he said, "We're not

talking about average Indians. There's at least two dozen Ghost Dancers wandering around out there!"

Gatewood said, "I've already notified the army by wire that Kamono is camped over on the Wounded Knee."

Longarm started to tell him he was a damned fool. But then he stopped to reconsider and said, "A troop of cavalry might be able to handle those three stubborn gals at that. At least the sight of army blue should make Kamono cautious."

As he headed for the door, he heard Comanche John say something to Kathy. He turned with a frown and asked, "What was that about Comanche lingo, Colonel?"

Comanche John said, "Kamono means 'ugly' in Comanche. I don't speak Sioux, but I can make it to the railroad depot in Comanche."

Longarm frowned thoughtfully. "I'm sure Wovoka and his followers are mostly Paiute. But hold on a second. Ain't Comanche a Shoshonean dialect?"

"I think so. Why?"

"Paiute is a Shoshonean lingo too. For a minute you had me sort of worried. The Comanche are the only tribe I know of who killed more whites than the Sioux, in the Shining Times."

Comanche John smiled and said, "I know. Quanna Parker bragged about that a lot. But I just came up from Texas, and the Comanche are settled down. Old Quanna got to remembering he was sort of white, once he found out he couldn't wipe his mama's people out. He signed a pretty slick peace treaty, partly with my help, like I said. The Comanche are in the real-estate business these days."

"The *what*?"

"Real estate," the colonel repeated. "Selling land to folks for folding money. The treaty gave them more prime range than they really needed, with the south herd gone anyway. The Comanche will sell you a quarter-section or a grazing permit cheaper than Uncle Sam would. So business has been brisk."

"I can see how it would be. But wouldn't even a

Texan be a mite nervous about living on a Comanche reservation?"

"Shucks, no. Quanna Parker was raised a gentleman by his white captive mama, Cindy Parker. Most of the sub-chiefs can read and write, and they know the advantages of good credit. If you cross a Comanche he can be as mean as hell, but he'll never break his word or a contract."

"Hmm, then it's safe to assume Wovoka's new religion won't convert many Comanche."

"No. I wouldn't worry about the Five Civilized Tribes in the Indian Nation, either. Like I said, I'm not really up on these north Plains tribes, but Wovoka's dream of uniting every Indian nation just won't work."

Longarm said they'd jaw some more about it later, and went out to saddle up and ride. As he was leaving the corral on a fresh bay pony, he spotted young Joseph and reined in. He asked the boy if he'd seen the white ladies leave, and Joseph pointed south.

"I told them Tatanka Iyotake was camped down near the reservation line. Everyone knows he's avoiding that crazy white lady who wants to marry him."

Longarm grinned and said, "I can't say she really has marriage on her mind, but I thank you anyway. They can't get in much trouble between here and Whiteclay."

But *any* trouble was too much, so he lit out to the south, feeling as broody as a wet hen. He wasn't certain how one man was going to make three females mind him, but he'd worry about that after he found them still wearing their hair.

The morning air was crisp and the bay was willing, so it didn't take him long to run out of reservation to the south. The two wagons were nowhere to be seen. Longarm swore and decided that as long as he'd come this far, he'd ride into town and see if anyone had answered his wires from Martin.

As he reined in near the telegraph office, Longarm spied Melody Forsythe's big black van across the way. He tethered his pony and walked over to it. Melody wasn't in the seat, but he knew the van was her quarters on the trail. So he went around to the rear and knocked. Nobody answered. He stood there undecided. He had a blade on his jackknife that would open almost anything, but it was broad daylight and people were passing. He noticed the way the light was glinting on the black paint and squinted his eyes. The paint had soaked in less over some gilt lettering that had once read, LIBERTY, MO. COAL & ICE. He'd thought it was a delivery van instead of a converted hearse.

He shrugged and went across the street to the Western Union. He found Melody Forsythe inside. He touched his hatbrim to her and she said, "Oh, you're one of those men from Pine Ridge. I've just sent a wire to Washington about you."

"I figured you might, ma'am. What happened to the other ladies in the ambulance?"

"I don't know. Didn't they come back to the agency? We found no Indians in the direction some fresh boy told us to go. So Olga said she knew of a camp, and I decided to come into town. I'm afraid my caravan is too heavy for cross-country travel. I mean to hire a horse and sidesaddle here, and search for my father properly mounted."

"I wish you wouldn't, ma'am," he told her. "I know for certain that Tatanka Iyotake is safe and well, and there's some trouble on the reservation right now."

Melody said, "You forget, I lived among the Lakota for over a year. Unlike you, I have friends among the Indians."

"These new troublemakers ain't Lakota. They seem to be a mixed bag of Paiute and Cheyenne."

"I've never met an Indian I didn't like. I know how to get along with them. They're only savage to people who try to rob them."

He sighed and leaned heavily on the counter next to her. "Ma'am, when you were out here last, the Indian Ring was in the catbird seat and there was some sense in what you thought about the Indians being mistreated. But President Hayes has been trying, partly thanks to folks like you having pointed out some past errors. Wovoka's Ghost Dance ain't a response to injustice.

It's a crazy Indian's pipe dream. They haven't a prayer of making it work, but meanwhile, lots of folks, red as well as white, could get hurt. I want you to stick around and I'll ride you back to the agency as soon as I'm finished here."

"Will you escort me out to find Tatanka Iyotake?"

"We'll see. Why don't you go have a soda or something, and I'll be joining you directly."

She looked like she wanted to argue, and he didn't look forward to it. He could see why Tatanka Iyotake was hiding from her. She had a fanatic gleam in her widely spaced gray eyes. She must have decided he looked stubborn too, for she nodded and left him alone with the Western Union clerk. The clerk waited until she'd left to opine, "That lady is sort of weird, if you ask me."

Longarm said, "I didn't ask you. I am Deputy U.S. Marshal Custis Long, and if your wire is back up, there should be some messages here for me."

The clerk reached under the counter and pulled out a sheaf of yellow sheets as he muttered, "Jesus, I got a right to an opinion."

Longarm lit a smoke and studied the replies to his questions. He didn't see anything he could arrest anybody for. Texas said Colonel Comanche John was who he'd said he was. Like Buffalo Bill, he was a gent who'd done a little scouting and cowpunching before deciding it was less work to grow long hair and be a showman. A friend in Washington who was privy to patronage and willing to share information with a discreet lawman said that Agent Gatewood had no qualifications as an Indian expert, but that he was as honest as most party workers. Olga really was a registered nurse. The wire he'd sent an old friend in the War Department had been worded discreetly, and the reply had to be read between the lines, but it seemed Captain Kehoe had a clean record and wasn't given to butchering Indians as a hobby. In the past, he'd rounded up his share of reservation jumpers without the usual bloodshed. That was likely why he was over-age in grade and didn't have too many medals to wear.

Longarm threw his wires in the wastebasket and went out to look for Melody. Her van was still there, but she wasn't at the ice cream parlor or anywhere else he looked. He went to the livery, and the black stablehand said she'd just hired a Virginia walking horse and a sidesaddle. Longarm gave the stablehand a nickel, and headed out after her.

He didn't catch Melody; the army did. As he topped a rise just outside of town he spotted Melody ahead, talking to Kehoe and his troop. Longarm rode in and said howdy. Kehoe said. "We're on our way to the agency. This lady shouldn't be out here alone."

Longarm said, "I know. After we take her back and tell Mrs. Gatewood to sit on her, I'll show you where I last spotted Kamono."

"You mean he's back again?"

"If he ever left. Don't look at me like that. I don't know how he cut back through us, either. But he did. He's over on the Wounded Knee, trying to start a war. You'll be pleased to know that Sitting Bull and the other elders don't think much of the idea."

For the first time, Melody looked at Longarm like he hadn't just crawled out from under a rock. "You see? I knew my poor father wasn't behind all these rumors of another uprising."

Kehoe blinked, startled. "Your father, ma'am?"

Longarm said, "She's white, just a mite confused. She's the lady who's been raising all that hell about us butchering Indians out here. Miss Melody Forsythe, may I present Captain Kehoe of the Seventh Cav."

She sniffed and said, "That's ridiculous. Captain Kehoe's scalp was hanging on a lodgepole just next door, when I was living with the Indians."

Captain Kehoe sighed, but didn't explain. He was used to being mixed up with his namesake. He raised his gauntleted right hand and said, "Let's move it out. Will you escort her, Longarm?"

Longarm said he would, and fell in beside Melody as the column headed for the agency. They were about halfway there when Melody suddenly peeled off and started loping her walker to the west. Kehoe swore and Longarm heeled his own mount after her.

Melody's hired mount was longer-legged and moved fast, but Longarm whipped his pony with the rein ends and tore after her, wondering what in thunder she was trying to prove. Melody topped a rise and he was just starting to worry about the long legs on that well-bred walker when she suddenly reined in, covered her face with her hands, and looked like she was fixing to faint.

Longarm pulled up next to her and reached out to steady her before he spotted what she had just seen. Olga's canvas-topped ambulance was lying on its side, just over the rise. The team was gone and a blue-striped arrow was sticking up from the wagon bed. Two still forms lay in the tawny grass farther down the slope. One was wearing black and the other was in white.

Kehoe came up to join them, took one look, and said, "Oh, Christ!"

Longarm said, "Hold on to her, will you? I'm going down to scout for sign."

He rode down to the overturned ambulance, dismounted, and tethered the bay to a skyward rear wheel as he dismounted. He took a deep breath and walked downslope to where the two women lay.

Olga was lying on her back, staring up at the uncaring sky. She'd been scalped and they'd cut open her white uniform from brisket to groin, so it wasn't all that white anymore. Longarm took off his hat and said, "Damn it, Olga. It's your own fault, but I'm still mad as hell."

He moved over to where Penny lay facedown, with an arrow in her tiny back. They'd taken her hair too. She had her little fist still tightly closed on a lump of ballast rock. Longarm felt the prairie sway under him and he swallowed hard. But it didn't work. He walked over to the ambulance, braced himself against it, and threw up his breakfast. Then he drove a fist against the wagon bed, hard enough to break the skin. That didn't help either.

As he straightened up, he saw that Kehoe had left

Melody with his guide and ridden down to join him. Kehoe said, "That's not a Sioux arrow, is it?"

"No," Longarm croaked as he wiped sweat from his brow. "They must have been in a hurry, this close to town."

"Which way do you think they headed?"

"Due west," Longarm said. "But it's a false trail. It always is. They want us to follow them west. So we'll go east after we get rid of that fool woman."

Kehoe said, "I'll detail two troopers to escort her in. How much of a lead do you think they have?"

Longarm mounted up as he replied, "A damned short one, if they mean to go back to the Wounded Knee to brag. They'll have wasted time in a circle out to the west. Let's go get 'em."

As they rode up the slope together, Kehoe said, "I'll have my troopers tell Gatewood to send a burial detail back here. Are you all right, Longarm?"

"What are you talking about?"

"You look sort of strange. This is no time for a white man to lose his head."

Longarm's gunmetal-blue eyes had gone cold in the shadow of his snuff-brown Stetson. Kehoe could not have known that he was one of the few men to see this transformation and live to tell the tale. "I haven't lost my head. I'm about as pissed off as I know how to get, but I know what I'm doing."

Then he pulled the Winchester from its boot, levered it, and braced it across his knees as he added, white lipped, "First I aim to track those Ghost Dancers down. Then I aim to shoot every one of them in the guts."

They rode hard to the campsite near the Wounded Knee and found . . . nothing. Longarm dismounted to study sign in the trampled earth of the creekside encampment. There were footprints, horse and human, all over the place and mixed up like a can of fishing worms. He followed the semicircle of cold tipi fires as he studied sign. He could see the holes where the lodgepoles had been. He kicked a boot through the ashes of a dead fire, picked up a coal, and muttered,

"They doused these fires and lit out right after I did. They must have expected company."

Kehoe walked over from the sandy creekbed and said, "The wagon left no marks on the far side. Doesn't that say it has to be west of the stream?"

Longarm shrugged and replied, "I don't know what it means. I must be losing my grip. I can't find any wagon tracks at all."

"That's pretty spooky," Kehoe said. "Didn't you say you saw the big red wagon near here?"

"Hell, it wasn't *near* here. It was *here*. I stood on the tailgate, right over by that tree!"

They both walked over to where Kamono had set up his medicine show. There was a thatch of cheat grass carpeting the ground around the cottonwood. He knelt and parted some stems with his fingers before he said, "Here's a spot where the wheels must have been pressed harder down. We wound up with quite a crowd on the wagon bed, at the end."

He found a square depression and said, "This was left by the two-by-four they braced this corner of the tailgate with. I told you they had a powerful magnet hidden by draped buffalo robes."

Kehoe said, "Yeah, but where did the damned wagon go after the show?"

Longarm stared at the trampled ground between them and the tipi ring and said, "Only one way it could have gone, if it didn't cross the creek. Kamono must have driven off before the others broke camp. All the scuffing and dragging lodgepoles about must have covered his damned wagon tracks."

"He still had to leave this area. There have to be tracks leading in as well as out of this abandoned camp."

Longarm said, "I know there *have* to be, but there *ain't*, damn it!"

"Damn it indeed," Kehoe said. "I don't believe in flying wagons."

"Neither do I. It's what the folks in the magic business call misdirection. Kamono somehow slickers folks with that fool wagon. We see it here and we see it there, but it's never where it's supposed to be."

"All right. How in hell does he do it?"

"If I knew that, I'd catch him. I think I'll have another jawbone session with this witch I know. She steered me right on one of Kamono's carnival tricks. Gypsies, tinkers, and such leave town in a hurry a lot. There might be some tricks the average lawman doesn't know, since they never catch a crooked road show, once it's left."

"I thought you were going to help me trail that war party, Longarm."

Longarm said, "I did just that, until we ran out of trail again. You boys go on hunting if you like. Before I chase my own tail all over, I mean to study on this misdirection shit. Somebody has misdirected hell out of us and it's getting tedious."

Kehoe said he meant to track down Sitting Bull, at least. So Longarm warned him to treat the old man decently as he peeled away from the column. He didn't stress it much. He knew Kehoe was a fair-minded officer for one thing, and wouldn't catch Tatanka Iyotake for another.

He rode through the half-built substation where the Indians had captured him, since it was not far out of his way to the main agency.

He wasn't surprised to find no Indians there. He poked through the cabin where he'd been caught napping, but found nothing to get excited about. He could see that the Indians had taken advantage of the Great White Father by salvaging while Gatewood had his construction crew called in for safety. There were double-headed scaffold nails in the grass, and some of the cabins had either been pulled apart or not quite put together when the job was postponed. There were boards in the grass all around. He picked up a double-headed nail and put it in his pocket for sentiment. As a boy, he'd put double-headers on the railroad track for fun. When a train rolled over one and flattened it out, you wound up with what looked like a tiny sword, about the right size for a fairy knight on a white-rat charger. One summer he'd wound up with a fruit jar of fairy swords. He'd never found any use for the fool things, but kids were like that.

He mounted up and rode back to the agency. They'd just brought the bodies in and everybody was long-faced about it. Even that sassy Melody seemed willing to believe there were *some* bad Indians about, so she'd likely not go running off to find her daddy right away.

Gatewood said he'd sent wires to the families back East and that Longarm was just in time for the funeral services over in the Indian burial ground. So Longarm fell in with the rest of the crowd as they followed the two caskets on the buckboard. He noticed a stranger in black and asked Gatewood who he was. Gatewood said he was Father Mahoney, a Jesuit who'd ridden in from the mission to the north. The priest had found a blue-striped arrow in his door that morning, and what the hell, nobody had been coming to services for a month anyway.

So the gals got a proper send-off. There were even a mess of Indians watching as they were lowered into the ground. The priest read the Good Book over them and one of the troopers who'd escorted Melody borrowed a horn and blew taps. It didn't do a thing for Longarm's feelings. He was still mad as hell, but his rage had give way to a dark, smoldering determination, and he was starting to think again.

He found himself walking back from the funeral with Kathy O'Shea.

He told her about the disappearing wagon and asked if she had any suggestions. She invited him into her own red wagon to look at her catalogues, but she said she was stumped. "I could make a birdcage vanish before your very eyes, but a full-sized medicine-show wagon would be a bit much."

He helped her up inside the wagon and said, "All right. For openers, vanish me a birdcage."

Kathy sat him down and rummaged through her clutter until she found a bamboo birdcage. She kept her back to him as she fiddled with it and said, "This

174

is one of my father's tricks too. I've always been too tender-hearted to do it with a bird inside."

She turned around, holding the birdcage in one hand. Then she whipped a black silk kerchief out of thin air and draped the cloth over the cage. Then she whipped the cloth away.

The cage was gone, all right. "Show me how you did that," he said.

"Professionals are not supposed to reveal their secrets," she answered haughtily.

He nodded and said, "I'm a professional too. So show me."

Kathy shrugged and pulled the folded-up birdcage out of her elbow-length loose sleeve as she said, "It's spring-loaded to fold into a small bundle like this. I have a length of black elastic tied to a shoulder bracelet. Do you want me to do it again?"

"No. I can see why you don't like to use a live bird. A cage is mostly air, surrounded by thin bars. Could you do that with something like a cigar box?"

She turned around to dig out a little table stand and set it on the floor between them. As she got out a painted wooden box, she showed him that it was empty and set it on the table, saying, "This is hard, working at such close quarters. You're supposed to be back a few yards. But I'll try."

She draped the cloth over the box, tapped it with a wand she plucked from somewhere, then lifted the cloth off. The box was gone and a vase of flowers was in its place. He saw that the flowers were made of wire and silk, but he said, "That's pretty good. How does it work?"

Kathy sighed. "I won't have *any* secrets by the time you're done with me." Then she lifted up what looked like a corner of the cloth covering the table.

Longarm nodded and said, "The box was lined with the same cloth you already had on the table. So when it collapsed out flat, it looked like the same tabletop. But where did those flowers come from? You didn't let me look long, but the box sure seemed to be empty when you flashed it at me."

Kathy removed the flowers and turned the collapsed box over. One panel was mirror glass. She said, "The flowers were folded into a wedge-shaped compartment. The mirror made the inside look square. I just had to let everything drop away and the flowers sprang into a full bouquet. All these tricks are pretty simple, that's why we don't like to explain them."

"Simple for you, maybe. But I see each one works a different way. Kamono can't yank that wagon up his sleeve with a rubber band, and I know he didn't fold it out flat under prairie sod. I figured maybe there was some common method to all this stuff."

Kathy handed him a catalogue of magic supplies as she put her gear away before sitting next to him. She said, "Every trick has to work a different way. The public would catch on if we repeated ourselves."

He started leafing through the catalogue as he muttered, "*This* public hasn't caught on much. That medicine man was using the trick you told me about electromagnets, so I'm sure he must have spent some time with a medicine show before he got religion."

He skimmed through the pages and found out where to buy a two-headed calf or a pitcher that could turn water into wine. But none of the props were anywhere near big enough. He handed it back to her with a puzzled frown and said, "I feel misdirected as hell. Nothing about this case makes any sense."

She asked, "Couldn't the Indians just be, well, *wild*?"

He shook his head. "Kamono thinks too fast on his feet for a simple idiot. There has to be a way for someone to make money out of all this play-acting."

She shuddered and said, "I'd hardly call what happened to those poor girls play-acting."

"Just the same, it was. This is the second time they left a Cheyenne calling card. I thought the first time they were just in too big a hurry to retrieve their arrows. But they left them for us to find."

"Are you saying you don't think those Ghost Dancers are Cheyenne after all?"

He nodded grimly. "I know they ain't. They can't all be sleeping in that one wagon, so they must have been using at least two of the tipis over by Wounded Knee Creek."

"That makes sense. But you said all the tipis were gone when you and the troopers arrived."

"They were, but the lodgepole holes were still there. The Cheyenne are funny Indians. They don't do a lot of things the same as most Indians do. Cheyenne set up their lodgepoles different. You could call them independent thinkers, I reckon."

Kathy's eyes widened. "Oh, I see! Kamono's Ghost Dancers are just pretending to be Cheyenne in order to have them blamed for what's been happening!"

"Blamed and ridden down by cavalry, which would tend to upset them into joining in another uprising. The Sand Creek massacre made the Cheyenne fight beside the Sioux the last time."

"Who do you think they really are, Paiutes?"

"No. They're green kids, but they ride like horse-Indians. I tried some Algonquin words on them, since Cheyenne is an Algonquin dialect. They didn't savvy a word. I know they don't speak Lakota either. I picked up a word or two that sounded like Ute. But that doesn't make sense. The Utes are horse-Indians, but they hate all the Sioux tribes worse than they hate us."

"Kamono is trying to unite the tribes, isn't he?"

"He says he is, but mixing oil and water would be easier. Hell, the Crow speak a Sioux dialect and they're still on our side! I can't see Utes, Snakes, or Shoshone joining up with the Lakota."

"What about Comanche? Didn't you say they speak a Shoshone dialect?"

He grinned and she asked what was so funny. He said, "You just passed a test. I was wondering if you'd disremember that."

She gasped, "My God! Are you suggesting the colonel and I are up to something?"

"It crossed my mind. But you wouldn't have shown me all these tricks if you weren't either dumb or innocent, and I don't suspicion that you're dumb."

She frowned and said, "We do have some Comanche in our main show."

"They're still there. I checked. I also know for a fact that when Wovoka approached the Comanche and Kiowa last year, they laughed him out of town. So I'll be surprised a mite if those Ghost Dancers turn out to have been sent by the Comanche Nation."

He took out his pocket watch and said, "Speaking of misdirection, I need your advice on some. I'm being watched by secret agents. How would I go about slipping away from here later tonight, with them thinking I'm bedded down?"

Kathy asked, "What do you mean, secret agents? Do you think one of the whites here at the agency is spying for the Indians?"

"They don't need a white spy. It's that innocent-looking kid, Joseph."

"Little Joe is spying on you? How do you know?"

"He's here. He doesn't belong here. He lives with his folks in Tipisota's camp, when he's behaving himself. He followed me and Simon Peter back here, and seems to be living pillar-to-post around the agency now. Doesn't that strike you as sort of odd?"

"Brrr. It does, now that you point out the obvious. You think that every time you ride out, young Joseph tells the Indians?"

"Sure. He's likely got other kids watching me too. They know I'm in here with you and they'll know when I leave, unless we can sort of misdirect them."

Kathy thought and said, "All right. After supper at the house this evening, we'll come back here to this wagon. We'll trim the lamp and let them think you're spending the night with me."

Longarm grinned and said, "I like your plan so far."

"Down, boy. You're not about to spend the night here. There's a trapdoor in the floor. After it's good and dark, you'll be able to drop between the wheels and—"

"That sounds good too. What about a mount?"

"They may be watching the stable and corral. Let's razzle-dazzle. You tie your saddled pony to the tailgate when I invite you in. Then leave it there all night. Meanwhile, since I assume you trust Gatewood, *his* horse can be tethered near the front door and—"

"Right! They won't be watching Gatewood. He doesn't go for moonlight rides all that much. But I've got an even better idea. I'll ride Melody Forsythe's big walker."

"Sidesaddle?" she asked, smiling lopsidedly.

"Why not? If a gal can stay aboard that way, a man ought to be able to. It's the last mount on the spread they'd expect me to ride out on."

Kathy laughed and said, "You *would* make a good magician! Do you think Melody will help?"

"I don't know. I don't aim to ask her. I'll get one of the troopers waiting here for Kehoe's troop to leave it near the house, sort of casual. Then I'll just wait until she's bedded down, and steal it."

Chapter 10

Colonel Comanche John shot the two of them a puzzled look as they passed him after supper that evening. The colonel was greasing an axle on his own rig, and Kathy just waved at him as she led Longarm by. Longarm was leading his agency pony. He helped Kathy up into her rig and tethered the pony. Then he took his Winchester in with him, as a sensible man would, and they shut the door.

It was dark inside. The sunset shone red through the frosted little windows on either side. Kathy lit a lamp and said, "Make yourself comfortable, lover. How soon do you intend to leave?"

He sat down. "Not too far this side of midnight. I want as many folks as possible asleep. Did I just get you in trouble with your boss?"

She grimaced. "Boss is all he is. We settled that a long time ago. I don't care what he thinks we're doing in here."

"Well, it's your reputation. I'll tell him later, if this works."

But Kathy laughed wickedly and said, "Let him brood. He has it coming."

"Oh? I didn't know you were sore at him, Kathy."

"I'm not sore. John's not really a bad sort. But, as I said, we had to settle a few things when I first came to work for him. He took it for granted that he'd hired me in every way."

Longarm said, "Well, you can't hold it against a man for admiring a handsome woman, Kathy."

"Just because a girl is born a tinker doesn't entitle every jackass to put a hand up her skirt!"

"*My* hands are in my lap, ma'am. Is it safe to smoke

around you? You look like you're fixing to explode, and I'm sure trying to avoid your fuse."

Kathy laughed bitterly and said, "You're right. I'm acting like a frightened virgin and I'll be damned if I know why. Do you always have this effect on women?"

"What effect is that? I'm just sitting here polite."

"Yes, and for some reason I feel like you can see right through my clothes."

"Look, if this is upsetting you, I'll just leave and figure out some other way to fool those pesky kids."

Apparently she didn't like that much, either, so she relented. "Don't go. I know it was my idea in the first place. I just hadn't considered . . . well, how long you were going to have to stay here."

He nodded at the little window across from them and said, "It's getting dark, but we have to kill at least four or five hours. You don't have a checkerboard, do you?"

Kathy laughed a little wildly, and said, "You really *don't* intend to get fresh, do you?"

He said, "Nope. It wouldn't be polite."

"I thought you were an experienced seducer."

"Well, such experience as I've had has taught me that women don't get seduced until they decide they want to be."

"Oh, you poor thing! I'll bet those two girls I saw fighting over you put something in your drinks, huh?"

He frowned and said, "Let's not be speaking ill of the dead. What did or didn't happen is between them and the angels now."

Kathy lowered her eyes. "I know. That was cheap of me. But you can't blame a girl for being curious, damn it."

He shrugged and said, "You and the cat can be as curious as you like. There's questions no lady asks, and if she does, no gentleman will answer them, so we'll say no more about it."

"You're trying to make me wonder, aren't you?"

"Nope. But for a gal who's skittish about men pestering her, you sure drone on about one subject. If you don't play checkers, how about a game of cards?"

She materialized a deck and they started playing whist on the seat between them. Kathy cheated something awful, but Longarm didn't say anything. They weren't playing for stakes, and it helped to pass the time.

After a while it got dark outside, and Kathy asked him what time it was. He said a little after nine and she fumbled the deal. "I don't know what's the matter with my hands this evening," she said. "I'm all thumbs."

"I noticed. Dealing like that could get a man shot in some places I've been. Why don't you just relax? I told you I was on my good behavior tonight."

"I'm not sure *I* am. Next to a fresh galoot, there is nothing as damned annoying as a man in complete control of his feelings. You do have feelings, don't you?"

"Yep, but I keep them under control, most times."

"I'll bet you wouldn't blink an eye if I ripped off all my clothes and threw myself at you."

He didn't answer.

"Well?" she said.

"Well *what*, Kathy?"

"For God's sake, I don't think I *could* get you excited."

"It's your deal," he said. "Try dealing from the top this time, just for the novelty."

Kathy said, "You may be shockproof, but we'd better think about shocking our little spies."

She reached out and snuffed the lamp. It was dark in the wagon, but he could see shadows by the moonlight through the frosted glass. She giggled and said, "If the colonel is watching, he'll have a fit."

"I noticed you enjoy teasing, Kathy."

"Oh? Are you saying I've been teasing you?"

"I don't know what you've been trying to do. It's your wagon, it's your deck of cards."

"We can't play cards in the dark."

"I know. You turned the lamp out."

She started to cry, so he reached out, gathered her in, and kissed her. She responded hungrily, then pulled away and said, "No. I don't want to!"

"Sure you do," he said, and kissed her again. He

182

knew she'd put up a better fight if he was wrong, and that he'd have to turn her loose. But meanwhile her lips were saying go while her vocal cords were saying stop. So he just went ahead. They didn't have all night, and he knew she'd be mad as hell if he left her hanging. Some gals were like that; they insisted that the man take the blame for what they wanted.

He got her half-reclined, and rolled his knees to the floor with his hips between her open thighs. The fandango skirt was no problem, but his gunbelt was, so he gave some ground with one hand long enough to unbuckle it and let it drop. He figured he might as well unfasten his buttons while he was about it. She asked what he was doing, and since there was no polite way to answer her, he kissed her some more as he got his free hand inside her skirts, moved them out of the way, and cupped his palm over her groin. He hadn't expected her to be wearing drawers, and she wasn't. Her fur was warm and wet as she twisted away from him and gasped, "Stop that! This is rape!"

"Sure it is," he soothed her, as he leaned forward and placed himself in position. The edge of the settee and common decency prevented him from going any further without a little cooperation.

She moaned, "Oh, if you don't stop I'll scream!" then moved her rump toward him to swallow him alive. "You brute," she hissed, "you're acting like an animal!" Then she locked her legs around his waist and started bouncing to meet him. She kept moaning until he almost wished he hadn't started. Then she suddenly forgot she was being mistreated and begged, "Oh, harder, faster!"

He cooperated with her request, and when they came up for air he asked, "Now that you've been victimized, can we take these damned duds off and do it right?"

"You bastard. That wasn't fair. You took me by surprise and deception."

He fondled her and said, "Yeah, I deserve to be castrated with a rusty can opener. But I still think it'll be better with our duds off."

She said it was indecent, but she didn't resist as he

undressed her, kissing the cloth away from delicate terrain, and while she had plenty of chances to break loose while he undressed himself down to the socks, she just lay there until he mounted her.

As he entered her again, she said, "I'll never be able to face you in the light. What must you think of me?"

He said, "Little darling, I think you were tailored to fit me by the angels."

"God, we are a snug fit, aren't we? 'Fess up. Am I as good as those other girls?"

"Honey, there ain't any other girls. There's just you and me and the moonlight. So let's just ride to glory. I got to get out of here in a little while."

So they did, and she didn't cry anymore until they'd worn out most of the possibilities and stopped to get their second wind. Or was it the third? Kathy's eyes were like a deer's in the momentary glow of Longarm's sulfur match as he lit a cheroot. She sighed, "I know what they were fighting about now. You really are incredible."

"Then why are you crying? Would it help if I said I was sorry?"

"No. Nothing you say has any meaning to you. You're a marvelous lover and you know it. But you just use us in passing. It never has real meaning to you, does it?"

He thought for a moment before replying, "I don't know who could be said to be using who, Kathy. Are you saying that the pleasure is confined to the male of the species?"

"God, no, you know you made me enjoy it. But damn it, it's not the same. I'll bet you'd do it to a snake, if someone would only hold its head."

He said, "I'd have to see your snake first. If you mean to suggest I can make love to a gal without messing us both up with dumb promises, I'll have to plead guilty. But I have to *like* the gal, as a person, if I'm to do right by her in bed."

Kathy lay silently in his arms for a time before she said, "Well, I sort of like you too."

He kissed her and asked, "Suppose I said that wasn't

enough? Suppose I said that if you didn't say you were crazy in love with me, I'd just go and slash my wrists?"

Kathy laughed and said, "We hardly know each other."

"There you go. Doesn't it sound silly, coming from a grown man? Us poor jaspers have to listen to it all the time."

She laughed again and said, "All right. I won't insist that you say you love me. But could you *like* me again before you have to go?"

Riding sidesaddle wasn't hard, it just looked ridiculous. Longarm had been right about the lines of the Virginia walker. Even riding a zigzag course to make sure he wasn't being followed, he got there well before dawn. His destination was the deserted substation by the Wounded Knee. He led the walker inside a roofless cabin and tethered it. Then he went across to what looked like it would be a school if they ever finished it, and climbed up into the little belfry. He had a dominating field of fire from cover and an extra box of ammunition in his side pocket. So all that mattered now was that his hunch might be right.

It was and it wasn't. The sky grew pink to the east and it started to get light enough to see. Longarm squinted down at the ground around the cabins and swore softly. The scrap lumber scattered across the grass had been trifled with. Half of it wasn't there anymore.

"Triple-titted sons of bitches," he muttered, and climbed back down to get the horse. As the sun peeked over the horizon he saw that things weren't quite as bad as they might have been. The grass was silvery with dew. So while they hadn't left tracks, their trail stood out as dark lines across the prairie. Longarm mounted up and followed, grinning wolfishly.

Once it became obvious where they were headed, he circled out to come in from the north east, where they'd least expect. Kamono was starting to repeat himself—a bad move for any magician—but this was no time for

185

a lawman to get overconfident. The odds were a mite steep.

He knew the livery rented the walker to folks who rode on open prairie a lot, so he dismounted and took a chance on its being rein-trained. He looked back once as he moved toward the creekbed on foot and, sure enough, the walker was staying put, with its reins dropped to the sod.

He heard hammering from the cottonwood grove in the draw ahead, so he got down in the wet grass and belly-crawled over the last rise with the rifle cradled in his arms.

Kamono and his platoon of Ghost Dancers were just down the creek from the last campsite. Most of the Ghost Dancers were just watching as Kamono and two helpers put the medicine wagon together on its sawhorse platform. They were making it out of lumber they'd left as apparent scrap near the construction site, of course. The reason Kamono's big red wagon left no wheelmarks was that it wasn't a big red wagon. It was just a big red misdirection that could be taken apart and scattered all around. Nobody paid much attention to a scrap of weathered-looking wood, particularly with its red side turned facedown. Two dozen riders could tote the other gear as they scattered after a meeting with the spirits. He saw some loaded packmules tied across the creek.

So, since he'd seen all there was to see and the range was about right, Longarm eased the Winchester into position, drew a bead, and let his breath half out before he squeezed off his first round.

Kamono never knew what hit him. As the medicine man dropped his hammer, Longarm nailed the two men closest to him before their leader hit the ground. After that, it got a mite harder. Even leaderless, all his targets started moving. He concentrated on the ones who were headed his way, cussing and shooting. Even though they'd seen Kamono put his medicine show together, they seemed to be sold on those bulletproof medicine shirts, so they must have been disappointed as hell when Longarm started dropping them. The ragged line charging up the slope hesitated as he tore gaps in it. Then one man broke and most of the others turned tail to follow him in panic as their faith wavered. But one stubborn cuss kept coming, singing his death song and shooting wildly from the hip. Longarm shot him right between a thunderbird and a magic turtle. He looked a bit disillusioned when he went down.

Longarm saw that the others were out of range as they headed for their ponies, so he bounded to his feet and ran down the slope, zigzagging to make up for not having a medicine shirt of his own. The odds were still over a dozen to one, but there were no takers. He nailed three more as they were mounting up, and then the Winchester's hammer clicked hollowly. He tossed the empty rifle aside and drew his sixgun, but they were riding out scattered and fast, so he lowered the muzzle to watch them tear-ass out of sight as if they'd just met Wendigo, Real Bear, and other awful devils.

He walked over to where Kamono lay, and rolled the medicine man over with his boot. Kamono was as dead as a turd in a milk bucket. Longarm said, "I would have liked to have a chat with you, old son. But since I seem to have made new Christians out of those kids you led astray, I'll just have to wrap up the loose ends without your help."

Something caught the corner of his eye, and Longarm glanced up at the skyline above the draw. A line of mounted Lakota were sitting their ponies, staring silently down at him. Longarm sighed and put his sixgun away politely. As he went to retrieve his empty Winchester, one of the Indians rode down alone. It was Tatanka Iyotake. Longarm picked up his rifle, keeping the muzzle pointed at the grass, and said, "Morning. Nice day, ain't it?"

Tatanka Iyotake dismounted and started to roll a smoke as he stared somberly at the bodies all around and asked, "Did you do this all by yourself, Longarm?"

"I cannot tell a lie. I did it with my little Winchester. Ain't I lucky none of them were Lakota?"

"Yes. That would have made me very cross with

you. Some of those young men up there on the ridge are wondering how we should settle this business."

Longarm struck a match with his thumbnail and held it out to light the older man's smoke as he said, "Well, you might point out that those medicine shirts these boys had on didn't work so good. If you aim to let me keep my hair, I'll show you how Kamono's magic tricks worked, and you can be the big hoo-rah in these parts again."

Tatanka Iyotake took a deep drag and said, "In the Shining Times, I never used children's tricks to make my people heed my council. They listened to me because what I said was true. My spirit name, Buffalo Bull Who Waits, was given to me in battle because I did not charge my enemies screaming like a woman about how brave I was. I waited for the best time and made the best moves."

"I know. Crazy Horse was a good general too."

Tatanka Iyotake sighed deeply. "He would have done better if he'd listened to me. His real name was Men Are Afraid of His Wild Horses, by the way."

He handed the smoke to Longarm, who took a drag and passed it back. Tatanka Iyotake said, "I don't know. In the Shining Times I always knew what to do. Things are more complicated today. I think maybe I will take Buffalo Bill up on his offer. Being in a circus might be more interesting than being in this jail. Is that crazy white girl still at the agency?"

"Yep. She says she didn't come out here to marry you. She has this committee back East, and she says they want to help you get a better treaty with the Great White Father. She says she can sue Washington for the money you never got for the Black Hills. They're digging gold up there now. That six million dollars Red Cloud originally asked for would be peanuts to the Great White Father and the gold miners."

Tatanka Iyotake grunted disgustedly. "I know Washington will never let us get our hands on real money. I have studied your people. Rich Indians would be too big a problem for them to cope with. How could they find

188

jobs for their politicians if we didn't need to be cared for, like children?"

"She was talking about that at the supper table last night. She said that while you folks are legally minors, she and her friends could be made your guardians and act for you in court. She says she could take your old claims as high as the Supreme Court, and that before they let that happen, the powers that be would settle with you. A quit-claim on the gold-mining properties would be worth a lot of money."

Tatanka Iyotake shook his head slowly. "I don't know what got into that girl. She was such a shy little thing when we took her captive that time. I adopted her because I could see she was afraid, and our women were teasing her. I made her my daughter and she always obeyed me, after we taught her to speak like a real person. After I sent her back to her people, she wrote me some nice letters for a while. But lately she's just gotten crazy. I wrote and told her we wanted to be left alone. People in Washington already say I am a bad Indian, and they keep trying to think up ways to have me killed. Maybe I will ride with Buffalo Bill for a while and let them see I am not a bad person. Go back and tell her to just leave us alone." The tired-looking, broad-faced, proud Indian inhaled deeply and let the breath out slowly. Then he looked Longarm steadily in the eye and said softly, "I have spoken." He turned and walked away, up the hill toward the blue sky.

Longarm made the peace sign for the others up on the slope to see, and legged it up the opposite slope to where he'd left his horse. His spine tingled all the way to the ridge line, but nobody shot him.

Chapter 11

The crowd had changed at the agency when he rode back. The three circus wagons were gone, but Captain Kehoe and his troop were there. As he rode in, Kehoe smiled crookedly and asked, "Do you often ride side-saddle, Longarm?"

Longarm slid down without comment, and as Melody Forsythe came out of the house and walked toward him grimly, he held the reins out to her and said, "I'm sorry I borrowed your horse without asking, ma'am. Where are the colonel and the others?"

Melody said, "They left just a while ago. They said it was a waste of time trying to recruit wild Indians that were really wild."

As she reached for the reins, Longarm snapped a loop of the handcuffs he'd taken from his pocket around her wrist. She gasped in surprise and reached for the steel loop with her other hand, so Longarm cuffed that one too.

Captain Kehoe was as surprised as she was, although he didn't scream the way she did. "Longarm, why have you handcuffed this lady?" he asked. "Because she's a killer," Longarm said, "and she's under arrest. I don't know who she is. We'll likely get it out of her before her trial."

The woman called Melody wailed, "Have you gone mad? Take these awful things off me this instant!"

The commotion had attracted Gatewood and his wife. Mrs. Gatewood ran up and gasped, "Can't you keep your hands off any woman, you animal?"

Longarm said, "Everybody just simmer down. I have just come from a discussion of this lady with Sitting Bull, and the last piece of the puzzle just naturally

190

fell in place. She's an impostor. Sitting Bull remembered her as a little white gal the squaws were teasing. This one's five foot seven or more if she's an inch, and the squaws only tease really pretty gals. No offense, ma'am. The real Melody Forsythe wrote thank-you notes after Sitting Bull sent her home unharmed and chaste, which was only reasonable. After that she likely married up or died or something. This gal knew the story and decided to be her. She knew Sitting Bull would avoid her, since he'd told her as much by mail. But she figured Tipisota or some other chief would sign himself and his people over to her as legal wards."

"You're crazy!" wailed Melody.

Captain Kehoe asked, "Why would any white woman want to adopt a tribe of Indians?"

So Longarm told him. "Two reasons. This Ghost Dance nonsense has a lot of other white folks nervous. So they'd part with cash for a quit-claim on lands the Indians might have enough claim on to cloud the deeds. Washington knows they did the Sioux out of millions, and folks are starting to say it was sort of ugly. So there's *another* settlement she and her confederates might get, and naturally, since the Indians are poor benighted savages, their white guardians would have to manage their funds a lot."

Kehoe nodded and said, "I see all that. But you said she was a killer, Longarm. Who in hell did she kill?"

Longarm stared hard at the prisoner as he said, "Olga and Penny. The three of them rode off to town together, remember?"

Melody tried to pull away as she screamed, "That's a lie! I left them on the prairie and rode into town alone!"

Longarm shook her into silence and said, "Sure you did. After you lured them off the trail and murdered them. You killed Olga first, because Penny had time to reach for one of her pathetic rocks. You likely shot them, then put some arrows in them and the wagon to throw suspicion on the Indians. Cutting them up like that was a neat ugly touch, wasn't it?"

Kehoe gasped and said, "Hold on! Are you saying we've been chasing a will-o'-the-wisp while all the time it was this innocent-looking witch?"

Longarm said, "Nope. Kamono was working with her. You'll find him and some other Ghost Dancers over in a draw I'll lead you to, after we get her locked up. Kamono was a real Indian, but him and his dupes were sent here to raise hell and get Washington in the proper mood to renegotiate with the Sioux. President Hayes is trying to balance the budget. An Indian war would be more expensive than buying off the Sioux again. Kamono had been taught some white man's magic to impress the Indians. Lucky for you, Sitting Bull wasn't impressed. I just talked to him, and if you'll leave him alone, it'll all blow over. He's fixing to go into a more harmless line of business."

He turned to Gatewood and asked, "I know you have a lockup. Do you have any Indian police handy?"

Gatewood said, "Yes. I just transferred a replacement for Simon Peter from another substation. I'll fetch him for you."

But Mrs. Gatewood suddenly snapped, "*I'll* take charge of this nasty slut! Come with me, God damn your eyes!"

She grabbed Melody by the hair and started dragging her off, kicking and screaming. Gatewood stared after them and said, "My old woman was right fond of Olga."

Kehoe laughed and said, "Well, we're not really needed here, Longarm. Suppose you show us where Kamono and his big red wagon are."

"I will, and you'll feel better about your tracking skills when you see how he misdirected us. I have never been so misdirected in my life."

"That makes two of us. But it's all over, right?"

Longarm shook his head. "No. The case is just getting interesting."

As he walked to the stable where Gatewood had put his pony and saddle after the Wild West folks had left, Gatewood said, "I know. You're going after the ones who shot Simon Peter! Melody couldn't have been the one who bushwhacked *him*!"

"Oh, I already shot the Carson brothers," Longarm said. "Simon Peter was wearing a badge and I learned the hard way that they were nervous about any lawman they didn't have bullied."

"Then who the hell *are* you still after, Longarm?"

"The son of a bitch behind it all, of course."

Longarm saw that he'd timed it close as he entered the Burlington yards with a Scotts Bluff lawman he'd picked up as a courtesy to the state of Nebraska. The sun was low and the Wild West show had been loaded aboard an eastbound train. But the train wasn't timed to leave for a good three minutes, and he saw Kathy and Colonel Comanche John talking on the platform near the last car.

As he and the Scotts Bluff law walked over, Kathy spotted him and came to meet him. Longarm walked her back to the colonel. Comanche John grinned and stuck out a hand. "We read about it in the papers. How long has it been now, a week?"

Longarm took the offered hand and shook it. "Almost. I had to ride over to the county seat in Martin to make sure I'd turned over all the wet rocks. There was a right helpful little gal working for the county clerk. She helped me so much I sort of lost track of the time. But I couldn't find a thing connecting any local folks to that mess on the reservation. So here I am."

The colonel said, "You should have gotten here earlier today. We just put on a good show."

Longarm looked him over, noting the fancy sixgun hanging from his white buckskins, and said, "I've already seen you bust balls. The show is over, Colonel. You're under arrest."

Comanche John's sixgun appeared in his fist too fast to be possible. He threw down on Longarm and the others, saying, "I don't think so, Longarm. I've got the drop on you and this train is about to leave."

Longarm shoved Kathy aside as he said, "Stand clear, honey. He might be fool enough to shoot."

Comanche John said, "I admire a man who can

face the facts of life. You're good, son, but as you see, I'm better."

Longarm stared morosely down at the muzzle pointed at his midsection. "You sure do draw pretty. But you're still under arrest. I searched Melody's wagon and found out she was your wife. Of course I already knew you'd taught Kamono all those shell games and loaned him some Comanche."

Kathy gasped, "What are you talking about, Custis? None of the Indians with the show are missing."

Longarm said, "I know. But old John here knows a mess of Comanche. Acting as an agent of the Comanche Nation a few years back made him so much money he could buy this whole traveling circus and leave some for them. So he had no trouble recruiting a mess of young bucks who wanted a chance to count coup. I wouldn't defend him, Kathy. He knew you'd cause more misdirection when he brought you along in a red wagon with your own magic act."

"You're pretty smart," sneered Comanche John as, up ahead, the locomotive whistle sounded the departure signal.

Longarm shrugged modestly. "It took me longer than it should have to figure it out. I was a step behind poor Simon Peter. I thought the C's he was interested in stood for the Carson brothers. But he'd likely figured out that those Shoshone-speaking Ghost Dancers couldn't be Utes or North Shoshone, either."

Longarm saw that the train was about to leave, so he said, "You'd best get aboard, Kathy. You and the other innocent folks will likely work out some way to stay in business."

Comanche John said, "They can have the show. I know you'll wire ahead, but I won't be aboard at the next station. I'll just ride down the line and sort of fade into the sunset."

Longarm said, "No, you won't." Then he turned to the lawman standing frozen at his side and said, "It's your town. Do you want to take him or shall I?"

"Are you crazy, Longarm? The rascal has the drop on us, and I've seen him shoot. He never misses!"

Longarm said, "Yeah, ain't that a bitch? All right, Colonel, you can drop that gun and grab some sky, for I've talked enough and it won't upset me much if I have to take you the unfriendly way."

The train started moving. Comanche John said, "I warn you, if you bat an eye I'll shoot!" Then he reached with his free hand for a grab iron to haul himself aboard.

Longarm drew his gun.

The colonel fired before Longarm's .44 cleared leather, of course, and the roar of his own pistol mingled with Kathy's screams as he fired three times at point-blank range, into Longarm's guts.

Then Longarm fired once, and the colonel's white buckskin shirt blossomed a big red rose over his heart as he let go of the grab iron and fell to the cinders like a wet rag doll.

Longarm stared down at the body and said, "It's just as well, I reckon. Proving some of it would have been tedious as hell in court. You're fixing to miss your train, Kathy."

The girl wrapped herself around him as she sobbed, "Oh, my poor baby, he's in shock! We have to get him to a doctor!"

The Scotts Bluff lawman came unstuck and gasped, "She's right, by God! He shot you three times! I know they say you're tough, but this is ridiculous! Set down and try not to breathe too hard while I fetch help!"

"I don't need a doc," Longarm told them. "It smarts a mite, but I ain't really hurt."

Kathy was fumbling at his vest and sobbing, "Oh my God, you're bleeding and you can't feel it! What ever made you take such a foolish chance? You knew what kind of a shot he was!"

Longarm chuckled and said, "Sure I did. Buffalo Bill uses the same kind of ammo when *he* busts glass balls and balloons all over the place. You're a magician, Kathy. Did you think he or any other man could shoot like that with real bullets?"

Her jaw dropped as she caught on. The town law was still puzzled. So Longarm explained, "He just came

195

from putting on a show, so I figured he had his revolver charged with fine birdshot. It's the only way he could hit the glass balls every time. He didn't know that I knew, of course, so he tried a desperate bluff. A man with that much at stake wouldn't have hesitated to shoot if he'd had solid bullets in that gun. I was surprised when he didn't surrender like I told him to."

The town law stared down at the nickel-plated gun near the dead man's hand and said, "Jesus! He must have been crazy!"

The train was leaving without Kathy, so Longarm put an arm around her as he holstered his weapon and said, "He wasn't crazy, just too used to fooling folks for his own good. He knew he faced a hanging and, what the hell, those last wild shots might have confused me enough to miss as he swung aboard the train."

Kathy had her hand inside his shirt. "You're peppered all over with birdshot," she said. "We have to get you out of those clothes and cleaned up. I can probably tweeze the balls out of you."

Longarm said, "You can tweeze my balls all you like, later. Is there a hotel here in town where a man can be treated in private?"

The local law grinned and said, "I know just the sort of place you folks have in mind. You did say I was going to share in the arrest report, didn't you, Longarm?"

"I did and you will. But I'm suddenly starting to feel mighty wounded. So if you'll point out that hotel and see about putting the colonel on ice, I'll make sure I spell your name right in my official report."

When they found themselves alone and undressed at the hotel, they found that Longarm's vest and hickory shirt had stopped most of the pellets, and there weren't enough in his hide to slow a grown man down enough to matter.

She made him lie flat on the bed and let her doctor him up anyway. She was giggling and twitching by the time she tweezed the last little grain of lead out, because of the way he was teasing her with his hands. She said, "That will have to do you, you randy rascal," and

196

climbed aboard him. It was nice to see she'd gotten over her initial shyness with him.

Later, as they rested up for another round, Kathy asked him, "What was that about a girl you met in Martin, you bastard?"

Longarm snuggled her head against his chest and said, "Oh, she was just a clerk who let me go through her files."

"I'll bet she did. Was she prettier than me?"

Longarm patted Kathy fondly. "Nobody is as pretty as you, honey."

"I'll bet you told her she was the best you'd ever had, right?"

He didn't answer. A man had to be careful in bed with a magician.

She sighed and said, "I suppose I'll be able to catch up with the show if I catch a later train tonight."

"There won't be another before morning," he informed her.

"I see. One night is all we'll have. By this time tomorrow you'll have forgotten all about me, and if I know you, you'll be saying the same sweet nothings to some other woman."

"Don't talk ugly about things that can be beautiful if you just let yourself drift with the here and now. I don't aim to forget you, Kathy. I never forget anyone as nice as you."

She cuddled closer, mollified. He hadn't lied. He'd remember Kathy's soft black hair and tawny body, just as he'd remember that saucy strawberry blonde's pale, rollicking rump. He blew a smoke ring at the ceiling and smiled up at it as he thought about that girl Kathy had just twitted him about. The one he hadn't met yet. He had no idea what she'd look like, but he was sure she'd be the best he'd ever had. They always were.

Chapter 1

Longarm hesitated for a moment before mounting the steps of the dressed-stone building. There was nothing about the solid three-story structure with its arched entryway at the top of a short flight of marble steps, that identified it as the building he was looking for, but it was the only one of its kind in sight, so he shrugged and walked up the steps. He looked for a knocker or a bell pull, but the double doors of dark brown oak with etched white panes of plate glass set in them had neither. Before he could raise a hand to knock, one of the doors swung open and a young-old woman wearing a black dress with white lace ruching at the high neck faced him.

"Marshal Long?" she asked. Longarm nodded, hurrying to remove his hat. "Mr. Bascomb's expecting you," she continued. "Do come in, please."

He stepped inside, and found himself in a long paneled hallway. The dull gleam of polished bronze doorknobs indicated rooms on both sides of the passage. Two flights of stairs rose just inside the entrance, one to his left and one to his right. Deep ecru carpeting cushioned his booted feet. The light was subdued, coming from small lamps suspended along the passageway in front of him. His hand tightened instinctively as he felt a tug at his hat. He looked down, saw the hand of the woman who'd let him in trying to take it, and somewhat sheepishly let go.

She said, "I'll put this in the cloakroom," and indicated a door under the left-hand stairway. "Mr. Bascomb's in room three, to your left down the hall."

"I see. Thanks, ma'am."

A discreet bronze numeral on its polished walnut

panel indicated the door to which Longarm had been directed. He tapped lightly and a man's voice called, "Come in."

Longarm entered to see Seth Bascomb rising from an armchair in a single, swift, unwinding move, unexpected in a man whose wrinkled face showed the erosion of a lot of years and whose hair and bristling, untrimmed mustache were snow white. Bascomb took a step toward Longarm, his hand extended.

"Longarm. Glad to see you again," he said. He pointed to the twin of the chair in which he'd been sitting, a deep brown leather lounger with a high back. Between the two chairs a low table stood bearing a bottle and glasses.

"You're looking good, Seth," Longarm said, briefly clasping Bascomb's wiry hand. The older man's grip, he noticed, didn't seem as firm as it used to be.

"Wish I felt like you say I look." Bascomb was already returning to his chair. He swept a hand toward the bottle. "Maryland rye. Help yourself."

Longarm settled into the easy chair. It seemed designed to cradle his big frame and hold him in complete relaxation. It might, he thought, be just about the most comfortable chair he'd ever sat in. "You not drinking these days, Seth?" he asked.

"No. Nor eating much, either." Bascomb watched as Longarm poured and sipped the rye. "Matter of fact, this case might be my last trial as federal attorney for Wyoming Territory. The doctor tells me I've got to take things easy from here on out."

"That why you wanted to sit down with me before court opens tomorrow? Hell, Seth, you don't need to worry about me forgetting what I'll testify to. I recall exactly what happened when Buck Pender killed that posseman up on Thunder Creek." Longarm had been taking out a cheroot while he talked. He stopped long enough to flick a match aflame with his thumbnail and puff the cigar into light. "Remember, I put the posse together. And I swore all of them in by the book, wrote their names down the way the rules say. Jim Cross was a legal federal officer when Pender gunned him down.

And if Pender hadn't tossed his gun away before I could swing my Colt around, he'd be a dead outlaw now, and we wouldn't be having this damn trial. Jim wasn't the first man he'd killed, you know."

Bascomb said, "I'm not worried about your memory, Longarm. I've had you on the stand too many times; I know you won't say the wrong thing." He paused and shook his head, adding, "Maybe I better say I don't worry about your saying the wrong thing in testimony given before the right judge."

Longarm frowned at the federal prosecutor through a cloud of blue cigar smoke. "The right judge? Hell's bells, Seth, Judge Leland—" He stopped suddenly and shook his head. "You saying Judge Leland's not going to try Pender?"

Bascomb gazed at him steadily. "I didn't realize you hadn't heard. Judge Leland died a month ago. The Justice Department sent out a judge from the East to sit until the President appoints a new one. He's from Boston. Name's Luther Evans. I've barely met him, he just got here a few days ago. From what I've heard, he's a stickler for details. And you're the only witness I've got who actually saw Buck Pender shoot Cross."

"Well, I remember it like it was yesterday. You don't have to worry."

Bascomb sat silently, thoughtful, while Longarm refilled his glass and sipped. Then he said, "You know, we take a little bit more relaxed view of court procedures out here in the West than they do back East, Longarm. I just want to be sure you'll go by the book, think twice before you say anything."

"Sure. I won't talk out of turn, Seth. I got a hunch this trial's one you set a lot of store by, seeing as how it's your last one. You'd like to win it, I guess, not go out a loser."

Bascomb smiled. "I'd call that a fair statement. Well, that's really all I wanted to say, Longarm. And now that I've said it, I'm going to bow out. I've left word here at the club that you're my guest this evening. Try your luck in the game room upstairs, if you like, have dinner in the dining room, whatever you fancy at the bar." A hint of a smile crinkled the corners of Bascomb's eyes. "I suppose you know the Astorian Club doesn't supply its members with female companionship, even though there are a lot of our members who bring their own ladyfriends here for privacy."

"You mean you're checking out this early? Damn, Seth, that doctor of yours really must've throwed a scare into you."

"He did. Well, not a scare, just a realization that if I don't follow his orders I'm in for real trouble. But don't let that bother you. Enjoy yourself. I'll see you in court tomorrow morning. Incidentally, if you don't feel like going back to your hotel tonight, all you need to do is tell the housekeeper, and she'll set up a bedroom for you for the night." Bascomb stood up.

Longarm rose and the two men clasped hands briefly. Longarm said, "Well, I appreciate the hospitality, Seth. Don't know as I'll use much of it, though. I'll finish up this drink, I guess, then go on back to the hotel."

"Nonsense. At least walk around the place. We're proud of the Astorian. There's not a club between Chicago and San Francisco that can touch it, not even in Denver."

After Bascomb had left, Longarm settled back into his chair and sipped his whiskey thoughtfully. The evening was late, and his first inclination was to finish the excellent rye in his glass, then go back to his room at the Stockman's Hotel in downtown Casper. He'd found Seth Bascomb's message waiting for him at the hotel when he'd checked in after his arrival from Denver on the notorious C&S Chugwater local just before dusk. Bascomb's note hadn't given him any clue as to the length of time he'd be expected to spend at their meeting, though, and Longarm hadn't stopped for dinner before taking a hack to the club. After a bit of reflection, he concluded that a meal at the famous Astorian Club would be a lot better than anything he'd be served at one of the cafes in Casper.

Long as Seth was nice enough to set up a good supper for you, old son, he told himself, *you'd be a plain jackass not to belly up to the table out here and dig in.*

204

It ain't every day you get a chance to set down and eat the kind of grub that rich folks enjoy.

Casper's Astorian Club was famous throughout the West. It was one of the oldest of a score or more of renowned establishments that had been erected by the cattle-rich, mine-rich, land-rich handful of men who'd tasted the luxury of private clubs and deluxe hotels in their travels, and had done their best to duplicate the facilities close to the isolated Western areas to which their business interests confined them for most of their time. The clubs were their refuges not only from boredom at home, but from the rough and raunchy saloons in which those who, through luck or ability, frequently faced the gibes and hazing of the far greater number of men who hadn't done as well.

With a satisfied sigh, Longarm settled back into the lounge chair and poured himself another sip of rye before going to the dining room.

Dinner measured up to his expectations, though he stuck to his favorite—steak and potatoes. The beef was moist and tender enough to cut with a fork, the potatoes fried to a flaky crispness that was unlike the usual soggy spuds cooked in long-used fat, the standard fare of main-street restaurants in towns the size of Casper. After dinner, Longarm went into the bar that adjoined the dining room for a top-off drink of rye. The barkeep looked at him with a half-frown, then snapped his fingers.

"Hell, I know you now. You're the U.S. marshal that's in town for the trial. Pender's trial. Let's see . . . Longarm, they call you. Mr. Bascomb mentioned you're a rye man."

"That's right," Longarm admitted. He took the drink the barkeep had poured for him, and lighted his after-dinner cheroot before sipping it.

"Well, I hope that bastard Pender gets what's coming to him," the barkeep said. "Jim Cross was a good friend of mine."

"I guess it's up to the judge and the jury now," Longarm remarked. "Nothing much I can do besides swear to what I saw when it happened."

"Yeah." The barkeep frowned. "But if this new judge from back East don't give him the noose, there's those around Casper who'll see that Pender won't last long."

"His kind usually don't." Longarm put his glass on the bar. "Well, I guess I'll get on back to the hotel and turn in. Not much else to do that I can see, tonight."

"You hit the games upstairs?"

"No. Didn't really expect to find games out here."

"Well, if you feel lucky, take the stairs on the left and go on up. Fellow never knows when he's hot until he tries his luck."

"Thanks. But I guess I'm wound up for the evening."

Longarm was opening the cloakroom door to get his hat when he saw the stairway. He hesitated, recalling the barkeep's words, and decided that as long as he was in the club, he might as well inspect all of its attractions. Instead of taking his hat, he closed the cloakroom door and mounted the left-hand staircase.

Like all the rest of the Astorian Club, the atmosphere of the gaming salon was quietly luxurious. Billiard tables, all idle, lined one side of the huge room. Individual gaming tables, widely spaced, were scattered around the perimeter of the area. Poker games were in progress at three of the tables, a spirited game of Pedro at a fourth, and a quiet game of whist at one isolated table in one corner. In the center of the room stood a roulette table, with a half-dozen players watching the croupier as he dexterously set the ball clinking onto the spinning wheel's cone. Past the roulette table there was a faro layout. The players were facing Longarm, but he blinked when he saw the back of the dealer—a woman, tall and slim, who wore her midnight-black hair in a low coil on her neck, with a high, jeweled Spanish comb sparkling above the crown of her head.

Old son, he told himself, *there ain't but one woman in the world wears that kind of hairdo.*

Taking his time, Longarm circled the gaming salon until he could see the face of the woman dealing faro. She was concentrating on the players at her table, and the chips they were stringing on the layout. Not until she'd called the turn and dropped the losing card on the soda beside the dealing box did she raise her eyes from the layout to glance around the room. By that time, Longarm had worked his way to a position where he was facing her over the heads of the poker players at their individual tables.

Her eyes locked on Longarm's and she froze, one hand in midair, for a long moment. Then she smiled. Longarm smiled in return. His eyes formed a question, and she nodded. Then she went back to the faro game. Longarm stood quietly until the case card showed and she pushed the dealing box to one side and announced in a tone which, though quiet, carried clearly to where Longarm stood. "With your permission, gentlemen, I'd like to close the table for a few minutes. I'll be back right away, though, and I hope you'll all stick around to buck the tiger some more."

Taking a cue from her eyes, Longarm edged along the wall to the stairway and hurried to the entry. The outer door stood ajar; that was the only clue he needed. He stepped outside into the cool, starlit night. He'd barely closed the door behind him when a pair of smooth white arms encircled him and whirled him around, and he found himself caught up in a long, impassioned kiss.

"You act like you're sort of glad to see me, Molly," he said when she finally released him.

"Glad! I'm so dammed tickled I could scream! It's so dark I can't really see you, but if you'll just stand still for a minute, I can feel you and see if you've changed."

Molly's hands played over Longarm's face, stroking his cheeks and chin, her fingers tracing the bold sweep of his mustache and running gently along his lips. Then he felt a hand at his crotch, exploring. His own hands were busy at the same time, running from firm, high breasts down spreading hips and along softly curving buttocks.

"You haven't changed a bit, thank God!" Molly said with a sigh. "Still the same Longarm. But it's been such a long time! How long? Two years?"

"A mite more'n that. I sort of figured I'd run into

you before now, but I guess when you were coming thisaway, I was heading thataway."

"Well, we've gotten together now. I hope you're not just passing through and moving on."

"I'll be here long as the trial lasts."

"Oh—I ought to've known. Buck Pender, of course. That's all I've heard about here at the club for the past week or so. And that reminds me, I can't stay away from my table too long. Where are you stopping?"

"At the Stockman's Hotel. Room 216."

"All right. The gambling room closes at midnight on weeknights. I'll see you as soon as I can get into town."

A quick kiss, and Molly was gone. Longarm stood outside in the cool night long enough to light a fresh cheroot before going inside to get his hat. He wondered what the custom was, whether he'd be expected to sign a club tab for his dinner and drinks, and went into the bar to find out.

"A tab?" the barkeep asked. "No, sir. Mr. Bascomb said you're his guest. If you're ready to leave, I can get the hackman to drive you into town."

"Well, I hadn't really thought about how I was getting back. But it'll sure beat shank's mare, even if it ain't very far to the hotel."

In his bare little room at the Stockman's Hotel, Longarm carefully hung up his Prince Albert coat on the first of the hooks provided in the corner opposite the bed, then hung his vest on the next hook in line, and eased off his stovepipe cavalry boots. He took his time in positioning his holstered Colt on the left upper headpost of the brass bed, where it would be in place for him to reach it easily with his right hand. He rummaged his traveling bottle of Maryland rye out of his saddlebags, took the glass that stood on the marble-topped nightstand, and poured himself a drink. Only then did he stretch out on the bed, his head propped up with both pillows, and lay back in comfort to wait for Molly.

She'd been the last person he'd expected to see in Casper, and he wondered idly what she'd been doing for the last two years since they'd parted in Boise, after he'd broken up the highgrading ring led by a member of the Idaho territorial legislature. Molly Melinda had been dealing faro in the gambling hall that was another of the legislator's secret ventures. She'd known more about her boss's business than he'd considered safe, and as Longarm's probing penetrated the legislator's illicit activities, the man had passed the word to shut Molly's mouth permanently. Longarm's intervention had saved her life, and their association had flared into something that went a bit deeper than the casual roll in the hay, quickly forgotten.

Stretched out, relaxing, his mind dipping into the past, Longarm had gone through three drinks and two cheroots before Molly slipped into his room.

"I got here as fast as I could," she said, locking the door before coming to sit on the bed beside him. "Even closed the table early, when play dropped off." She leaned over to kiss him. "If it had been up to me, I'd have come back to town with you."

"Guess if I'd been a real gentleman, I'd have waited for you." He grinned, passing her his half-filled glass and reaching down beside the bed for the bottle. "That fancy club's just a mite too rich for my blood, though. I reckon I could get used to it, but I ain't about to try, seeing as how I never will be able to afford to live like a nabob."

"You're enough of a nabob for me." Molly was unbuttoning Longarm's shirt and balbriggans. His chest bared, she began to rub her cheeks on the thick, bristling brown hair growing on it.

Longarm pulled her to him and kissed her, his hand caressing her breasts. "You're a fine girl, Molly. Only fault I can find with you now is that you got too damn many clothes on."

"Look who's talking!" Molly unbuckled Longarm's belt and began fumbling the buttons of his fly apart. "You knew I was going to be here. It seems to me you should've been ready for me."

"Hell, Molly, we always used to figure that getting each other ready was half the fun."

"And it still is."

Molly had freed Longarm now and was gently caressing him with her soft hands. "It's just as big and beautiful as ever." She shrugged her shoulders to help Longarm slip her dress down to her waist, and cradled his swollen shaft between her soft, pink-tipped breasts.

Rising above him, she let him slide her dress and shift down over her hips. With a quick kick, Molly flipped the garments to the floor. Longarm gently pulled the high Spanish comb from her hair, and her dark mane fell in a cascade over her face and curled in thick coils on Longarm's chest. He cradled her chin with one hand and drew her lips to his. Their tongues entwined, Molly straddled Longarm's thighs and slid her hips along them until she'd trapped his shaft between the corded layers of muscle on his flat belly and the soft, warm moisture of her crotch. Slowly she began to slide back and forth.

Longarm remembered Molly's ways. His calloused hands found her breasts and she leaned forward to let him take them between his lips, nipping at her nipples with his strong teeth until she began to pant and her body started quivering. She began to work her hips faster and faster, and he could feel her juices flowing hot on his belly and thighs. She prolonged her movements until he felt her body begin to grow taut. Then, with one swift move, Longarm released Molly's breasts, lifted her hips, and let her guide him into her. She dropped onto him suddenly, as he thrust upward.

"Harder!" she urged him. "Harder and deeper!"

His hands on her hips, Longarm lifted her and let her drop as he thrust upward, once, twice, then a third great upward heave, harder and deeper than before. Molly stiffened and shuddered, and her body writhed convulsively.

"Hold me now," she begged. "Pull me down!"

Longarm held her hips clasped to his while she reared up and shook spasmodically minute after minute until a deep, sobbing sigh came from her throat and she collapsed on his chest, gasping and panting.

"Don't wait too long," she whispered, when she

could speak again. "Or have you forgotten how I like for you to do it?"

"I ain't forgot," he assured her.

Molly was still straining to breathe, inhaling in great, convulsing gulps, when Longarm rolled them over in the bed. He withdrew almost completely, then drove into her fiercely, again and again, thrusting quick and deep until once more her body began to tremble. He did not stop, but pounded steadily, Molly's fingernails digging into his back, her legs locked high around his hips. Even when she stiffened and shuddered, Longarm did not stop, but kept driving into her until her spasm eased and she lay limp, her arms sprawled lifelessly. He could feel the muscles of her thighs quivering around his waist, and slowed to a gentle stroking for a while until Molly stirred and opened her eyes and looked at him, her face a white island in the sea of her dark hair that curled in wild disarray over the pillows.

"Are you ready for me now?" she asked softly.

"About as ready as I'll ever be."

"Let me have you, then."

Longarm knelt above her, his knees straddling her lax body, and moved forward. Molly raised her head enough to reach his slick, throbbing erection and her lips enclosed him, drawing him into her mouth. He was tender and sensitized now. He could feel each movement her tongue made, traveling over and across him, and he shivered lightly as the warmth of her mouth and the gentle, pulsing pressure of her distended lips combined with her tongue's continuing caresses.

Running his hand back along Molly's soft hips, Longarm found her moist pubic hair and slid his fingers between her thighs. He felt her body stiffen between his knees, and her encircling mouth tightened around him as he gently stroked the warm wetness of her other lips. Her tongue's motion grew rougher and faster in response to his rubbing. Longarm felt himself tightening into orgasm as she continued to work her lips, trying to pull him deeper into her mouth.

He held back as long as he could endure the nearly unendurable tugging pressure of her lips, until his

211

fingering brought Molly's hips into twitching motion, until he felt her hot juices flowing around his stroking fingers. Then he let go. His hips thrust forward as he gushed in shuddering release while Molly's throat moved convulsively and her hands pressed him to her until he was drained. Molly sighed contentedly, holding him deep in her mouth until she felt him begin to grow flaccid.

Longarm dropped beside her on the bed. She snuggled against him, and they lay side by side in satisfied exhaustion, Molly's head cradled on Longarm's muscular shoulder until she stirred and raised herself up on an elbow.

"You're still the longest-winded man I've ever found," she smiled. "I've known a few men who can bring me off twice, but you're the only one who can hold out while I go three times and still stay up until I finish you off the way I like to."

"And you sure have got one hell of a way of finishing a man off," he told her. He picked up the bottle on the floor beside the bed and was fumbling around trying to find the glass when she took the bottle from his hand.

"Never mind the glass," she said. "I'll drink out of the bottle. Then I'll take a puff off that cheroot you're going to light, and we can catch up on what's happened since we said goodbye in Boise."

"That's going to cover a lot of territory."

As though he hadn't spoken, Molly went on, "And by then we'll be ready to start all over and make up for some of what we've missed."

Longarm grinned. "You got things all planned out, I see. Well, I don't have to show up in court until nine o'clock tomorrow morning, and there ain't a better way I know of to pass the time till then."

Chapter 2

Even before selection of the jury began at Buck Pender's trial the next morning, Longarm could see that a clash of wills between Seth Bascomb and Judge Luther Evans was inevitable.

Bascomb had hailed Longarm in the courthouse corridor on the way to the courtroom. "I'd appreciate it if you'd sit with me at counsel's table today," the federal prosecutor said. "My clerk's not feeling very well, and he won't be on hand. And damn it, I feel lonesome at that big table without company."

"You don't think this new judge will mind?" Longarm asked.

"He'd have no reason to, at least not during the *voir dire*," Bascomb replied. "It's a bit less formal than the actual trial, and that won't begin until the jury's empaneled and the court's heard the defendant's plea. But just to make it look better, I'll give you a pad and pencil, and you can make a note or two now and then."

"Hell, I'm just glad to oblige you, Seth. You treated me to a might fine evening out at that club of yours. I owe you."

"Nonsense. You just sit there and look wise, and nothing's going to be said."

Something was said, though not directly to Longarm, by the narrow-faced, thin-lipped judge. It was Bascomb to whom Evans directed his criticism, within minutes after the court had been called to order.

"Mr. Bascomb," Evans said sharply, his voice a nasal, grating twang. "I am not accustomed to seeing counsel in my courtroom carrying firearms. You will

213

instruct your associate to remove his weapon, or to remove himself from the courtroom."

Bascomb stood up. "Your Honor, this gentleman is not associated with me as counsel. He is a deputy United States marshal whom I have asked to assist me in taking notes because my assistant is ill."

"That is of no importance whatsoever. My order still stands."

Bascomb leaned over and whispered to Longarm, "You heard him. You mind sliding your gun in the drawer there, just to make the damned old Yankee buzzard happy?"

Longarm reluctantly slid his Colt from its cross-draw holster and placed it in the drawer of the counsel's table. Bascomb looked questioningly at the judge, who nodded. Then, after Bascomb had taken his seat, Evans turned his attention to the chief bailiff, who had pulled a chair up behind the one occupied by Buck Pender at the defense counsel's table.

"Bailiff, I see the defendant is wearing handcuffs. You will remove them."

Leaping to his feet, the bailiff protested, "But, your honor, this man's dangerous! He's got to be cuffed for the—"

"Bailiff!" Evans interrupted sharply. "It should not be necessary to remind you that your function is to carry out the instructions of the court. It would be extremely prejudicial to the defendant's case for him to be shackled during the *voir dire*, while the jury is being selected, or during the trial."

Longarm was watching Buck Pender's mean, slash-mouthed face while Judge Evans was delivering his reprimand to the bailiff. He saw Pender's grin begin then, and grow wider and more smug during the few moments required for the bailiff to follow the judge's orders.

Bascomb whispered, "I hate to think about what that old fool's going to say next, but I've got a pretty good idea of what's coming."

Evans said, his voice even sharper than usual, "I notice that the bailiffs are carrying revolvers. So are

214

most of the veniremen and many of the spectators. Chief bailiff, you will impound the weapons worn by these people—as well as your own and those of your assistant bailiffs—and return them to their owners after court has adjourned at noon."

At Longarm's side, Bascomb was on his feet. "Your honor!"

"I have not finished my instructions, Mr. Prosecutor," Evans snapped, "But I will defer doing so until you have finished speaking. Go ahead."

"Your honor," Bascomb began, "with all deference to the court, weapons are as much a part of the everyday clothing of the men in this courtroom as are their shoes and trousers and shirts. With all respect, I suggest that they be allowed to make their own disposition of their guns, and I ask for a brief recess until they can do so."

Bascomb stopped, and Judge Evans asked, "Are you through with your remarks, Mr. Prosecutor?"

"Yes, your honor. Except to repeat my request for a recess to allow the men with weapons to dispose of them as they wish, and return to the courtroom unarmed."

"Your request is denied, Mr. Bascomb." The judge cleared his throat, but his hawking cough did nothing to remove the grating nasal bite from his voice as he said, "In taking note of Mr. Bascomb's request, I have been told that it is the custom in this section of the country for almost all men to carry weapons. However, a court of law is a place to exercise reason, not marksmanship. I do not propose to have my courtroom turned into an armed camp. Bailiffs, you will collect the weapons, including that of the United States marshal."

Longarm watched the bailiffs as they made their way around the courtroom. In addition to revolvers being worn openly in belt holsters, several of the spectators surrendered pocket pistols. So did two or three of the prospective jurors. Surprisingly, the court reporter handed over a small pocket pistol, causing Judge Evans to frown angrily. At last the bailiff came to the table where Longarm and Seth Bascomb were seated. Longarm opened the drawer and handed over his Colt, but did not offer to give the bailiff the derringer that nestled in his right-hand vest pocket at the end of his watch chain.

From somewhere, one of the bailiffs had managed to produce an empty box. The confiscated guns were laid in the box. Judge Evans nodded with approval. "You men may claim your weapons when court recesses at noon. And you will not, let me emphasize, you *will not* bring them into my court again, or I will be forced to find you in contempt." He looked at the defense attorney, then at Bascomb. "If counsel is ready, we will now proceed with the *voir dire.*"

Selection of the jury ate up the rest of the morning and most of the afternoon. Buck Pender almost insultingly ignored the verbal sparring between his attorney and Bascomb as the choice of jurors dragged on. He spent most of the time gazing out the courtroom windows. Then came the formalities of charge and plea, with Pender casually returning a drawled "not guilty" when it came time for him to speak. Bascomb, visibly exhausted after the long session of questioning prospective jurors, made the required formal statement outlining what the prosecution proposed to prove. Pender's attorney reserved his opening statement, and Judge Evans adjourned the court for the day.

Walking down the corridor to the door, Bascomb said to Longarm, "Well, my guess is that we've lost any chance of sending that damned killer to the gallows."

Longarm frowned. "How's that?"

"Why, that Yankee judge pulled my teeth. Pender sitting there without handcuffs, the business of disarming everybody—all that's reduced this to a trial for petty larceny, not murder."

"Now damn it, Seth, Pender killed Jim Cross and I watched him do it. Ain't my word going to be worth anything when I get up in the witness stand and testify to what I saw?"

"Sure it will. And I don't doubt the jury's going to

find Buck Pender guilty. But I'm afraid they won't bring in a hanging verdict."

With raw disbelief in his voice, Longarm asked, "You mean just because of that business with the handcuffs and guns?"

"*Just* because of that. Pender's an animal, and a dangerous one, not just a petty thief. How many men has he killed, Longarm?"

"Oh, maybe seven or eight, besides Jim Cross."

"And neither you nor anybody else can testify to that in this trial. As for that byplay with the guns, Evans apparently still doesn't realize that what I said is true, that damned near every man in the territory carries one at least part of the time. Hell, I do myself, when I'm traveling."

"From the way Judge Evans acted, I got the idea he doesn't really approve of a man carrying a gun. Even somebody like me, who's upholding the law," Longarm said thoughtfully.

Bascomb nodded. "That's city thinking. Back East, there's a policeman on every corner to protect folks. Here, we've got to look out for ourselves." They were outside the courthouse now, on the sidewalk. Bascomb said, "If you'd like to have dinner at the club again this evening—"

"No, thanks, Seth," Longarm replied. "It ain't that I wouldn't enjoy it, but—"

"But you've got other plans?" The attorney smiled. "All right. I'll see you in the morning, then."

When he left the Stockman's Hotel for the courthouse the next morning, Longarm not only left Molly Melinda sleeping in his room, he left his holstered .44 Colt Model T in care of the desk clerk, with a request that it be kept for him in a locked drawer.

Word had apparently spread that the meat of Pender's trial was coming up, for the courtroom was crowded. Seth Bascomb was already sitting at the counsel's table when Longarm came in. He motioned him over.

"I did some thinking last night," Bascomb said. "I'm

going to call you to the stand at once, and you're going to be the only witness I'll put on."

"Whatever you say, Seth. I guess I'll have to wait outside, like always, till you're ready for me?"

Bascomb nodded. "Yes. But you won't have to wait long, so don't go wandering off. You'll be called in as soon as court convenes."

Longarm found a place in the hall on the bench that was reserved for witnesses. He wondered, as he tried to make himself comfortable on the straight-backed hardwood seat, why it was that nobody who made courtroom furniture seemed to know enough about human anatomy to design the benches to be comfortable. He was still squirming, trying to find a position that fitted his frame, when the bailiffs brought Pender down the corridor. They stopped outside the door to remove the outlaw's handcuffs and take off their gun-belts.

Pender grinned wolfishly at Longarm, his broad mouth twisted to show a gap in his stained teeth. Longarm fixed his gunmetal-blue eyes on the killer. Pender returned the stare only for a moment before turning his head aside.

As Bascomb had promised, Longarm was called to the witness stand as soon as the court convened. Under the prosecutor's questioning, Longarm went through the events of the day, almost ten months earlier, which had led to the murder of the federal posseman by Buck Pender. The defense attorney registered objections from time to time, but Longarm was no stranger to the witness box. He kept his testimony brief and well organized, his replies prompt and unhesitating. By midmorning his evidence had been completed.

"Will you cross-examine now, Mr. Goodhue?" Judge Evans asked Pender's lawyer.

Goodhue stood up. "If it please the court, yes, your honor." He started toward the witness stand, all eyes in the courtroom following his progress.

Even Longarm did not notice Pender bending forward, slouched low over the chair just vacated by Goodhue, until the killer stood up, brandishing a nickel-plated revolver.

"Don't nobody move!" Pender shouted, his voice overriding the thud of Goodhue's footsteps on the uncarpeted floor. The gun in the outlaw's hands was aimed squarely at Judge Evans. "Looks like I got the only gun in the place," Pender went on, flashing his wolf-like grin. "I guess I got you to thank for that, Judge."

He started toward the bench, his revolver's muzzle centered unwaveringly on the judge, even when he swiveled his head snakelike from side to side to keep the rest of the courtroom under observation. In front of the bench, Pender stopped. "Come on, Judge, hurry up! You've helped me this far, now you're going to be my pass outside too. Shake a leg now! You and me are leaving!"

Force of habit, stronger than unpleasant and unaccepted reality, prompted Judge Evans to command, "Bailiffs! Restrain this prisoner!"

From force of habit, the bailiffs began moving toward Pender. The outlaw unhesitatingly gunned down the chief bailiff, who toppled forward to the floor, clutching his belly. A stir swept the courtroom as, here and there, men sprang to their feet.

Pender turned his back to the bench and faced the courtroom. He waved his pistol. "Everybody set down!" he barked. "There's five shells left in this gun! Who's going to get the next one?"

Slowly the scraping of feet and the buzz of voices subsided as the spectators and jury members settled back into their seats.

"All right, your goddamned honor!" Pender snapped at Evans. "Get your ass out of that chair and come along! We got to go!"

Longarm, in the witness stand at the end of the bench, had kept silent and motionless. He knew that Pender was aware of him, knew from the killer's record that there would be a bullet in his heart or brain at once if he attracted the outlaw's attention by so much as moving a finger. He froze in his chair, waiting for a chance.

"Go where?" Judge Evans gasped.

"Shit!" Pender snorted. "A man smart as you're sup-posed to be ought to know the answer to that! You're my ticket out of here, Judge! And if anybody gets in my way while we're leaving, you'll be a dead man! So will whoever tries to hinder me!"

"Now be sensible!" Evans said. Shock or fear sent the judge's grating, nasal voice a tone higher than usual, and put an even rougher edge on it. "You know you can't get away with this!"

"Like hell I can't!" Pender retorted confidently. "I'm doing real good so far. I'll take my chances on making it the rest of the way. Now let's move!"

"I refuse to be abducted from my own courtroom!" Judge Evans said.

Longarm reluctantly gave the judge credit for stand-ing his ground in the face of what must have been the first threat of this kind that Evans had ever faced.

"You've got nothing to say about it," Pender told Evans. "So suppose you just come along, quiet and peaceful. And you better tell these men in here not to try anything, or I'll drop you right now and make it out on my own!" He stepped up to the bench and shoved his revolver into Judge Evans's chest.

Actual contact with Pender's revolver seemed to con-vince Evans that he had no choice. He clenched his jaws, then nodded. "Very well. I'll go with you."

"Tell everybody to stand clear while we get out," Pender ordered.

Evans raised his voice. "You men heard him. I'm going with him. You hold your places, and I'm sure you won't be harmed."

Pender divided his attention between the spectators and the judge while Evans sidled behind the witness stand where Longarm sat.

Longarm had been busy figuring his odds. Pender had five shots left in the revolver. Longarm decided the outlaw was too cagy to use a bullet on him until the very last moment, when he was almost out of the court-room. Until now, Pender had done nothing except glance his way now and then, in the certainty that Longarm had no weapon.

Judge Evans reached the corner of the witness stand and started around its end toward Pender. Longarm tensed his leg muscles while he watched the judge's reluctant progress. When Pender turned to look over the courtroom, Longarm moved.

With a single leap, he flew over the edge of the witness stand, drawing his derringer in midair. He landed between Judge Evans and Pender, and as his feet hit the floor he pushed Evans down. In the same motion, he triggered the derringer almost in Pender's face. The outlaw fired, but he was still swinging his revolver around to cover Longarm, and his finger tightened on its trigger in his dying reflex. The slug from the pistol plowed harmlessly into the floor.

Longarm stepped over the outlaw's still body and kicked the revolver away. He was only half aware of the explosion of pounding footsteps and the chorus of voices raised in the courtroom as the gunfire broke the spell that had kept its occupants frozen. He bent over Judge Evans and helped the jurist to his feet.

"You all right, Judge?" he asked as Evans gazed at the confusion in the courtroom. Automatically, the judge's hands were smoothing down the ruffled silk of his judicial robes.

"I—yes, of course I'm all right, Marshal!" Evans snapped.

His eyes took in Pender's body sprawled on the floor, the outlaw's features obscured redly now by the blood streaming from the dime-sized hole that the big slug from the derringer had punched between the man's eyebrows. Then Evans's gaze shifted to the derringer, barely visible in Longarm's big hand, and the gold watch that dangled from the chain connecting the watch to the weapon.

"Marshal Long," Evans said, "I distinctly forbade weapons in my courtroom. Do you remember that?"

"I sure do. It was a damn fool order to start with, but I guess you found that out the hard way. It damn near got you killed."

Evans's face reddened. "Marshal Long! You're forgetting my position! And your own, I might add!"

Seth Bascomb, recovered now from the shock of the swift-moving events, sprang to his feet. "Your honor! I respectfully suggest—"

"Be seated, counselor! You're out of order!" the judge ordered.

Habit sat Bascomb back in his chair. Evans, his jaw set angrily, his nostrils distended whitely, made his way to his own chair on its raised platform. He sat down and rapped his gavel angrily.

"Bailiff!" he called.

For a moment the assistant bailiff, who was bending over his wounded colleague, paid no attention. Evans pounded the gavel until the bailiff looked up.

"Bailiff, disarm this man and place him under arrest!"